ONE OF THE MADDING CROWD

One of the

DAVID. W. DUTTON

Madding Crowd

DEVIL'S PARTY PRESS, MILTON, DE

ONE OF THE MADDING CROWD

Copyright © 2018 by David W. Dutton.
Front cover photo by Kiselev Andrey Valerevich.
Cover design by David Yurkovich.
All rights reserved.
This is a work of fiction. Any similarities between actual persons,
places, or events are entirely coincidental.
ISBN: 978-0-9996558-0-1

DEDICATION

To Marilyn, for her unwavering support and patience.

It was the best of times, it was the worst of times.

Charles Dickens

ONE OF THE MADDING CROWD

Prologue

THE ENGLISH NOVELIST AND poet, Thomas Hardy, understood the world in which he lived. I wish I could say the same of mine. Mid-twentieth century America was much like Hardy's Victorian England ... a self-confident world consumed by its own busyness.

The small, coastal town of Martin's Neck appeared to be a little different from any other town of its time; seemingly, it was part of the general milieu which comprised our nation. Only in later years did I begin to realize how different my personal niche actually was. Even now, with much of my life behind me, I have difficulty understanding and coping with its reality ... or what passed for reality.

As a young adult, I began to view this microcosm with different eyes. In many ways, our lives were divorced from the outside world, much like the characters in Hardy's 1874 novel, *Far From the Madding Crowd*. Still, we could not avoid being affected by national and international situations and trends. I suppose it was this duality I found so hard to understand. We lived our lives with one foot in isolation, the other as active members of Hardy's "crowd." The two worlds were constantly at odds, each trying to replace the other. Both forces were equally strong ... and equally unsuccessful. As a result, we were caught in the middle, torn apart by conflict.

Our ancestors had created and fostered a world designed to form a cocoon around its inhabitants. In doing this, they constructed their own definition of reality from which there was no easy escape. As such, this world endured from generation to generation. With the growing complexity and strength of our global society, one would have expected this microcosm to slowly collapse and disappear, but this did not happen. Instead, it remained solid, holding its inhabitants securely.

That we found it hard to escape society's grasp should not be viewed as any weakness of character. Quite the contrary. Most were strong, forceful people with high ideals and aspirations. Some tried to escape, but few succeeded. Some escaped for a time, only to be wooed back again. Most viewed any alternate life as an anathema not to be considered. All were victims, willing or unwilling. The tragedy, it seems, is that no one recognized the truth.

In retrospect, our lives were filled with pain, upholstered with the best that life had to offer. We lived our lives fully, disastrously, and sadly ... and accepted life without understanding what was really happening. I suppose I should be happy about this fact since there was nothing anyone could have done to change things. In that sense, we were all making the best of an impossible situation.

It frightens me to acknowledge these realities ... to finally reach a measure of understanding. It frightens me to see our own children continuing the traditions thrust upon them–traditions which are so much a part of their lives that they don't realize their existence. It frightens me to have this knowledge and know there is nothing I can do to reverse what has happened or to prevent it from happening again. This fabrication is cyclical, self-perpetuating, and insidious–an ever-present monster which dines with us daily.

First, you must understand I am mad ... not in the sense of being angry, or, as is politically correct, having a mental health condition. Like many, I have successfully hidden this affliction for years and will probably continue to do so. Sure, I've seen my share of psychiatrists and psychologists over the years–who hasn't? It's simply that each engagement has resulted in being *cured* or learning to *cope*, or whatever buzz word is in vogue at the time. This has nothing to do with my madness. I was born with it and have fostered it diligently for many years. It has grown and matured and reached a sophistication that cannot be matched. It is a marvelous thing, this madness. It almost has a life of its own. It is almost a separate entity. Yes, it is a very dear part of me, a friend of sorts–the kind of which one does not approve but loves in spite of his or her faults.

You must read this story with these things in mind because they color everything that follows. I would love to be able to tell you exactly what happened, but I can't. I can only tell you what I remember. Good or bad, with this you will have to be satisfied. Besides, there is no one else who even suspects the truth, let alone understands it. This pathetic treatise is as close an account as will ever exist.

Please read with tolerance, remembering that these were and are real people. They have the same fears, hopes, and faults inherent in us all. Most of all, they are kind, loving individuals who only wanted the best for those around them despite what actually happened. They cannot be blamed, only pitied. They were and are victims of a life fashioned exclusively for them, a life from which they could not escape. Please remember that, above all, they are human with all the frailties which accompany that condition.

Now, the story as I remember it ...

1

In the Beginning…

OUTWARDLY, MY FAMILY WAS little different from any other. By *family*, I mean my extended family, comprised of parents, grandparents, aunts, uncles, cousins, etc. Our family tree reads like something from King James with enough *begets* to stagger the mind. It is so extensive that the circles it contains makes one dizzy to the point of wondering if someone is a thirty-first cousin or an aunt thrice removed. I suppose this is typical of any American family that has resided here for over fourteen generations. One of our lame family jokes is that we inter-married to keep the money in the family, except that no one now knows what happened to the money.

Money. It never seems to have been a problem where our family was concerned. Of course, ostensibly, there has never been enough of it, but isn't that true of every family? Regardless, we, as a family, have seldom wanted for anything we needed or desired. Even today, money flows from one member of the family to another, depending on where it's needed. There is nothing formal or legal about these transactions. They simply happen. In many ways, it's as if there is a single pile of ready cash from which any member is free to draw. Likewise, there is never a paying back of monies used. Somehow this system works; though I'm not sure why or how.

Beginning in the late 1600s, our ancestors worked tirelessly to create a society exclusive enough to make most people jealous, and my family was not alone in this endeavor. Martin's Neck, nestled in the crook of the Mid-Atlantic seaboard, was filled with families who did the same. It was a prosperous area filled with merchants, farmers, shipbuilders, and sea captains, each of whom pursued and won their fortunes to secure a niche for their burgeoning families. As a result, big houses were constructed along the narrow streets of the little town, and a level of luxurious living was established that would never wane.

As Martin's Neck grew, streets and buildings bore our family names, and most areas of endeavor and progress were linked with one or more of our representatives. The bulk of our family fortune was produced through shipbuilding, banking, and mercantile investments. By the early 1800s, three branches of our family—the Powells, the Fredericks, and the Greys—owned the town's three major shipyards. The ships they produced pumped large sums of money into family coffers. In later years, the stock market helped magnify our holdings, enabling future generations to continue the lifestyle to which all had grown accustomed. These investments financed college educations, fancy automobiles, vacation homes, and travel.

As with most small towns, kind married kind, and, by the dawn of the twentieth century, there were few families who were not related through marriage. Hence, the circle of our family grew and grew. Great uncles and cousins twice removed were as much a part of the family as first cousins and grandparents. Each was an important part of the family infrastructure, each a component of a well-synchronized machine set in motion generations before.

Any social function involving the whole family was a huge affair. As a child, I remember our annual New Year's dinner, which was always hosted by Lillian Powell Harrison, my second cousin twice removed. Although Cousin Lillian had relocated to Boston when she married, she still maintained a large house in Martin's Neck. She opened this rambling, yellow edifice each summer and over the Christmas holidays. Strangely, I cannot remember having ever seen Cousin Lillian's husband at these affairs; I expect he felt intimidated by our family, as was perfectly understandable.

Cousin Lillian's gigantic dinner party was always a treat. The big house glowed with candlelight and bustled with servants busy with preparation. On the day of the party, the gigantic dining room would be filled by two banquet tables spread with food. I have no idea how many people attended these functions, but the children, of which I was one, were always sent to the library to pour over *National Geographic* magazines in anticipation of dinner. As a treat, net stockings filled with candy hung from the mantel in the drawing room. These were always taboo until after dinner, and their promise kept us on our very best behavior.

Summer always marked a shift of residence for many people. This phenomenon, for the most part, predated my memory, but as far back as the late 1800s and early 1900s, people closed their houses in town and moved to the beach. The shore was a mere fifteen miles away, but the air was better, and life was much less formal. My mother remembered these years well and spoke of them with much delight. The "beach," so to speak, was divided from the mainland by a wide canal that had to be crossed by a foot bridge. Every family maintained a garage or stable on the mainland side and carried whatever they needed across the foot bridge to their cottage. These "cottages" were large, cypress-shingled affairs built on the bay front. In comparison to the homes in town, these structures were plain and required much less attention. They boasted large windows, which allowed the sea breezes to circulate through them. This time away was a break from the stiff formality of everyday life.

This phenomenon continued when my Uncle Fred and Aunt Harriet Powell built in new cottage in the early fifties. This became a family gathering place and figured largely in all family activities for almost forty years. By then, the old footbridge had long been replaced by one suitable for vehicles. The sprawling residence was the setting for many of my memories with my cousin, Tom. One of my favorite remembrances of the house was my own bachelor party. As was the norm, this involved much drinking and carousing, and culminated with the groom being thrust into the bay.

During my early childhood, life was a dream from which I would not awaken until I was approaching my teenage years. Sadly, I realize that only now. While this time did not prepare us for what awaited, the memories help sustain me when life becomes difficult. Even now, I would not trade those times for anything of monetary value. They shaped who I am today, good or bad. They helped establish my personal values, no matter how unrealistic. They showed me the power of family, position, and wealth, in spite of how much those powers twisted my later life. Above all else, they brought me together with Tom Powell, my closest and dearest friend and cousin.

Tom and I were like princes of the kingdom. No door was closed to us. Wherever we went and whatever we did was greeted with approval and acceptance., except, perhaps, by our parents. As far as everyone else was concerned, we could do no wrong. Or so it seemed to us. Only now, in retrospect, do I realize that we did not consciously recognize this gift. And in not recognizing it, we never abused it. We simply enjoyed our status and accepted it as our due. As children, our birthright brought us little things: there was always change for Popsicles, library fines were dismissed, unexcused school absences were tolerated. In later years, it meant free alterations at the tailors, waived speeding tickets, and underage cocktails at restaurants. The latter always impressed the girls. But again, we never abused any of it. Tom and I were good kids, golden boys in the true sense of the word. Our world expected the best from us, and, true to our heritage, we supplied our best. Our grades were the best, our clothes were the best, and we were polite to the extreme. We were the dream of every girl's parents. Only in later life would we falter. I began a downhill spiral, and Tom was close to follow.

Through it all, we did our best to perpetuate the charade forced upon us by our family.

2

Summer 1957 – George Sawyer

TOM AND I WERE seated at his kitchen table, immersed in our coloring books, when we heard distant footsteps.

"Boys, this is George Sawyer," My Aunt Harriet Powell indicated a slight, black-haired boy of seventeen. "He's coming to live with us. George, allow me to introduce you to my son, Tom, and my nephew, Marc."

Tom and I smiled with a degree of uncertainty. What was this all about? Where had this boy come from, and why was he going to be living here?

Of course, it wasn't my worry. At ten years of age, I was only a sometime guest in the house. Tom would have to deal with this interloper on a daily basis.

"Let me show you your room," Aunt Harriet said with a smile as she ushered George out of the kitchen.

Aunt Harriet was a statuesque woman with thick, blond hair. One would have never classified her as pretty, but she certainly was striking. Between her height and a penchant for large hats, she was something to behold, and someone you didn't think of crossing. Seeming to sense this, George followed, swallowed up by the house that would be his home for many years to come.

"Who's he?" I asked, skeptically, after they'd left the room.

Tom shrugged, studying his coloring book. "Somebody Mom's got to help around the house."

"A servant?"

"Nah, I don't think so." He looked up at me with eyes that showed confusion. "Mom says he's not." Tom returned his attention to his coloring book and began to color. "He's supposed to cook and clean and keep the fires going." He selected another crayon. "I don't know …"

I studied him for a moment. "Did you know he was coming?"

Tom shrugged again. "I guess so."

I was confused. "Is he, like, a brother?"

Tom looked at me in disdain. "Of course not! He's just here to clean!" He paused, thinking. "He's like Carl and Annie, and Lizzie."

Carl lived and worked for the Messick sisters. Annie had been with Aunt Dinah Lank for years. Lizzie now lived on her own, but for years had been with Aunt Harriet's mother, Elena.

I nodded. "From The Settlement?"

"Yeah."

"Slow, like them?"

"That, too."

"Oh."

The Settlement probably had a proper name, but everyone simply referred to it as that. It was a government-sponsored home for individuals, especially children, who'd been diagnosed with mental difficulties and had nowhere else to go.

Tom threw down his crayon and closed the coloring book. "Let's go outside. I'm tired of this!"

Tom was two months my elder, so, as was usual, I followed his lead. From the kitchen through the long, screened porch, and into the big backyard. "What do you want to do?"

Tom ran across the yard and threw his lanky frame onto a swing suspended from a huge walnut tree that abutted the stable. With a firm push, he was airborne. "Don't know! What you wanna do?"

I flopped down onto the thick lawn and leaned back against the tree trunk. "I don't know." My eyes strayed to the overgrown tangle which marked the neighboring yard. Within the undergrowth and towering trees, the huge house reared its tall chimneys and many dormers in defiance. The place had always fascinated Tom and me, but we were forbidden to trespass there. Perhaps that was part of the magic.

"Well," I sighed, "we could always go over to Hancock's." The Hancock family had owned the old house for years, but it had been vacant as long as we could remember.

Tom began dragging his feet with each pass. "Mom would have a fit!"

"Yeah." I nodded, as he continued to break his swing. "We could get Freddie to go with us."

Fredrica "Freddie" Clifton was our age and only lived two houses away. Her mother was a cousin, or something, to the Hancocks, and acted as a sort of caretaker for the property. Although Freddie wasn't allowed there either, she considered anything and everything as fair game. She also bore the dubious honor of being our fourth cousin, somewhere along the line, as well as our partner in crime.

Tom jumped from the swing and took off in a run. "Race ya!"

I followed as well as my short legs would allow. Eschewing the obvious route of the driveway and sidewalk, Tom cut across the driveway and lawn to the south, through the high privet, across the adjacent lawn, skirted a fish pond, and finally barreled through a wall of hollyhocks into the Clifton's rear yard. I was a good ten steps behind. By the time I cleared the hollyhocks, Tom was already knocking at their back door.

"Whadya want?" The voice was clear and defiant.

I looked up to see Freddie leaning over the balcony railing of the big, white house. Overweight, with erratic, red pigtails, she was a force not to be taken lightly. Although she was somewhat younger than both of us, Tom and I stood in awe of her. At our age, we would have found it difficult to believe she would grow into a strikingly pretty woman with a beauty that would rival that of her mother. The latter was clearly depicted in Mrs. Clifton's coming-out portrait, which hung over the grand piano in their drawing room. Both Tom and I were amazed that such a gorgeous creature could "go to fat" as Freddie's mother had.

"Hey!" Tom yelled, stepping back so that he could see her. "Whatcha doin'?"

"Lookin' at you!"

"Hi, Freddie!" I yelled, joining Tom in the driveway.

"Dare you to jump!" shouted Tom mischievously.

"Big deal!" In spite of her weight, Freddie scrambled over the railing to the porch roof and then dropped ten feet to the lawn. Pushing her pigtails aside, she ran to join us. "What's up?"

Tom looked nervous. "Your parents home?"

"Nah," said Freddie with a shake of her head. "Just Bertha."

Bertha Hancock was Freddie's grandmother and she lived in the Clifton's home. A short, stubby woman, she drove an automobile by looking through the steering wheel rather than over it. Eccentric and overbearing were the least of her qualities.

"Wanna go to Hancocks'?" asked Tom with a smile.

"Sure!" Freddie turned and ran toward the house. She opened the door to the screened porch and yelled. "Mom-Mom! I'm goin' over to Tom's!" Without waiting for a reply, she slammed the door and ran back to us. "That covers things. Okay, let's go!"

We retraced the path forged by Tom but did not pause at Tom's backyard. Instead, we shouldered through the bushes that bordered Tom's yard and waded through the weeds and tall grass until we reached the wide veranda. Pressing our noses against the huge, bowed windows, we could view the shadowy interior as we had done so many times before. For us, each time was like the first. The mystery of the great house never waned.

"Let's go in!" said Tom, stepping away from the window.

With only a moment's hesitation, the three of us ran the length of the porch and jumped to the ground. Hugging the house, where the grass did not grow as high, we skirted the north wing until we reached the kitchen door. Freddie and I stood aside as Tom firmly kicked the bottom panel of the door and waited for it to swing open. As caretakers, Freddie's parents seemed to leave a lot to be desired.

"You first," I said, looking at Tom.

"No, it has to be Freddie," Tom answered. "Otherwise, we're breaking in."

Freddie pushed the door open and entered the kitchen. "Like no one's done that before!"

Ignoring the grungy kitchen, we followed Freddie into the dining room. Like the rest of the first floor, it was filled with furniture.

"I love this couch!" I flopped down on an enormous Chesterfield sofa upholstered in faded, green velvet.

"Yeah, we know," Tom replied, crossing into the drawing room. Without stopping, he walked through the room, crossed the wide foyer, and entered the library.

Freddie followed, stopping at the large double doors which led to the white-paneled room. "Mommie says we're not allowed to play the piano."

"Yeah, right!" Tom answered. "We're not supposed to be in here anyway."

By the time I joined them, Tom had opened the big box-grand and was fingering the keys. "Damn! Wish I had a piano!"

"Why don't you ask your parents?" said Freddie, growing impatient.

"Ah, they'd never go for it."

"I'm going upstairs!" I shouted as I bolted for the wide staircase.

"Don't go in the front room! The floor's rotten!" warned Freddie.

"Yeah, we know," answered Tom, closing the piano.

Freddie and Tom followed as I ran ahead. The narrow sitting room on the second floor opened onto the roof of the porch by slender glass panels that flanked a larger window. By the time Freddie and Tom reached the second floor, I was already standing outside.

"Jump!" Tom yelled.

"No thanks." I turned to him and smiled. Fearful of heights, I could only jump with much goading by my peers.

I looked up at the towering trees, their leaves beginning to stir erratically in the freshening breeze. In the distance, beyond the heavily forested front yard, the sky was beginning to darken.

"Storm's coming," I said, as I lowered myself to the flat roof. Swinging my feet over the edge, I leaned back, arms extended behind me. "Could be a big one."

"Hope so," said Freddie, flopping down beside me. "I love a good storm."

Tom lowered himself to the roof next to us. "Want a cigarette?"

"Sure!" we chimed. Both Freddie and I knew that Tom's parents had just returned from a shopping excursion in New York. That meant only one thing to us–cigarettes. The finest chocolate wrapped in real cigarette papers emblazoned with a trio of delicate gold bands. Sold only at Schrafft's at 61 Fifth Avenue, they were made available only to us when our elders ventured northward in search of quality goods and entertainment.

Tom withdrew a narrow plastic cigarette case strikingly similar to those carried by adults. A young gentleman in the making, he passed it to Freddie first. She might be sort of a tom-boy and our playmate, but she was still a girl and destined to be a lady.

As we enjoyed our "smoke," thunder rumbled in the distance. The western sky was black now. A jagged bolt of lightning forked through the sky and disappeared behind the screen of trees. More thunder followed.

"Wow! Look at that!" Freddie breathed.

"Yeah. Cool." Tom feigned flicking an ash from his cigarette.

"Here comes the rain." He unfolded his lanky frame and stood as the first drops splatted against the porch roof. "Better get inside."

Freddie and I followed suit. Within moments, we stood inside the second-floor sitting room, our noses pressed against the window pane. The wind rose, then howled. The rain beat against the glass in a discordant tattoo. Small twigs skittered across the porch roof and disappeared off the edge into oblivion.

It was dark in the house now. No light or candle penetrated the deep shadows. Behind us, a dimly shrouded stairway. We were alone. Just the three of us, and the storm.

3

August 1958 – Christabel McCafferty

FREDDIE'S GREAT UNCLE HAROLD Wilkinson had built the big, white Colonial next to Tom's parents' in the early 1920s. Following the death of Harold's wife, Eunice, in 1955, the house had gone on the market. Now, it sat empty and neglected. It was simply too large by contemporary standards, as most home buyers were building more modest and convenient houses. Too much upkeep was the common description for such architectural dinosaurs.

Freddie, Tom and I lounged on the thick grass beneath a widespread oak in Tom's side yard. It was too hot to do anything but seek the cool shade of the tree. Too hot to go exploring. Too hot to climb trees or explore the cavernous stable behind the Hancock house. Too hot to get into mischief.

"Wow! Look at that!" I said, coming to attention.

A sleek, jet-black Lincoln suddenly turned into the driveway next door. Fancy cars always impressed me. Tom, not so much. Tom's father bought a new car every year, and I was a bit jealous of that fact as well as the fact that they were always oversized, expensive models. My father was more conservative and saw little need to waste money if the car he was driving was "perfectly fine."

"Oh, yeah." Freddie stretched to catch a look. " Mommie said that someone was looking at Uncle Harold's house today."

"You know them?" asked Tom, running his fingers through his thick, blond hair.

"Nah, someone from out of town."

The vehicle slowly crunched its way up the gravel drive before stopping in the parking area behind the house. The driver's door opened, and a large, red-haired man unfolded from the car. For a moment, he paused, gazing up at the house.

"Well, this is it." He seemed to be addressing no one in particular. For several long moments he studied the rear facade and then stuck his head back into the car. "Don't you want to see it?"

Several minutes passed before the passenger door opened and the red-headed stranger was joined by a dour-looking woman. A small hat with a feather perched on her dark-brown hair, which she wore in a severe bun at the nape of her neck. "It's awfully big." Her voice was low and gravely.

The man grinned. "Yeah. I like it."

The woman stared at the man in silence.

"Christy, honey, don't you want to peek inside ?" The man smiled in self-satisfaction.

The feather on the hat quivered as the woman jerked her head to face her husband. "Have you purchased it already?" We could tell she was not pleased.

The big man shrugged. "I put some money down on it. Didn't want it to get away."

"Then you've already made up your mind." It was a statement rather than a question.

"It's refundable. I mean, if you really don't like it."

"As if that's going to make a difference."

At that moment, one of the Lincoln's rear doors swung open. There was a pause, as if the occupant was uncertain about becoming part of the conversation. Then she emerged, deep-brown eyes blinking to adjust to the sudden burst of sunlight.

Christabel McCafferty was stunning. Not really pretty, but striking. There was something about the way she stood there in the car park, one hand pressed to her hip, the other shading her eyes. It was almost as if she was resigned to her fate. And perhaps she was.

Christabel was our age. She resembled neither of her parents. Short, unlike her father; fair, unlike her mother. Blond, nearly ashen, hair. Features finely chiseled in an almost classical way. Christabel lacked any of the coarseness displayed by her parents.

Christabel looked up at the big house and showed no response whatsoever. Suddenly she looked over at the three of us, still lounging in the shade of the tree. Her face showed no recognition, no acknowledgment that we even existed. She stared at us for only a moment and then turned away.

Sighing, Christabel took a deep breath, and began to follow her parents toward the house.

4

Fall 1958 – Christabel Again

I DIDN'T SEE CHRISTABEL McCafferty again until the start of school.

Although she and her parents were in and out of the house during the ensuing weeks, Tom and I did not encounter her. With school fast approaching, he and I were whisked off to Philadelphia for a week of shopping, dining, and live theater.

But Freddie had seen her. She'd actually met and talked with Christabel. The day after the McCafferty family moved into the big Colonial, Freddie's mother had made the obligatory, *welcome to the neighborhood* visit. She had insisted that Freddie accompany her.

When Tom and I pumped Freddie for information, it came forth in a tsunami of disjointed facts and opinions. Once you pressed Freddie's PLAY button, there was no stopping her.

It was August, and the three of us were perched in the top branches of the huge boxwoods that defined what had once been a formal garden behind the Hancock house. This was strictly forbidden because the huge bushes were too fragile for our weight. So much for rules.

Tom stretched one leg along a branch. "So what's she like?"

Freddie feigned contemplation. "Kind of snooty." She paused, searching for the right word. "Aloof."

I sprung to Christabel's defense. "Maybe she's just shy."

"Nah." Freddie shook her head, red pigtails flying. "Snooty. They moved here from Washington. She's a city girl. You can tell that by the way she dresses."

Tom looked perplexed. "Why'd they move here?"

"Her father's retiring. He's some sort of diplomat or something."

"But why Martin's Neck?" Tom persisted.

"Don't know."

Tom grew sarcastic. "What *do* you know?"

Freddie crossed her arms and glared at him. "She's adopted. German war orphan, whatever that means."

I was enthralled. "She told you that?"

"Nah, her mother told Mommie. She never mentioned it to me. Her parents were in Germany or Belgium or somewhere like that after the war ended. That's where they got her."

"Sounds like they bought her," I sneered.

Tom laughed. "Two cartons of cigarettes."

Freddie said nothing but continued to glare at us.

"What else?" Tom prodded.

"She seemed nice enough to me. I felt like she wanted to be friendly but just didn't know how. I guess it's hard moving into a new place where everyone's a stranger."

Freddie was right. Moving into a new place would be challenging in the best of situations. Moving into Martin's Neck was difficult on a level all its own. Assuming that she and her parents would "fit in" was a long shot. One simply did not move into Martin's Neck and instantly become part of the community. It was as if those who moved here were never to be heard from again. Martin's Neck society was static, closed, and, for the most part, cold. At the very least, you had to be born here. It was kind of an unspoken rule. Only if one's parents and grandparents had been born here did one truly belong. This fact did not bode well for Christabel McCafferty and her parents.

The school year began on Tuesday, September 2, the day after Labor Day, as was the tradition. Dressed in our best back-to-school attire, we trudged to the big, brick schoolhouse, its entrance flanked by tall, ivory columns. Like many buildings in Martin's Neck, the school had been built to impress.

Christabel McCafferty was in Freddie's class. I guess that was a good thing, but I had secretly hoped she and I would be classmates.

On that first day, I saw her briefly in the hall, albeit at a distance. Still, I knew it was her. It was in the lunch line that I got a really good look at Christabel once again.

Her class was ahead of mine in line and had already turned the corner leading into the cafeteria. This provided me with a clear view of Christabel for several minutes when the line stalled. She stood talking to Freddie and a couple of other girls as we waited. She looked older than the rest, but that was probably because of her attire. She wore a straight, tweed skirt below a crisp, Ship and Shore blouse. A simple pendant adorned her throat. Unlike many of the girls, Christabel's ashen hair was not pulled back in the obligatory pony tail, but left to fall softly to her shoulders. I remembered my first impression of her and knew I was right. No, she wasn't exceptionally pretty, but she sure had style. I couldn't stop staring. When she smiled at something Freddie said, I felt all warm inside. Was this the girl for whom I had been waiting? Suddenly, at age eleven, my world seemed full of possibilities.

The line began to move, and I lost sight of Christabel as she rounded the corner. Then the sound of her laugh reached me. I kept my place in line and followed Christabel, hoping to hear her musical laughter once more.

5

November 1958 – Cousins

THOMAS JAMES POWELL III, "TJ" for short, my grandfather and patriarch of the Powell family, suffered a stroke and died shortly before Thanksgiving. The holiday was a gloomy one that year. We all went through the motions, but a definite void seemed to invade every facet of our lives.

The "ladies," a group of black women of good family, came to my grandmother's house to prepare and serve the lavish dinner. Drinks were poured into the finest crystal while black hands passed silver trays loaded with tempting hors d'oeuvres and crudités.

While the adults mingled and chatted in the drawing room, we cousins found refuge in our grandmother's morning room. As cousins, we were five in number–Franklin, Howard, Tom, Jane, and me. I always thought it strange that five siblings would each only have one child. I suppose that says something about the love and nurturing our parents received as children, or lack thereof. Beyond an occasional game of checkers with my grandfather, my maternal grandparents always seemed distant and preoccupied. In later years, we would compare notes and draw the same conclusions–our grandparents really didn't enjoy being parents, let alone being grandparents.

The five of us were a mixed bag. Tom and I headed the list, children of the two eldest Powell siblings, Frederick and Victoria, respectively. My Aunt Valerie, the next in line, bore Jane, who, at seven, was the youngest of our quintet. Howard was the son of my Uncle Tom,

Thomas James Powell IV. I always thought it strange that Uncle Fred and Aunt Harriet named their son Tom when the naming right clearly belonged to Uncle Tom and Aunt Caroline. Lastly, there was Franklin, the youngest of us boys by two years and son of the youngest of the Powell offspring, Uncle John and his wife, Melissa.

The door of the morning room opened as Regina Dodd shouldered her way in. She carried a large tray loaded with glasses of punch and an oversized platter of goodies.

Regina had been my nanny during the first months of my life. Reports have it that my mother demanded Regina do everything for me. This included bathing, diapering, feeding, and generally mothering me. After eighteen months of this, Regina finally confronted my mother, asking, "When are you going to learn to take care of your own child?" No one seems to remember my mother's response, but Regina left that day, dumping me into the arms of a woman who had no idea of what it meant to be a mother.

Regina set the snack tray on the coffee table and smiled. "You kids enjoy this. I put it all together by myself."

A chorus of "thank yous" erupted as Regina passed around the cups of fruit punch. Regina was our favorite of the ladies because she always gave us a kiss and a hug whenever she saw us. Her affection wasn't confined just to the walls of our family homes.

"Now one of you call if there's anything you need." She flashed a soft, wide smile and closed the door behind her.

Tom picked up a cracker smeared with some sort of cheese spread and looked at me. "Whatdidya get from Pop-Pop?"

I swallowed my punch quickly. "Money."

Tom and Howard laughed. Jane and Franklin sat with surprised looks on their faces.

Howard snorted. "We *all* got money."

"I got a box," said Jane innocently.

Franklin looked across at her. "A box?"

Jane smiled. "A pretty box. With shiny things all over the lid."

Tom nodded. "Mother of Pearl. That was Pop-Pop's jewelry box. He bought it on their trip to Turkey."

"I remember it." What child wouldn't? As Jane said, it was covered in little, shiny triangles arranged in an intricate mosaic. It virtually sparkled whenever the sun caught it.

Tom continued, "I got his Waterman desk set. It's cool! Green marble with my birth date on it. Mom says it was given to him when he served on the Levy Court to commemorate the birth of his first grandchild." Tom smiled. "That would be me!"

Not to be outdone, I interrupted. " I got his diamond cufflinks."

"And I got his pocket watch," added Franklin.

Tom turned to Howard. "What about you?"

Howard shrugged. "Sapphire shirt studs. Don't see what good they are."

I laughed. "They take the place of buttons when you're really dressed up."

"So?" Howard wasn't convinced.

"So you'll get plenty of use out of them when you get older."

"Yeah, sure," he scoffed.

Jane picked up another cracker. "I bet they're pretty."

"I guess so."

Tom laughed. "Well, think of it as money in the bank. If you ever get hard up, you can always sell them."

That occasion came more quickly than we could have imagined. In January 1959, Howard's father filed for bankruptcy. No one saw it coming, least of all, us children.

Uncle Tom owned a large car dealership on the outskirts of Martin's Neck. He sold *only the best*: Cadillacs, Buicks, Oldsmobiles. Somehow, dealing in high-priced, luxury automobiles had not paid off as well as he had hoped.

Within the family, the whole affair was quite hush-hush, something not to be discussed at the dinner table. My Grandmother Powell was heard to utter, "Thank God TJ didn't live to see this." The remarks of Uncle Tom's siblings were less compassionate. It wasn't so much the money as the social disgrace of it all. Powells simply didn't do things like that. They were different from other people and above common problems like bankruptcy.

Under the guise of righting wrongs, Uncle Tom and Aunt Caroline sold their big house and moved in with our Grandmother Powell. As a solution, it was far from satisfactory.

Aunt Caroline managed to survive on a day-to-day basis under the ever-watchful eye of our grandmother. Knowing Grandmother Powell, she probably blamed Aunt Caroline for the whole thing.

Poor Howard didn't fare as well. Grandmother Powell kept him trapped tightly under her thumb, directing his every move. Whenever he came to my house or Tom's house to play, he never wanted to go back home. Of course, in this case, home was simply a cold pile of bricks, both inside and out. Finding a place of true refuge or sanctuary was not easy in the Powell family.

In the end, the whole mess sorted itself out. Suddenly, there was money again. Debts were satisfied. Uncle Tom bought a sleek, Bauhaus-style home on a large parcel of land just outside of town, and he and his family made a hasty exodus from my grandmother's foreboding pile. All within a short span of four months.

When the Powell families put their collective minds together, things got done, no matter who tried to get in the way.

6

1959 – Dancing

THE WINTER OF 1959 was like any other in a small town. The holidays were behind us, and the cold, dark winter loomed ahead. As kids, we didn't let that bother us. Collectively, we made sure there was always something happening. This year led to a series of weekly parties that moved from house to house among our classmates.

We were a close-knit class ... only fifty-five in number. Most of us had been in school together since kindergarten. Occasionally, someone like Christabel McCafferty would move into Martin's Neck, but most of us were children of the old guard. We were friends; our parents were friends; our grandparents were friends. There was a certain comfort and solidity to such a life. Our teachers all knew us and our families. If they were new to Martin's Neck, they soon learned. We knew what was expected of us and typically delivered. That's not to say we didn't make a few unscheduled excursions into the forbidden, though most of that would come later. For now, in the sixth grade, we played our cards close to our chests.

Friday nights were reserved for parties. This left Saturday nights free. The local movie theater always showed double features on Saturday night, and these were not to be missed. Besides, Friday night seemed like the logical extension of the final school day.

The setting for most parties was the basements of our parents' homes. Most basements in Martin's Neck had been converted into rec rooms or TV rooms and, as such, made the perfect place for social gatherings. The locale also provided a perfect way for our parents to chaperone without having to attend.

Our gatherings were largely what one would imagine. Plenty of chips, pretzels, and sodas ... and music. Music was always being played from a newly acquired record player or a parent's more sophisticated hi-fi system. With music, came dance. There was always dancing, and our generation was hooked on it.

Tom and I, like many of our peers, had learned the basics from our ballroom dance classes. The rest was absorbed by watching *American Bandstand* and *The Grady and Hurst Show*. The end result was that everyone danced until they could dance no more. And then they danced some more.

It was at one of these parties that I finally came face to face with Christabel McCafferty. She was standing alone, sipping a soda–from a glass, of course–and watching the dancers. I sort of sidled up to her and stood, following her gaze upon the dance floor. When the silence became too awkward, I finally summoned the courage to speak.

"Hi."

She turned and looked at me. There was no smile, simply an appraising stare.

"Hello."

Seeming to lose all of my social graces, I stammered. "I'm Marc."

She looked away and down at her drink. "I know."

"You live next to my cousin, Tom."

"Yes."

"I've seen you there." Our conversation was quickly spiraling from awkward to just plain silly.

"You have?" She looked at me archly, as if suddenly aware of a newly discovered stalker.

"Yeah." Another pause. "When I've been over to his house."

The awaited response never came, and I stumbled ahead. "You know Freddie Clifton, don't you?"

"Sure. She lives two doors down."

"She's my fourth cousin, or something like that."

Christabel smiled to herself. "That's nice."

Once more at sea, I foundered. "Feel like dancing?"

"Okay." She set her glass on a nearby table and then turned to face me. It was then that she really smiled.

My smile was instantaneous. I held out my hand, and she took it. We walked onto the dance floor and slipped smoothly into a Lindy

Hop to the strains of Bill Haley and His Comets. It was the most natural thing in the world. It felt good. More than good, actually. It felt perfect.

I sent Christabel twirling away from me and then drew her back. She smiled and then laughed—a lilting, musical sound. It was obvious that she loved to dance. And I loved to dance. Especially now. Especially with Christabel McCafferty.

7

1959 – Beatrice

TOM AND I WERE more like brothers than cousins–a closeness that would remain for the rest of our lives. Rarely did a weekend pass that we did not spend time together, either at his parents' home or mine. Although we had fun whenever Tom spent the weekend at my house, we enjoyed much more freedom while staying at his.

Uncle Fred and Aunt Harriet were the social pillars of Martin's Neck society. When not entertaining at home, they were traveling. It was common practice for them to suddenly decide on a Friday afternoon to run off to Philadelphia or New York for the weekend. When these excursions were planned in advance, Tom and I were usually left in the care of Tom's grandmother, Elena Cookman. On spur-of-the-moment departures, we would be left at home in the care of George Sawyer.

George had been with the Powells for two years now and had recently turned nineteen. He had graduated from dusting and cleaning to overseeing the washing and ironing, and he handled most of the meal preparation. Aunt Harriet treated George with some condescension, but still seemed perfectly comfortable leaving us in his care whenever the occasion arose. She never seemed to question the suitability of her decision and neither did my parents. Of course, being Powells, they were of a like mind and shared the same distorted outlook on life.

With George in charge, Tom and I had free rein to do whatever we wanted. If something went awry, George would have to answer to

Uncle Fred and Aunt Harriet upon their return. He was older and was supposed to know better.

On one such day, Tom and I hoofed it down the hill from his house to the little business district of Martin's Neck. Our favorite haunt was The Mercantile, a huge store that sold everything imaginable. Of course, such an establishment had a wonderful toy department. On this particular day, Tom and I were in the market for balsa wood fliers, one of our favorite, regular purchases. These little airplanes were a delight. With various adjustments to the wings and tail, they would perform either long, straight flights or fascinating loop de loops.

As we trudged back up the hill, our purchases in hand, the first rain drops began to fall. Picking up speed, we raced to the house and cleared the doorway just as the real deluge began. Laughing at our near miss, we stood at the open doorway watching the rain while acknowledging that "flight school" would need to be cancelled for the day. Balsa fliers did not hold up well in the rain.

"What we goin' to do now?" I asked with a sigh.

Tom smiled and closed the door. "You'll see."

I followed him through the kitchen and then the big dining room until we reached the long drawing room at the front of the house. It was a sizeable area, nearly thirty feet in length, populated with Aunt Harriet's assortment of camelback sofas and wing chairs. The mahogany tables glowed in the fading light, and the dour portraits stared blankly at our intrusion.

Tom turned to me and smiled. "Whatdya think?"

"Your mom would have a fit if we broke anything."

Tom tore into his package and began assembling the little plane. "Aw, we're not gonna break anything."

Sitting beside Tom on an oversized Sarouk rug, I busily attacked my plane. Tom was done first and ran to stand in the large, bay window. Deftly, he lifted the plane and sent it soaring down the length of the room. Without an accompanying breeze, it floated lazily above the furniture, just missing the bottom of the large, crystal chandelier.

Standing, I laughed at his effort. "You're gonna have to do better than that." I launched my glider and watched as it clipped the high back of one of the chairs before crashing pathetically to the floor below.

Retrieving his plane, Tom laughed. "Watch this!" He stood again in the big bay window and hurled the tiny glider with all his force. The wings were set for a straight flight, and the toy aircraft flew swiftly toward the mantelpiece. For a moment we held our collective breath as the plane narrowly cleared the assortment of lusterware on the mantle. Beatrice was not so lucky.

Beatrice was a staid but beautiful woman whose oil on canvas portrait presided over the fireplace. She wore a draped, rose-beige garment, and her hair was hidden by a matching turban. She had occupied this place of honor for as long as I could remember.

Mouths open wide, Tom and I watched as the little plane collided with the canvas, bounced off the mantle, and fell to the marble hearth.

"Oh, shit!" Tom ran toward the fireplace. Commandeering a footstool, he climbed up to investigate the damage. "Oh, shit, shit, *shit!*" He fingered the narrow hole in the canvas.

"What you two doin'?"

George Sawyer stood at the doorway to the dining room, a dish towel in his right hand, a scowl on his face. "Wait till Miz Powell sees that!"

Tom's head snapped around. "Who's gonna tell her?"

"Me!" There was taunt mixed with pride in his voice.

Tom jumped down from the stool. "You do, and I'm gonna tell her you sneaked out last night to go drinking and left us alone."

George's face turned red. "Did not!"

"Did, too!" sneered Tom.

"Can't prove it." George insisted, feeling a bit smugger.

Tom laughed. "Don't have to. Who's she gonna believe? Me or you?"

Defeated, George turned quickly away. "There's still goin' to be hell to pay."

Of course George was right. There was hell to pay, and Tom and I were the ones to pay it. Aunt Harriet noticed the rip in the canvas immediately and quickly laid the blame where it belonged. George said nothing; he didn't have to.

The portrait of Beatrice was removed from her place of honor and shipped to a Philadelphia artist for repairs. She returned eventually, but not to the drawing room, having been deemed "damaged goods." Rather, Beatrice was relocated to the first-floor guest bedroom and hung above the fireplace, her honor forever soiled.

Over fifty years later, I pawed through Aunt Harriet's belongings at a local auction house. Following her death, everything was to be sold. All the "good stuff" was displayed in the main auction barn. The contents of the attics and cellars had been relegated to a lesser venue to be auctioned at a later, less auspicious date. It was there that I found the heavily carved walnut frame that had once encased Beatrice's portrait. Tattered remnants of the canvas still clung to the edges of the wood where the painting had been cut from the frame. I had no idea what had happened to this family possession, and I never would.

Always a woman of mystery, Beatrice had simply disappeared without ever divulging her secrets.

8

Summer 1959 – Granny Steadman

FREDDIE AND CHRISTABEL SAT at the long trestle table that dominated the center of the Clifton's big kitchen. They busily attended to the last of their homework when the telephone on the wall suddenly rang out.

Freddie threw down her pencil and rose to answer the phone. "Clifton residence." A pause followed.

"Well, Mommie and Daddy went to Philadelphia last weekend to visit Aunt Mary and Uncle Harold Thayer." Freddie paused again, thinking. "So I spent the weekend with Mary Elizabeth Farmer and her parents while they were away."

Another pause. "No, Mom-Mom Bertha hasn't been anyplace." Freddie looked at Christabel and rolled her eyes. "You, too. Bye."

Freddie racked the receiver and shook her head. "Jeez, Louise!"

"What was that all about?" Christabel asked.

"Weekly newsletter. Mrs. Steadman ... Marc's grandmother."

Christabel looked confused. "Newsletter?"

"Gossip column." Freddie laughed and took her seat.

"You mean for the paper?"

Freddie nodded. "Every week. Regular as clockwork. Mrs. Steadman calls to see what everyone has been doing."

Christabel was astounded. "And they print that stuff?"

"Every week. Regular as clockwork." She laughed, and struck an affected pose. "Did you know that Miss Fredricka Clifton was the weekend guest of Miss Mary Elizabeth Farmer at her parents' home on Chelsea Boulevard."

"You're kidding!"

Freddie shook her head. "Nope. Every week in the *Martin's Neck Chronicle*. Takes up a whole page."

"Oh, my God! This is the boonies!"

"No, my dear Christabel, it's what we call the society page. Rest assured, Washington doesn't have anything on us."

Christabel returned to her schoolwork. "I still don't believe it."

"Read it some time. It's always good for a laugh."

"Yeah, as if anyone cares."

—

Granny Steadman kept her finger on the pulse of Martin's Neck, and she was a force not to be taken lightly. She knew everyone and most of their family history as well as their current business. Residents often went out of their way to avoid her for fear of what might show up in her weekly column. Nothing was sacred, and more than a few inhabitants had discovered items of their dirty laundry displayed within the pages of the *Martin's Neck Chronicle*.

But while the adults, my mother included, treated her with a cautious, hands-off attitude, the younger sect loved her. In contrast to my Grandmother Powell, she was warm and loving. Most importantly, Granny Steadman was fun. She was a great storyteller with an imagination that thrilled our young minds.

My grandfather, Phillip Steadman, had died long before I was born. Granny Steadman had raised my father for most of his teenage years. Now considered a grand dame, she presided over her world from her big, white Victorian house that sat perched at the corner of Magnolia Street and Sheffield Avenue.

As a young child, I spent many hours with her while my father worked and my mother attended to numerous social obligations. I would lay reading on the divan in her study or play with my toys in the center of the Kerman carpet while she sat at her desk, dialing, talking and then recording her findings, as if compiling the written history of the known, free world. In her own way, I guess she was.

It was on those days when Granny Steadman declared a "holiday" that she truly bloomed. The weather had to be perfect: the right amount of sunshine, the proper breeze, the perfect temperature. She would greet me at the door and say, "I think today is a day we need to spend at the campground. Why don't you run around and see who wants to go? I've already got the basket ready."

A boy on a mission, I would run from house to house marshaling the troops. "Granny's goin' to the campground today. Wanna come?"

Rarely was there a negative response. After making my rounds, I would return to her corner, neighborhood kids walking along side or trailing behind. Sometimes as few as five; often as many as fifteen. Somehow, she always packed enough food in her basket for any size army of hungry mouths.

On those excursions, Granny always wore the large, straw garden hat reserved for the journey. It was forever complimented by a long, flowered, cotton dress and Granny's "sensible shoes." Sensible they may have been, but they were nonetheless heels, though shorter and wider than her dress heels. Together our caravan would set out down Mulberry Street, Granny clutching a tall walking stick, we kids sharing the burden of the basket with eager hands.

The campground was an old, Methodist camp meeting place situated on the north bank of the Martin's River. It consisted of a series of rough tent-like cottages arranged in a circle around a large, open tabernacle. The entire site was shaded by tall pine trees that kept the area cool even on the hottest days. The campground was a forty-five-minute walk from Granny's corner. But even the walk was fun. We'd run ahead, chasing butterflies before scampering back to stoop and pick Queen Anne's lace. We would watch birds and hunt for turtles along the way. On those days, the whole world was a Louis Carroll-fueled land of adventure and surprise.

Leaving the dusty road behind, we found refuge among the tall, cool pines. The tents sat in their solemn circle, doors and windows shuttered. The big tabernacle brooded about its loss of importance.

None of this mattered to our merry band. The first hours were filled with games and much whooping and hollering. We played all our favorites: kitty wants a corner; red light, green light; and, of course, tag and hide-and-seek. When our energy waned, we'd all collapse on the benches of the tabernacle. Granny would bring forth the big wicker basket and dole out her collection of goodies. Granny was not a gourmet. She disdained my mother's luncheon spreads that were better than many peoples dinners and instead was known for "just plain cookin'." The picnic menu never changed: sandwiches of potted meat, Kraft Cheez Whiz, or peanut butter. These were washed down with

Kool-Aid, at least two different flavors from which to choose. The whole was topped off with Oreos or Nutter Butters ... whichever happened to be on sale at the time.

With lunch behind us, we would yawn, stretch, and begin to relax, making ready for what would soon follow. Granny was a storyteller supreme who could keep us mesmerized for hours. Many of the stories we had heard over and over, but it made no difference. We greeted them like old friends come for a visit. She would often launch into one of our favorites. It was the continuing saga of a group of treasure hunters whose dirigible had crashed in the jungles of darkest Africa. We sat transfixed as the story of their struggles and exploits unfolded once again. Of course, there were new stories as well. How she could come up with so many was a mystery. My one regret is that I never wrote them all down.

By late afternoon, we would wind our way back to the corner of Mulberry Street and Sheffield Avenue. Granny's hat might have begun to droop a little, and her step may have been a bit slower, but she still kept up the pace.

In later years, especially after her death, Granny Steadman would be remembered for many things, but I think these childhood adventures remained the most vivid in our memories.

9

1960 – Victoria Powell Steadman

MY MOTHER HATED GRANNY Steadman. As a child, I had no knowledge of this fact, but, now, in retrospect, I know it was true. I'm not sure why she hated her. My guess is that it happened after my mother moved in with Granny.

My parents were married during the second World War. My father was in the Navy at the time and finding and establishing a home was not part of their immediate plans. Granny Steadman lived alone, whereas Grandfather and Grandmother Powell still had children at home. I don't know whose idea it was that Victoria Powell move in with Granny Steadman, but it was a match made in hell.

Of course, Grandfather and Grandmother Powell were not exactly pleased with my mother's choice of a husband. Although arranged marriage was not practiced in Martin's Neck, it had been long assumed that their darling Victoria would marry Isaac Hobson. Isaac was the only child of a wealthy, land-owning family that resided outside of Martin's Neck. My mother and Isaac had been an on-again, off-again item for several years, until she got to know my father. Apparently, after that, poor Isaac never had a chance. My mother knew what she wanted and would damn well have it. And she wanted Marc.

Matthew Steadman was certainly a nice enough young man, but the Steadmans were not the social equals of the Powells. I have no idea how such rankings were established, but they definitely did exist. Grandfather Powell had been a banker, and I guess there was a certain prestige associated with that title. Grandfather Steadman had captained his own schooner and plied his trade up and down the Eastern Seaboard. Still, he was classified as a working man.

Cap Steadman, as he was known, died when my father was sixteen. Granny Steadman never remarried; she raised her son by herself. I suppose that in the scheme of things, everyone thought my mother would be some sort of help to Granny or, at the very least, would provide company for her.

Thus it happened that Victoria Powell Steadman moved into Granny's sizeable, old Victorian house on the corner of Magnolia Street and Sheffield Avenue. Her arrival was accompanied by a large upright piano and a massive wardrobe, and she was quickly ensconced in Granny's front guest room with its ornate oak furnishings. How the tiny closet accommodated all my mother's clothes was a mystery that remains unexplained.

No one ever talked about that time in my parents' lives because it was certainly not a happy one. My mother was in a constant worry about my father's safety while still trying to maintain a somewhat normal life. She entertained at bridge on a regular basis, lunched with friends, and found a job as a secretary working for a local manufacturing company. Whenever my father's ship was in port, she'd dash off to the Philadelphia Navy Yard to see him.

―

At home, life continued in a restrained silence punctuated with occasional angry outbursts when something contradicted my mother's wishes or schedule. Two vastly different women, residing in the same house, simply did not work.

Physically, they were direct opposites. Granny was tall for her time, gaunt with graying blond hair that she wore in a severe French twist at the back of her head. Mother was short and petite with a head of shoulder-length, thick black hair.

Even their church affiliations differed. Although they were both Methodists, Granny was an active member at the smaller, less prestigious church at the bottom of the hill. Mother, on the other hand, had been born and raised in the big, fancy Methodist church at the top of the hill. Why this should make so much difference, I will never understand. Yet, it did.

As with church, their whole value structures were in contrast. My mother was all about show, nice clothes, and social functions. Granny was the opposite. She wore the same dress, day after day, never caring what other people thought. She also spent most of her time at home. Granny was politically active in the Democratic Party, which was a continuing embarrassment to my mother. The Powells had been staunch Republicans for generations.

In later years, my mother reflected upon what she referred to as "a callously painful incident." In retrospect, I still don't know why it was such an issue for her, but I guess it simply underlined her heated relationship with Granny.

Given my mother's concern for the opinions of others, Granny's drawing room, where my mother did most of her entertaining, had suddenly become an issue. The room was nice enough. The furniture, carpet, and drapes were of good quality. It was simply dated and stuffy.

In an effort to brighten her surroundings, my mother ordered a bolt of English, cabbage rose-covered fabric from a merchant in Philadelphia. Slipcovers were in vogue, and the colorful print would much improve the overstuffed sofa and chairs. Being Victoria Powell Steadman, she knew exactly what she wanted. Unfortunately, the upholsterer she hired was very busy at the time. Thus, the bolt of fabric languished in the corner of Mother's bedroom.

Sometime later, my mother rushed off to Philadelphia to see my father for several days. Granny, in an effort to ease some of the tension, decided that she was more than capable of constructing the desired slipcovers and set to work. When my mother returned, Granny met her at the door smiling.

"I have a surprise for you."

Being naturally suspicious, the comment alarmed my mother as she followed Granny into the drawing room. She stood in stunned silence. The sofa and two arm chairs now sported bright, colorful slipcovers.

"What have you done?" My mother was livid.

Granny was immediately confused. "I thought you'd like them."

"Well, I don't!" My mother took a step toward one of the chairs. "They're all wrong!"

"What's wrong with them?"

She leaned down and grasped the end of the dust ruffle. "The ruffle. It's all wrong!"

Granny was perplexed. "Why?"

My mother turned and glared at her. "*Why?* Just look at it! It's supposed to be gathered and flouncy. You've done a box pleat. It's all wrong. It looks terrible!" My mother stormed out of the room and up the stairs leaving Granny alone with her disaster.

A box pleat seems like such a small thing, but it's over such issues that wars are fought. It was yet another battle lost by my mother to Granny's good intentions. Still, the box pleats remained until I inherited the house upon Granny's death. They stood as a constant reminder of blood shed over petty grievances.

10

Summer 1960 – Burton's Brae Beach

THE SUMMER OF 1960 marked the end of our childhood summers in Martin's Neck. Uncle Fred and Aunt Harriet's beach house was finally completed, and the rest of our summers would be spent with them at Burton's Brae Beach. Although we missed being at the center of things, Tom and I loved the beach. It seemed that we spent every summer there together, swimming in the bay, walking along the sandy shores, building sandcastles and lighting bonfires on an almost daily basis.

Powell Cottage was the last house at the southern end of the beach community. Beyond that, the dirt roadway stretched through a forest of thick, scrub pine and culminated at a large, vacant cottage that was the sort of place from which ghost stories grow. Legend had it that Dr. Fleming had built the Victorian pile as a vacation home for his wife, Josephine, only to learn later that she was having an affair with their architect. In a fit of rage, the doctor ultimately killed Josephine and then took his own life. Since then, the house had sat shuttered and silent, accessible only to those who knew its secrets. The rest of the land was untouched and uninhabited. It became the perfect place for our never-ending adventures.

Uncle Fred had purchased an old army jeep, which, despite our youthful ages, became our main source of transportation. On any given day, Tom and I would jump into the vehicle and head for the abandoned Fleming cottage. There we would leave the jeep and set out on foot.

It was a typical sunny afternoon as Tom careened to a stop and killed the engine. The jeep's motor sputtered and coughed before finally dying. Taking a deep breath, Tom smiled. "What you want to do today?"

I shrugged. "Might as well check out the old jetty." I jumped from the jeep and joined Tom on the driver's side. Together, we set off through the sand-entrenched pines until they fell away to reveal the wide, sandy beach. From midway of the beach, the rocky structure of the jetty extended out into the bay. Heavy weathered beams formed the framework holding in place the large granite stones. It was a treacherous piece of construction, just perfect for climbing and exploring. Midway down its length a large, reinforced concrete foundation was all that remained of the original beacon. Bent and rusted rebar punctuated the uneven concrete. Still, it was the perfect vantage point as far as we were concerned.

Carefully, we wound our way down the rocky length until the foundation platform was within reach. Grabbing a twisted piece of rebar, Tom pulled himself up, grasped the edge of the platform, and hauled himself up onto the flat surface. As the shorter of the two, I had a more difficult time, but Tom's strong grasp soon had me sitting beside him.

It was a glorious day. The sky was a clear, crisp blue, devoid of humidity. The gentle waves lapped at the rocks closest to the water. Around us, gulls and terns wheeled and cried, upset that we had usurped their post.

Tom stretched and leaned backward. "So, what's going on?" The tone of his voice was calm and friendly, not wheedling or prying.

Caught off guard, I shot him a glance. "What do you mean?"

"Something's up. I can tell. You're too quiet. What's on your mind?"

I shrugged. "Nothing."

"Christabel?"

I laughed. "Christabel is *always* on my mind."

Tom's laughter joined mine. "Don't I know it?"

"That obvious, huh?"

A snicker from Tom. "Just a little."

Silence ensued. The gulls and terns continued their chorus. The sun ducked behind a fluffy, white cloud, sending a shadow their way.

"So, what is it? She giving you a hard time?"

I shook my head. "No, it's not her."

"Who then?"

I sighed. "Mom and Dad."

"What about?"

I paused, searching for the right words. "They want to send me off to military school."

"No way!"

"That's what *I* said."

"How'd they take it?"

"They ignored me. As usual."

"Are you going?"

"Not if I can help it."

Tom sat and stared at me. "Where is this place?"

I shrugged. "Connecticut or New York. Somewhere like that. It's called the Dewey Academy. Named after some naval hero."

"Jeez!"

"Exactly."

"What brought all this on? I thought they only sent bad kids to places like that." Tom laughed. "You do something really bad I don't know about?"

"Don't I wish." I sighed. "Nah, Dad says it'll make a man out of me. Good discipline, good values, all that bullshit."

"Yeah, right." Tom paused. "What did your mom have to say?"

I snorted. "Just what she always says ... nothing. As far as she's concerned, my dad never made a wrong decision in his life. She just follows blindly along."

"You gotta be shittin' me!"

"Plus she'd like to get me away from Christabel."

"Why?"

"Ah, she's always saying we're too young to have a real relationship."

"How long has this been going on?"

"There've been rumblings for months, Tom."

"And you're just telling me now?" His tone was hurt and angry.

I shrugged. "I kept thinking it would pass."

Tom paused again. "I bet your granny doesn't agree with you going."

"Doesn't matter what she thinks. She has no voting rights in our house. Dad's the captain of that ship."

"So I've noticed."

There was silence again. I didn't want to talk about it, but I had to talk to someone. Tom was my primary confidant. He alone would understand how I really felt. But, like me, he was also powerless to do anything about the situation.

"I don't want to leave my home, all my friends. I was really looking forward to starting junior high here at Martin's Neck."

"Me, too. It wouldn't be the same without you."

"Damn, damn, and double damn!"

"Have you told Christabel?"

I shook my head. "No. I kept hoping they'd have a change of heart, but they're heartless."

"She's not going to be happy."

"That makes two of us."

"Three."

I wanted to cry. Everything suddenly seemed so hopeless. "What the hell am I going to do, Tom?"

Tom sighed. "I don't know, but we've got to think of something."

11

Fall 1960 – Desperate Measures

THE REST OF THE summer passed in a foggy haze. Every day and every night were colored by the impending change in my life. Where was the answer? Where was the way out?

Good to his word, Tom thought up a variety of scenarios to get me out of my predicament. None of them held water.

Tom leaned back against the tall, Victorian headboard of his bed. Christabel and Freddie lounged at the foot, and I sat perched on the edge to Tom's left. Summer was over. Powell Cottage had been closed for the season. The day of my departure loomed menacingly, and still, no plan had been hatched.

Tom stretched and yawned. "I say you take the train to Miami. Go live with Uncle Leland and Aunt Charlene."

"And how am I supposed to get to Wilmington to catch the train?"

"Take a bus. Hitchhike."

Christabel shook her head. "Tom, be reasonable."

"The moment I'd arrive in Miami, Uncle Leland would be on the phone to my folks."

Freddie rolled over onto her back and stared at the ceiling. "Parents are such pains in the ass!"

I laughed. "Mine sure are."

Tom snickered. "Mine aren't. They're never here."

Freddie glared at him. "You're lucky! My parents kowtow to Bertha Mae like she's the Queen of Sheba."

Tom laughed. "The Queen of Sheba was black."

"Black, white, who cares? Bertha Mae controls the purse strings, and that's all that matters. They even turned over the master bedroom to her. Now *they're* sleeping in a guest room on the third floor."

Christabel looked at us with disdain. "You ought to be thankful. You should see my father when he's drinking. Nasty, nasty, nasty."

Freddie turned to look at her friend. "Why does your mother put up with that?"

"She's too busy smoking cigarettes and fighting depression to care."

"Sounds like great fun," Tom said.

"A real hoot."

Freddie sat upright and sighed. "We're not much help, are we?"

I offered a weak smile. "I don't think there's much help to be had. Mom and Dad have made up their minds. Enrolled me right after we visited the school last month. Already been fitted for my uniforms."

"Uniforms. Yuck!" Christabel twisted her face into a scorn. "I hate uniforms."

Tom laughed. "I thought all girls liked a guy in uniform."

"Not when you've seen as many as I have. Back in Washington, our house was overrun with uniformed staff. Most of them were a bunch of jerks."

I sighed. "Then I ought to fit right in."

Christabel glared at me. "Don't you dare say that!"

I shrugged. "This whole thing is depressing the hell out of me."

"Marc Steadman!" George Sawyer's voice echoed up the rear stairway. "Your father's here!"

I jumped off the edge of the bed. "Got to go. Can't keep the old man waiting."

Christabel rose and kissed me lightly on the cheek. "Call me tonight if you can."

"I will."

Freddie wrapped her arms around me and laid her head on my shoulder. "You take care, sweetie. Everything's going to be all right."

"I hope so."

"Marc! Get a move on!" It was my father's voice this time. "Your mother's waiting on us for dinner!"

I navigated the narrow, steep stairway that serviced the wing in which Tom's bedroom was located. My father waited at the foot, just outside the door that led into the dining room.

"About time."

"Sorry."

I followed him through the dining room and the big kitchen beyond to the driveway where his truck awaited. The white pick-up sported the Steadman and Son logo. My father owned and operated a large building supply company and a construction company, each bearing that name. The plan was for me to eventually become a part of that conglomerate. I was less than enthusiastic about the idea.

———

Dad and I rode in silence. Our once amiable relationship had quickly become strained with the burden imposed by the Dewey Academy. Where once our house had been somewhat of a family home, it now felt uncomfortable and cold. Gone was the occasional bantering, the sharing of local news and gossip. I had gone from being the golden boy to being the problem child in one quick step.

"Marc, I just don't understand why you don't want to go to Dewey. It's a great place for a young man to grow up."

Any argument was futile, but I launched into one anyway. "I like my life the way it is."

"I understand that, but part of life includes growing up."

"Can't I grow up here in Martin's Neck? With my friends?"

"That's not the issue."

"It is for me."

My father shot a look in my direction. "Careful, young man. I don't like that tone."

"Sorry."

"You have to recognize that your mother and I want more for you than what Martin's Neck has to offer."

"What's wrong with Martin's Neck?"

My father sighed. "Nothing. Martin's Neck is just fine. But you need ... broadening. You need to understand the world before you can be a viable part of it."

"Whatever."

"There's that tone again."

"Sorry."

Dad turned into the wide, paved driveway. In the distance, the lights of the rambling house glowed in the twilight. My parents had built the house on thirty acres of forest left to my father by my Grandfather Steadman. As was my mother's wish, the house was a large Cape Cod-style structure with an overactive thyroid that reminded me of the Raleigh Tavern in Williamsburg. The main body of the house boasted a wide front porch and seven dormer windows. To the left, a dormered wing housed the master suite. To the right, another dormered wing housed the garages. Behind the whole was another wing containing the kitchen, great room, and a screened porch. My rooms were above the garage, a fair distance from my parents' enclave. The entire dwelling was furnished with eighteenth-century antiques and expensive reproductions: Chippendale, Queen Anne, Hepplewhite, Sheraton, Adams. You name it, we owned it.

My mother insisted that our evening meals take place in the formal dining room—by candlelight, of course. Tonight was no different. Our once-lively conversations were now replaced by silence. The meal was fine, but I had no appetite. I messed and fiddled with my food, moving it from one section of the Wedgewood plate to another.

Mother looked over her upraised fork. "Aren't you hungry?"

"Guess not."

"Then why don't you asked to be excused?" My father's voice was gruff.

I stared solemnly at him and paused. "May I be excused?

He didn't return the stare but concentrated on the food in front of him. "Yes, you may."

I laid down my fork and pushed back my chair. Without further comment, I exited the dining room to the rear hall that housed the staircase to my rooms. My suite was comprised of a bedroom, a study, a dressing room, and bath. Even here my mother's influence was apparent. What thirteen-year-old chooses a maple, four-poster bed and a Queen Anne highboy?

The bedroom was dark and unwelcoming. Its atmosphere wasn't going to help my mood. I sought refuge in my study and stretched out on the wide window seat. *Call Christabel. Call Christabel.* "Call me tonight, if you can," she'd said.

I reached for the wall phone and dialed her number. She answered on the third ring.

"Hello."

I sighed. "It's me."

"How are things?"

"Tense. I was pretty much asked to leave the dinner table."

"Oh, Marc. I'm sorry."

"Don't be. It was obvious they didn't want me there."

"You don't know that."

"I talked a bit with my father on the way home. He's not budging."

"Did you expect him to?"

"No. Not really."

"My father's the same way. Once he's made up his mind, there's no turning him around."

The conversation stalled.

"What am I supposed to do?"

Christabel sighed. "I don't know. What can you do? They're your parents."

"Tell me about it!"

"It doesn't seem to me that you have any options. If they want you to go, then how can you stop them?"

"I guess I could dig in my heels and throw a hissy fit. Go screaming and yelling as they drag me to the front door of the school." I laughed. "They'd love that."

"We both know you're not going to do that."

"I feel like it." I paused. "I just feel like screaming and screaming and screaming. It's like no one's listening to me. No one cares about how I feel."

"I care."

"You don't count."

"Thanks a lot." Christabel feigned indignation.

"You know what I mean."

"Yeah, I do."

"I just don't understand why they won't listen to me. Can't they see I'm going to be miserable if I go away to that school?"

"They think they're doing what's in your best interest." Christabel paused. "I don't want you to go. But maybe they're right."

My temper flared suddenly at her remark. "Oh, please! Not you, too! Jesus! Cut me a break!"

"Marc! I don't agree with what they're doing, but how do you expect to change it? You may have to try and make the best out of a bad situation. What other choice do you have?"

"Well, thanks for nothing!"

"Marc."

"I'm looking for help here, and you go siding with my parents!"

"I'm not siding with your parents. I don't want you to go. I just don't see any way around it."

I suddenly felt deflated. All hope seeped out of me, puddling at my feet. "Yeah," I sighed. "You're right. It's hopeless."

"Don't be that way. Things might look better in the morning."

"I'm not counting on it. I'm running out of time."

"I love you, Marc."

"Love you, too."

"Call me in the morning." The lightness in her voice was forced. "Maybe we can get together with Tom and Freddie. Spend all Saturday together."

"Yeah ... my last act of freedom."

"Will you do that?"

"Call you? Sure."

"Tomorrow, then."

"Yeah, tomorrow." I rang off and racked the receiver. God, I was doomed! I lay back against the cushions of the window seat and stared at the ceiling. What to do? Where to run? Where to hide? It was a brick wall. There were no answers. No escape. Only the inevitable. The parting. The end of one life and the start of another.

The hollowness inside me rose up and consumed me with one, mighty gulp. Doomed. That was the only word for it. Doomed and damned. And damned again. I'd never felt so alone, so bereft of understanding and compassion. It was as if my very existence had been negated, my very fabric wrenched asunder and scattered aimlessly at my feet.

Did no one care? My eyes flooded with tears, and I blinked in a half-hearted effort to contain them. Angrily, I brushed aside my tears. Damn it! It wasn't fair!

I jumped from the window seat and strode into the adjoining bathroom. I needed something. Something to calm me down. Something to help me sleep. I stared at my haunted reflection in the mirror. My eyes were red, my hair a mess. The look on my face was one of desperation. I was trapped. There was no way out. Simply a dead end. Was this what it had come to?

I opened the medicine cabinet and stared at its contents. I assumed there wasn't enough alcoholic content in my aftershave and colognes to achieve drunkenness. I considered going downstairs to raid my father's liquor cabinet, but realized it would do no good.

Slowly, I withdrew a plastic vial of pain killers leftover from when I had broken my arm the previous summer. I'd avoided taking them at the time because they made me feel lightheaded and unbalanced.

Opening the bottle, I shook a few of the pills onto the palm of my hand. One or two should help. I popped them into my mouth and dry-swallowed. One or two, hell, try three or four. I did, but needed a glass of water.

I began to feel better. At least I told myself so. Two more, and then I would quit. When I tapped the vial, five pills rolled out onto my palm. Two or five—no difference, I reasoned. Down the hatch.

I stared at my reflection. What was I doing?

Helping myself. That's what!

I tipped the pill bottle again and emptied its contents. Five more pills. Without hesitation, I palmed the drugs, washing them down my throat. There! Finished! That'll show them!

With determination, I switched off the light and left the bathroom. In my bedroom, I sat on the edge of the bed and kicked off my shoes. Laying back on the quilted coverlet, I rested my head on the pillows and closed my eyes.

Maybe I wouldn't see Christabel tomorrow after all. Maybe tomorrow wasn't going to come at all.

12

Fall 1960 – Aftermath

THE ONE GOOD THING about coming from a family with money is that you can create your own history when the need arises. My parents took every advantage of that power. What was known behind closed doors as Marc's "accident" became publicly known as mononucleosis. How they pulled that one off, I will never know, but they were experts in the art of societal subterfuge.

My mother had discovered my unconscious body and the empty pill bottle the following morning when I didn't show up for breakfast. An ambulance was called. I was rushed to the hospital where my stomach was pumped and I was plied with gallons of fluids. Needless to say, their medical team's efforts were successful.

Of course, I was subjected to a continuous barrage of questions and consternation from my parents and my doctors. Why had I done it? Was it an accident? What was I thinking? Didn't I know pain killers were dangerous?

My God! Were they even listening? Of course they weren't.

In the end, I claimed ignorance and allowed it to be classified as an accident. Still, my mother demanded I see a psychiatrist, an ordeal that continued for several weeks until she was satisfied that I was in my "right mind."

School was out of the question. I was recovering from "mononucleosis," after all. Though as a result of this faux diagnosis, I became a virtual prisoner. Under my mother's ever-watchful eye, days passed with monotonous regularity. I read. I napped. I watched television. It was a boring existence, but one I had requested. Now I had to pay the price.

My only respite was in phone conversations with Tom, Freddie, and Christabel. Sure, I had lots of calls from friends and classmates, but Tom, Freddie, and Christabel were my support group. Even with them, I perpetuated the charade. I think Tom suspected something was afoot. He had probably heard whispers within the confines of the family. Regardless, he never actually broached the subject, although he hinted at it.

"How ya doin?"

I lay on the window seat, the phone's receiver cradled between my shoulder and cheek. "Not too bad. Bored."

"Mom says you're not allowed to do anything."

"Damn little."

Tom laughed. "A real vacation."

"Yeah, right! Some vacation. I'm sick of it."

"Beats going to school."

"Easy for you to say. I still have to do all the work."

"Do you know when you'll be returning?"

"The doctor says end of October, beginning of November. I can't wait."

"Be careful what you wish for."

"Hey, let's see how you like being cooped up with only your parents to talk to."

"I'd be stuck with George," Tom chuckled.

I laughed, too. Uncle Fred and Aunt Harriet could never stay put long enough to care for a sick child. Like so many other things, that task would be delegated to George Sawyer, and the idea of George, as nurse maid, was ludicrous.

A silence prevailed for several moments before Tom continued. "I guess this solves the problem of you going away to school."

"I hope so. It's definitely too late for the fall semester. I guess I'll just have to wait to see what Dad has up his sleeve for the winter."

Dad had gotten the message, but whether he'd actually heed my suicide attempt remained to be seen. He never alluded to it. My mother, on the other hand, read the message loud and clear.

One afternoon, shortly after my "accident," I walked downstairs in search of a snack. As I exited the rear stair hall, I heard sounds from across the other end of the house. There was no mistaking the anger of my parents raised voices. Cautiously, I crept through the dining room, the foyer, and formal living room until I was in close proximity to Dad's study.

"I'm his father, and I think I know what's best for him!"

My mother issued a sarcastic laugh. "So much for that! You see where that's gotten us!"

"You actually believe he took those pills to keep from going to Dewey?" My father's tone was dismissive. "Be realistic, Victoria. He'd never do anything like that!"

"Well, something happened. And I'm not about to go through this again!"

"I don't think you need worry about that."

"And I'm not!"

My father paused. In my mind's eye, I could see him scrutinizing my mother's face. "What are you trying to say?"

"I don't know if it was intentional or not, but, for now, I don't want any further mention of the Dewey Academy in this house!" A pause. "Do you understand?"

"I understand that you're upset." Dad answered.

"I'm more than upset! I'm scared!"

"I think you're overreacting."

"The psychiatrist said it could have very well been intentional. We both knew he didn't want to go."

I thought I discerned a deep sigh from my father. "Okay."

"You promise?"

I assumed he nodded, because my mother soon continued. She started to backpedal. "I know you were only doing what you thought was good for him, but maybe we need to rethink that."

"Whatever you say." I could tell my father was far from convinced. He simply wanted the conversation to end.

"Maybe in a few months ... next fall perhaps."

My father issued no audible response. There was a shuffling of papers, a scraping of chair legs across the floor. My mother's interview was officially over. I beat a hasty retreat back to my room. The last thing I wanted to do was face them at a time like this. Still, for the moment, victory was mine. Time would tell as to whether my father intended to follow through on his promise.

13

1961-1962 – Golden Years

FOR THE NEXT TWO years fortune smiled on me. I was, once again, the golden boy of fame and fable. Everything around me was wreathed in the finest haze of gold; shimmering, glowing, sparkling. I was leading the charmed life. And I had Tom, Freddie, and Christabel at my side.

At home, life gradually returned to our idea of normal. My father seemed to finally relax. My mother returned to her days of bridge, luncheons, and shopping. My accident quietly slipped into the past. As one can imagine, my family had the innate ability to reclassify any unpleasant memory as simply a myth. That was fine by me.

From time to time, the brightness dimmed. Perhaps I wasn't as good as the rest of my family at manipulating the forces that drove my life. God knew, I tried; I had the best of teachers. Certainly, my accident demonstrated that. Still, I seemed to lack a firm grasp on my destiny. It was something that slipped away every once in a while. I was simply going to have to do better.

Christabel and I remained an item for most of that time, but I was not without competitors. Dan Welch, who we had known all our lives, suddenly set sights on Christabel, and she on him. She confronted me with the horrible truth at one of our many school dances.

It was the night of the Fall Harvest Fling. The auditorium was decorated with the obligatory array of pumpkins, dried corn stalks, and scarecrows. The band was a cover act that played both current hits and older tunes. It was a night that promised to be fun. Or so I thought.

Christabel wasn't herself. Half the time she "didn't feel like dancing". That, in itself, should have raised a red flag for me. Still, I kept pushing, trying to improve her spirits.

"But you love this song," I insisted.

"That doesn't mean we have to dance to it."

"I'd like to."

"Well, I wouldn't."

I stared at her across the table. "What's wrong with you tonight?"

She didn't smile. "Nothing."

I reached out and held her hand in mine. She didn't pull away, but her hand remained motionless. No returning grasp. No warmth.

"Tell me."

With that, she withdrew her hand and curled it in her lap. "Dan asked me out."

"So?" I laughed, which was probably the wrong response.

"I said okay."

My stomach clenched. My throat was suddenly dry. Surely, this couldn't be happening. "Why'd you do that?" I couldn't mask the distress in my voice.

She stared at me across the table. "Because I wanted to ."

"Why?" I was dumbfounded.

"Marc, you're the only boy I've even been with since I moved here." She paused. "I guess I just want a change. See if we're doing the right thing."

The first spark of anger licked my brain. "You're not going to give me that 'We can still be friends' bullshit, are you?"

"Can't we?"

"No. We cannot."

"Why not?"

I pushed my chair away from the table. "If you want to see Dan, then do it. But don't expect me to play along. I'm not going to stand on the sidelines waiting for you to get your head back on your shoulders."

"Marc, don't say that."

"What do you want me to say?" I leered at her, anger distorting my face. "That I'm happy for you?" I stood. "Come on, Christabel, this is the real world, not some soap opera."

For the first time, her anger began to rise. "You're the one making it into a big deal!"

"This isn't a big deal? Well, thanks a lot!" I turned and quickly exited the auditorium. Behind me, the band was playing "Run Around Sue."

—

I was hurt. I was angry. Most of all, I missed Christabel. I missed our long nightly phone conversations. I missed dancing with her. I missed her smile. But I wasn't about to let her know any of this. I was too proud for that.

Instead, I started seeing Mary Elizabeth Farmer, if only to prove to Christabel and to everyone else that I was all right. Mary Elizabeth's father owned an electrical contracting firm that did a lot of business with my father's construction company. Her parents weren't in the same social stream as mine, but our liaison was perfectly acceptable.

Mary Elizabeth wasn't a great dancer. She certainly knew all the steps, but her heart wasn't in it. Improvisation was out of the question. Whenever I tried, she would reply, "For God's sake, Marc, if you want me to follow you, stick with the steps!" or words to that effect. Enough said.

School dances were fun, but cellar parties were the best because they were largely unchaperoned. Although the host's parents were always at home, they rarely ventured down the basement stairs during the course of an evening, which gave us free rein. Close dancing, petting, and necking in a dark corner became the norm. Mary Elizabeth was good at all three.

Tom and Freddie were ever present. Freddie rarely came with anyone in particular. She had yet to bloom. Tom, on the other hand, was always on the arm of one girl or another. Usually, it was either Leigh Armbruster, Marie Grover, or Sue Anne Michaels. Each tall and leggy. Each a perfect match for Tom.

Needless to say, our group wasn't much of a group right now. Christabel and Freddie remained close friends and confidants, but Christabel shied away from Tom and me. Whenever the three of us were together, I would gently coax Freddie into talking about Christabel, but she rarely felt inclined to reveal any of Christabel's confidences.

—

Fall gave way to winter and winter to spring. In early April 1962, our school marching band traveled to West Virginia to perform in the Apple Blossom Festival. Most children in Martin's Neck were expected to pursue music as part of their education and an indication of their social standing. We were inducted early, usually in the fifth grade. I played the trombone; Freddie, the flute; Christabel, the clarinet; and Tom, the trumpet. It was simply something one did whether one liked it or not.

We were housed in a large, rambling, Victorian inn on the side of a mountain. It was the perfect location for a good time.

The parade had gone well. We had placed first in the competition and were more than ready to celebrate our victory. A group of us was camped out in the main lounge of the inn, talking, laughing, and generally having a good time. Freddie was regaling us with a funny story when I saw her stop and stare across the room. I followed her gaze. Christabel stood at the base of the staircase, tears streaming down her cheeks.

I watched as Freddie left the group and rushed to Christabel's side. She slipped an arm around Christabel's shoulders and whispered in her ear. Finally, Christabel nodded, and Freddie led her across the lounge, through a pair of French doors and out onto the wide porch that overlooked the valley below. The door closed behind them.

Not my problem, I assured myself, and turned back to the group.

A few minutes passed before Freddie was standing by my chair. "You need to come out here." She motioned toward the porch.

"Why?"

"She's a mess. She wants to talk to you."

"What happened?"

"She'll explain." Barring further conversation, Freddie turned and walked across the lounge.

I sat for a moment, uncertain, but wanting to know what was happening. Finally, with a sigh, I followed Freddie onto the porch. It was empty except for Christabel who sat on the end of a chaise lounge, crying softly.

I stood looking at her. "What's wrong?"

Christabel brushed away stray tears and stared back at me. Her bottom lip quivered. Instead of speaking, she sadly shook her head. How the hell was I supposed to deal with this?

We were in a stalemate, with no one speaking.

Finally, Freddie spoke up. "Christy, tell Marc what happened."

Christabel shook her head and brushed away more tears.

"How can I help, if you won't talk to me?" I sat beside her on the chaise.

She sobbed softly.

I placed my hands over hers. "Whatever it is, it can't be that bad."

She flared momentarily. "How would you know?"

"Then tell me."

She sat staring at her lap. "It's Dan. He tried ... he was kissing me ... my blouse."

"What?" I stood quickly. "That son of a bitch!" I started to leave, but she grabbed my hand.

"No! It's not his fault. He's drunk."

"You've got to be kidding!"

"Ralph Morrison stole a bottle of vodka from the bar."

"Jesus Christ! That's no excuse!" I pulled away from her.

"Marc, no! You'll only get us all in trouble. We were all drinking."

Freddie stood with her hands on her hips. "That's really smart. What were you thinking?"

Christabel shook her head sadly.

Freddie looked at me. "Well, I'm going to let you two sort this out. I don't need to be a part of this mess."

I nodded to her.

Freddie placed her hand on Christabel's shoulder. "You stay here with Marc, sweetie. You'll feel better in a little while. You'll see." Freddie kissed the top of Christabel's head and then left.

For a moment, we sat in silence. I took Christabel's hand and brought it to my lips. "You'll be fine. Just take a minute."

"You're so sweet to me."

"You'll be fine." I had no idea what to do next.

Finally, Christabel sighed and squeezed my hand. "Can we go for a walk? I just want to get out of here."

"Sure. It's a beautiful night."

We walked, finally coming to rest on a rocky terrace that overlooked the valley. The lights in the village painted a picture postcard. Its serenity seemed to dispel Christabel's anxiety, and she snuggled close to me on one of the wicker settees that adorned the terrace.

"Cold?"

She nodded.

I walked back to the porch and found a large afghan draped over one of the chairs. Back on the terrace, I tucked it around Christabel's

legs and pulled the rest over our bodies as we huddled closely together.
"Better?"
"Much."

The morning sunlight flooded the valley. Here and there wisps of smoke snaked from several chimneys. The sudden burst of light woke me immediately. Christabel lay snuggled at my side, her breath slow and even. I kissed the top of her head and smiled. There was something really good about all this, and I felt a serenity that I had seldom ever experienced. I felt older, more in charge, more in control. I felt a new power within me. It was a strange sensation, and I was initially unsure whether to welcome it or run from it.

By the summer of 1962, Christabel and I had been seeing one again regularly since that night in West Virginia. Our night together, on the rocky terrace, had sort of cemented our relationship in a way I didn't really understand. Still, I didn't question it. I was merely happy that it had happened.

With summer came the opening of Powell Cottage and the yearly shift in our base of operations. Freddie and Christabel remained in Martin's Neck while Tom and I focused on Burton's Brae Beach. Christabel's mother was overly protective, always expecting the worse to happen. I guess that was symptomatic of her ongoing battle with depression. As a result, Christabel was rarely allowed to spend time with us at the beach. She was largely restricted to the confines of the big, white house and her mother's watchful eye.

There was something different about this summer. I guess part of it was that we were getting older. At fifteen, every day seemed ripe for adventure, and there was always much to do.

For starters, there was a crowd of new, young faces. Several cottages had been built over the year, and it seemed that each boasted at least one teenager. As a group, we would congregate at Burton's Store, which was the hub of activity for the little beach community. It wasn't anything fancy, but it had a snack bar, a juke box, and several pinball machines. Best of all, it had a big dance floor that we put to good use whenever we gathered there.

That's where I met Sandy Davidson. Her parents had just built a cottage four doors down from Uncle Fred and Aunt Harriet. She was a pretty girl with dark-blond hair and a good figure. It wasn't that I was enamored with her; I simply liked her looks. She was fun and easy to talk to. She also loved to dance.

Tom disapproved of our relationship, but he kept his mouth shut. His allegiance was to Christabel, but he wasn't about to tell her about Sandy. Freddie, had she known, would have told Christabel immediately. Girls are like that.

The summer proceeded at a leisurely pace. Besides gatherings at Burton's Store, there were long walks on the beach, many by moonlight. There were bonfires on a regular basis where Sandy and I sat cuddled together, telling ghost stories and dreaming about the future.

———

Disaster struck on the Fourth of July.

We had been planning our celebration for weeks. Of course, there would be a bonfire, but bigger and better than all the previous ones. There would be hot dogs, marshmallows, and sodas. There would music, compliments of Tom's newly acquired radio. There would even be sparklers and fireworks, garnered by one of the guys who lived in Virginia where such items were legal. It promised to be a great evening. And it would have been if not for one small glitch.

We chose the beach in front of Powell Cottage for our gathering. Everything was going according to plan. The radio spouted Jan and Dean and The Beach Boys. Sandy and I sat side by side, my arm around her shoulders. It was great.

"Well, who do we have here?" The sarcastic tone of Freddie's voice floated out of the darkness.

Tom jumped to his feet. "Hey! What are you guys doing here?"

Freddie smiled. "Mommy and Daddy are down visiting the Burkes so we tagged along. Didn't know you were having a beach party."

Tom stammered and began introductions. I had removed my arm from around Sandy's shoulders, but it was too late. Christabel had seen me; had seen *us*, and there would be hell to pay.

There was no denying it.

14

August 1962 – Reprise

THE SUMMER SLID DOWNHILL after that. Christabel and I weren't speaking to one other. I was in a royal funk. Even Sandy shied away from me after the Fourth of July incident. Who could blame her? I had neglected to mention Christabel to her, a more than intentional oversight.

As if things couldn't get any worse, my father summoned me to his office one evening after dinner. My mother sat in one of the leather wing-backed chairs sipping crème de menthe over ice. The whole scene did not bode well.

My father motioned toward the other chair. "Have a seat."

Hesitantly, I sat, casting a quick look at my mother. Her face was expressionless.

My father shuffled some papers on the desk in front of him and then looked up at me. "Your mother and I have been talking, and we feel it's time you reconsider the Dewey Academy."

Panic stricken, I looked to my mother for help. There was nothing there.

"You've had some time now to adjust to the idea, and you're older. We think the time is right."

I was speechless. I was at a loss. My mind slipped and then started again. This couldn't be happening.

"We don't want any hysterics. Not like last time. As I said, you're older now. You should be able to see the benefits of going there."

"But Dad …"

My father raised a hand. "Give it a chance. If you still feel the same way by the end of the semester, we'll give it some consideration."

Yeah, right! Then it would be one more semester, then another. Consideration meant one thing ... doing things my father's way.

I looked at my mother in desperation. "Mom, you know how I feel."

My mother set her glass on the little table beside her. "Yes, I do. But I think your father's right. The experience will be good for you. You may not think so now, but in the future, I think you'll view it differently."

I let out a huge sigh. "I don't believe this. I thought this was settled."

My father smiled smugly. "*Tabled* is the better word. We wanted to give you time to get back on your feet before bringing it up again."

I shook my head slowly.

"You've had over a year now. Things have been going your way. You seem happy."

"*I am happy!* That's why I don't want to go."

My father paused. A pensive look crossed his face. "Maybe you're *too* happy ... too complacent."

I exploded. "Jesus H. Christ!"

"Marc!" My mother's voice was shocked.

"Young man, you will not talk like that in this house!" My father's words bore no breech.

I stared at the floor in front of me. "Sorry, Sir."

"I should hope so." He shuffled the papers on the desk top. "The fall semester starts in three weeks."

Three weeks! Sweet Jesus, what was I going to do?

"I've had our tailor send them your current measurements so we don't have to make a special trip for uniform fittings."

Oh, whoopee! Like I gave a damn.

"We'll take the train to New York on the fifth of September, and then a car out to the school. Your mother and I will see that you have everything you need. I've opened an expense account at the local branch of our bank in Pelham Bay. If you have any problems, all you have to do is contact Giles Merchant at their branch office. He'll take care of anything you need." He smiled smugly.

All wrapped up in one neat, little package. He looked so self-satisfied with all he'd accomplished. The world was his oyster right now. Good for him. The son of a bitch.

Silence filled the study. My mother resumed sipping her drink. My father ordered the papers in front of him into a neat stack that he set purposely to one side. "How does that sound?"

I hesitated for a moment. "Like I don't have any say in the matter."

My father smiled. "You've been very clear about your feelings, but, as parents we do have the right to do what we feel is best for you."

"So you say."

"Lose the tone."

"Sorry."

My mother rattled the ice shards in her glass. The green liquid glowed and flowed around them. "Your father and I want you to be happy. We know it's going to be hard leaving all your friends, but that's also part of growing up."

"Why can't it wait until I go to college?"

"College is a rough road," my father interjected. "We want you to be well prepared for it when the time comes. Dewey will help achieve that. It has a wonderful reputation. Most of their graduates go on to lead quite successful lives."

Like I cared. I was being ripped out of my comfortable life and thrust into a harsh, military environment that offered me little chance for happiness. I'd heard the tales about military schools. Early to bed, early to rise—all that bullshit. Hard work, long hours, unquestioning obedience. The whole gamut. It wasn't for me.

My father took my silence as mute acceptance. He laughed. "Someday you're going to thank me for this. Trust me."

15

September 1962 – Dewey

MY FATHER WAS AS good as his word in that everything went according to his well-laid plans. We took the train to Pennsylvania Station in New York where we were met by a sleek, black, Cadillac limousine. As a family, we were quite a sight. My mother had done her best to mimic the style of Jackie Kennedy, complete with a tailored wool suit and pillbox hat. My father looked every inch the successful businessman in his gray tweed overcoat and its fur collar. I followed suit in a tailor-made jacket and trousers in shades of dusty teal and a French-cuffed shirt with aquamarine cufflinks. If nothing else, you had to give us credit for knowing how to dress.

The big car wound its way through the congested city streets until it reached East Side Drive. Once on the New England Expressway, it began to eat up the miles. We rode in silence, each of us absorbed in our personal thoughts.

Finally, the car slowed and then pulled through a pair of tall, wrought-iron gates. The Dewey Academy had once been a country estate built during the Gilded Age. The original house, now the administration building, sat surrounded by an assortment of newer buildings overlooking Long Island Sound. There were cars and people everywhere. Suitcases sat cheek to jowl with duffle bags on the curbs.

Our driver maneuvered the limousine into a tight parking spot meant for two cars. We were greeted immediately by an upperclassman who was assigned to help us.

"Cadet Bradley Charles, class of '63." He extended his hand to my father. "I'll be your guide for the day." Having greeted my parents, he turned to me. "Cadet Steadman, welcome to Dewey. We hope you will be happy here." A sly smile crossed his handsome face. I didn't like that smile, not one little bit.

Cadet Charles grabbed my two pieces of luggage. "Just follow me."

We followed him through the throng and into a three-story brick building that housed my dormitory room on the second floor. It was a large room, big enough for a trio of cadets. There was a set of bunks, a single bed, three desks grouped below a large window, three chairs, and three chests of drawers. Uniforms filled the large closet awaiting their new owners. Apparently my two roommates had yet to arrive.

The upperclassman set the suitcases next to one of the bunks and then removed his hat. Running his fingers through a shock of blond hair, he turned to my parents and smiled. "There's a reception for parents at the admin building. It's just a short walk from here."

"But, we were going to help Marc unpack and get settled." My mother's voice showed uncertainty for the first time. I hoped she was feeling guilty about bringing me to this hell hole.

The sly smile returned. "I'm sure he can manage. Can't you, Cadet Steadman?"

"Yes."

"*Sir*," he corrected.

"Yes ... Sir."

"You go along and enjoy the reception. You'll have time to visit with him again before you leave."

My father took my mother's arm and guided her toward the door. "We'll see you in a bit, son."

I glared at Dad as they left the room. Great. Just great! Leave me here with this guy who's so full of self-importance. Talk about the lamb awaiting the slaughter.

Cadet Charles sat on the edge of one of the desks and smiled. He wasn't overly tall, but he was built like a football player. The sly smile was disturbing.

"Steadman, huh?"

"Yes ... Sir."

"What kind of a name is that?"

I shrugged. "English, I guess."

"Your dad rich?"

"No, not really."

"*Sir*."

"Sir."

"That your dad's car?"

"No. It's a Carey, Sir."

"I don't fuckin' believe you, Steadman."

"It's a Carey. It brought us from the train station, Sir."

His voice took on a feigned, southern accent. "You all from the south, Cadet?"

Who was this jerk, and what was he getting at? "South of here, Sir."

Charles continued his southern drawl. "Does your daddy still ride the plantation on a big white horse?"

"My 'daddy' is a contractor," I sneered. "But my uncle still rides his plantation in a red Oldsmobile Tornado."

Charles laughed. "Just how old were you before you learned that 'damned Yankee' was two words?"

My temper flared. Cut me a fucking break! I smiled sweetly. "*Is it*, Sir?"

Charles laughed again. "Good one, Steadman. Good one. I think you and I are going to get along just fine."

Somehow, I doubted that. If first impressions meant anything, ours would be a stormy relationship at best.

"I'm your RA, so you'll be seeing a lot of me."

Yeah, whether I liked it or not.

Two other guys my age suddenly entered the room, followed by two more upperclassmen and an assortment of parents and luggage. Edward Andrews was a tall, gaunt young man who was in need of several pounds to fill him out. Christopher Robinson was shorter than I, with a thick build and a mass of copper red hair. They both appeared to be as much at sea as I was.

Edward's mother fluttered around him and his luggage while his father stood silently behind the bank of desks. Mr. Robinson watched as Christopher grabbed his suitcase and plopped it onto the single bed. The three upperclassmen stood off to one side, talking in hushed voices and laughing among themselves. For several minutes, confusion reigned as we endeavored to make some sense of the pile of luggage and belongings.

Finally, with the parents dispatched to the reception, we were alone with the three upperclassmen. Silence enveloped the room as they each stood smiling at us like the proverbial cat and its mouse.

Charles took the lead. "Stand at attention."

The three of us looked at one another. The upperclassmen laughed. Charles, the loudest of the three barked, "They don't have a fuckin' clue!"

One of the other cadets stepped forward. "Side by side, heels together, arms at you sides, shoulders back, head straight, eyes forward."

We did our best to follow directions. Charles walked slowly around our little group. "Not too bad. How does it feel, cadets? It better feel really good because you're going to spend a lot of time like this. Understand?"

I nodded.

"What's that, Steadman? I didn't hear you."

"Yes, Sir!"

My roommates chimed in behind me.

"Good." Charles continued to slowly circle us. "Now, you've got about a half hour to finish unpacking. At 13:00 hours, all new cadets are to report to the quadrangle. There, you will stand at attention while the commodore gives his bullshit welcome speech. Understand?"

In unison, "Yes, Sir!"

"Once the old blowhard finishes, you will be released to say goodbye to your parents. After that, the fun begins." The sly grin resurfaced. I didn't feel one bit better about it.

Charles joined his classmates at the doorway. "Okay, at ease. We'll see you all at the quad."

The three of us looked at each other uncertainly. What in hell had we gotten ourselves into?

As the upperclassmen began to leave, Charles turned at the last minute and looked directly at me. "And Steadman?"

"Sir?"

"You and I will be talking." He smiled with feigned sweetness. "You and I will be talking a lot."

When they had left, Ed turned and looked at me. "What was that about?"

"Just busting my balls," I replied.

Christopher laughed ruefully. "I'll say! He's got a real hard-on for you."

Didn't I know it. And what was I supposed to do about it? Talk about being off to a good start! I felt trapped with nowhere to run. I was on my own now, and I'd have to take care of myself. Lucky me.

16

Fall 1962 – Bradley Charles

BRADLEY CHARLES WAS A true martinet. He ruled our dormitory with the strictest of hands and broached no infraction, no matter how small. The first-year cadets lived in constant fear of him, and he seemed to glory in that fear. The older cadets respected him and considered themselves fortunate to be able to call him a friend. Those not so fortunate gave him a wide berth. He was a god.

Bradley Charles looked like a god as well. At nearly six-feet tall, he was powerfully built. His thick, blond hair and bright-green eyes would hold anyone in awe. He simply had a presence, and he used it to his own benefit. He was in charge, and you had damn well better remember it.

He also lived up to his promise, hounding me day and night, week after week. Whenever I sought refuge in a corner of the library, Bradley Charles would be at the next table watching me. He was a constant visitor to our room, always on the lookout for some infraction for which we could be punished. At drill, he was forever at my shoulder, barking orders and ridiculing me when I messed up. My life had become a nightmare from which I could not awaken.

Chris Robinson closed and secured his suitcase. "Why don't you report him to the commodore?"

I laughed. "Lot of good that would do. He'd just come down harder on us."

Ed Andrews nodded. "Yeah, we got enough trouble as it is. Besides, who's going to believe you? He is the RA after all. He's never busted us for anything we didn't do."

"Right." It was a no-win situation. Charles played by the book. Every misdemeanor for which we had been punished was valid. Sloppily made bunks, messy desks, unpolished shoes, and wrinkled uniforms were all punishable offenses. Bradley Charles never missed a beat.

Chris set his suitcase on the floor next to his bunk. "And just think, you have him all to yourself this weekend."

This was the first weekend in which first-year cadets were allowed to leave school. Chris and Ed were both headed home to visit their parents. I was not so lucky. My parents were in Florida visiting Uncle Leland and Aunt Charlene, so I had nowhere to go. I was stuck. In fact, I was one of the few cadets who would be remaining at Dewey. Most of our dorm would be vacated, the library would be closed, and the mess hall would only be available for fast food twice a day. What fun.

Chris and Ed finished packing their bags and left. They were among the last to leave. With their departure, the dorm took on an empty, ghostly feel. Miles of empty hallways and vacant rooms stretched in every direction. I was alone and had never felt so much so.

I turned on all the lights in our room, brightening the otherwise dreary day. Clouds obscured the sky and cast a pall over the quadrangle outside our window. Occasionally, a lone cadet scurried across the quad, clutching his heavy pea coat close for warmth against the brisk wind. While the rest of my classmates were off to warm homes and loving families, I was stuck here. Alone. Lucky me.

I wiled away the afternoon reading and listening to the radio. Nothing helped. I was still alone. At 17:00 hours, I donned my pea coat and headed for the mess hall that sat at the head of the quadrangle. There were only a handful of cadets at the long dining tables. Dinner was unimpressive: hamburgers, fries, sodas, a cookie for dessert. As I was finishing my meal, I sensed someone standing across the table from me. I looked up and encountered Brad Charles' sly smile. This time it bordered on a sneer.

"Whatcha doin', Steadman?" He rested one foot on the chair across from me.

"What's it look like?"

"*Sir.*"

So we were going to play this game. "Sir."

"All alone are we?"

I hated his self-satisfied air and didn't rise to the bait.

"Mommy and Daddy out of town?"

I nodded.

"Touring the continent this week?"

"Florida. Sir."

"Ah, sunny Florida. Don't you wish you were there?"

I didn't reply.

Brad paused and then removed his foot from the chair. "Well, enjoy your dinner." Even that came off as a snide comment.

I simply nodded.

"Maybe I'll see you later."

Was that a threat?

Night. The room was dark; the blinds were drawn. I couldn't see a thing. And suddenly, I couldn't breathe. Something covered my mouth and nose. I shook my head, attempting to free myself. The pressure only increased. I began to panic. I twisted frantically, but the pressure now covered my whole body. I was trapped. I couldn't move. I tried to yell, but the hand blocking my mouth wouldn't let me. It slipped a little, allowing me to draw a breath through my nose. Again, I tried to wrest myself free, but again failed. I was no match for whomever was holding me captive.

I sensed the faint odor of alcohol as my captor placed his cheek next to mine. Even slightly slurred, Brad's voice was unmistakable. "Don't you even think about yelling."

I froze. What in God's name was happening?

Slowly, Brad removed his hand from my mouth. In an instant, his lips covered mine. I squirmed, trying to move my head on one side, but failed.

Brad stared at me through the darkness. The feeble, ambient light reflected off his cold, green eyes. "Don't make a sound. Not one sound."

I didn't know what he was threatening, but I knew I didn't want to find out. I twisted my body again and tried to push him off me. He slapped me hard across the face. Only once, but it was enough. I lay still, staring up at him. I could taste blood as it trickled from my split lip. No doubt about it–I was outmatched.

"Ah, Steadman, I've had my eye on you from the very beginning." His smile was nasty, lascivious. "We're going to be seeing a lot of one another after tonight."

He kissed me again, and my brain shut down. I was lost.

17

Fall 1962 – Lost Weekend

MILKY SUNLIGHT TRIED TO break through the clouds above the quadrangle, but it kept losing the battle. The quadrangle was empty, and the brisk wind from yesterday sent leaves skittering across the concrete pavers. I sat at my desk, gloomily watching them.

I didn't feel like eating. I didn't feel like doing anything. My lip was sore. My body ached. The hot shower had helped, but it wasn't enough to restore any sense of well-being. I had scrubbed myself until my skin was red, but I could not rid myself of his smell. God damn him.

I rose from my chair and crossed to my bunk. Angrily, I stripped the stained sheets and stuffed them in the blood-marked pillowcase. How dare he?

I slowly opened the door, half afraid I would see his smiling face. The hallway was empty. I took the two short flights down to the laundry and threw the soiled linens into a washer. Once it was going, I sat on a low stool and stared at the machine blankly. What was I supposed to do now?

I couldn't let him get away with this. Should I tell the commodore? But what evidence did I have? It was his word against mine. There were no witnesses, only my split lip, which could have happened any number of ways. Who was going to believe me, a first-year cadet? Of course, Ed and Chris would believe me, or at least I thought they would. Why wouldn't they? What did I have to gain by lying? Still, we were roommates; we could easily be accused of conspiring against our

RA in retaliation to his strictness. Brad's position and reputation made him almost untouchable. What was I to do?

I needed a plan. That much I knew. My father often said, "You've got to have a plan." But the plan remained to be determined.

The rest of the day passed slowly. I was reluctant to leave my room for fear of encountering Brad in one of the long, empty hallways. At midday, I ventured down to the first-floor lounge and grabbed some snacks and a soda from the vending machines and then hurried back to my room. I wasn't about to risk running into him at the mess hall. The last thing I needed was to see that creepy smile of his.

I spent the afternoon thinking and planning, and ran all sorts of scenarios in which revenge was the main event. None of my schemes made any sense at all. None were the least bit feasible. They were simply wanderings of an addled mind. Still, I needed a plan; I wanted a plan. No. That wasn't right at all. Right now what I wanted was revenge. I just didn't know how to obtain it.

By the time the day slipped away, I was exhausted. Still no closer to a plan, I undressed and made ready for bed. I looked at my bunk and shivered. How could I sleep there after what had happened? What if he came back again tonight? There were no locks on the door. Grabbing one of the desk chairs, I wedged it under the doorknob as I had seen done on television and in the movies. Hopefully, that would serve as a deterrent.

Feeling a bit more at ease, I climbed into bed and lay staring at the underside of the bunk above me. Sleep was a long time coming.

Sunday was little different from the day before. The clouds seemed lower, and the wind felt colder. I had slept fitfully, but had awakened feeling marginally better. Although my dreams had been peopled with many faces, mercifully, none of them were Brad's.

I grabbed my swim suit and a towel and then headed for the mess hall for a late breakfast, early lunch. I wasn't about to let Brad Charles hold me captive another day.

Sunday morning swims had become a ritual for me and my roommates, and today it seemed like a good idea to continue it. Maybe the cool water would refresh or cleanse me in a way that the hot showers had not.

The locker room was empty, but that was no surprise. I changed, grabbed my towel and headed for the pool. A single towel lay draped over one of the benches. In the pool, a lone swimmer completed a lap and began another. I turned and placed my towel carefully on a bench.

"Hey, *Studman*."

I turned quickly, my eyes meeting Brad's. They glinted electric green, and his dreaded smile curled his lips.

"Nice day for a swim. Being Sunday, I figured you'd be here even without your entourage."

"Stay away from me, you son of a bitch!"

Brad continued to smile. "Hey, no reason to be so antagonistic."

I grabbed my towel and turned away from him. "I've got plenty of reasons!" I walked quickly toward the door that led to the locker room.

"Hey, Steadman, come back here!"

"Go to Hell!" I shouted over my shoulder.

I heard splashing as Brad exited the pool.

In the locker room, I quickly threw down my towel and opened my locker. Grabbing my shirt, I turned to see Brad standing, watching me. "Hey, man, I'm sorry."

I thrust one arm into a vacant sleeve. "Sorry, my ass!"

Brad grabbed my shoulder and forced me to face him. "I said, I'm sorry."

I pushed him away from me, sending him against the row of lockers.

He laughed. "Boy, you must really like your sex rough." Then he hit me squarely in the stomach with a fist.

I doubled over in pain. Brad grabbed my right arm and twisted it behind me, forcing me against the lockers. The locker vent pressed into my face while I tried unsuccessfully to free myself from his hold. The only sound I could manage was a muffled, "No."

He penetrated me, and I began to cry. Not from any pain, though there was certainly discomfort, but from the sheer humiliation of the act. He grabbed me with his free hand, and, when he came, so did I.

Brad laughed softly to himself, his breath hot against the back of my neck. "Feel better now?"

I couldn't speak. I couldn't fight. All I could do was cry.

Brad rested his chin on my shoulder and whispered in my ear. "You're mine now. Remember that, Steadman." He paused awaiting my response.

I offered none.

"Do you hear me?" He increased the pressure on my arm. "This is just between you and me. No one else. Understand?"

I managed to nod.

He kissed the nape of my neck and laughed softly again. "Good boy."

Brad released me, and I slid to a heap on the floor. Wedged between the bench and the lockers, I rested my head on my knees and cried. I cried for myself. I cried for my parents. I cried for Christabel who was no longer mine.

18

November 1962 – Trapped

UNFORTUNATELY FOR BRAD, FINDING a way to be alone with me did not prove to be as easy as he may have thought. I had two roommates, and we were always together. I made sure to never visit the library (or anywhere else for that matter) alone. There was safety in numbers, and I was going to play that card to the hilt.

Of course, I told no one; not even Chris and Ed. I suppose I should have, but I didn't. I was scared of Brad Charles and what he might do if I told anyone. And while I could have reported him, what proof did I have? Brad was the model cadet, respected by his peers and superiors alike. It would take more than my say-so to convince anyone differently. I was the victim, and I had no power. He was right; I was his, and would remain so until I could do something to upset the status quo. What that might be, I had no clue. I only knew I wanted revenge. I wanted it badly.

—

Brad's attitude toward me softened after that weekend. It wasn't obvious, and most people would never have detected it. Still, I could sense it. He remained the consummate martinet, punishing us for each and every military code violation, but there was a change in his attitude toward me. No one else seemed to notice this, and I wasn't about to mention it.

Brad did manage to be successful twice within the next few weeks. Both times occurred on weekends when the school was practically deserted. My parents were still in Florida, and I had no one to go home to. I thought about going to Uncle Fred and Aunt Harriet's, but they had joined my parents in Florida. There was simply nowhere to go. As much as the idea appealed to me, it didn't make much sense logistically. Therefore, I was left to Brad's mercy and paid the price both times. The first time, I fought him, but it was useless. The second time, I simply gave in and accepted my fate. God, I hated him. Somehow, he was going to pay. It was only a matter of figuring out how and when.

I needed a plan if I was ever going to free myself of his grasp. But, think as I might, no viable plan came. And, it was not for the want of thinking. I could think about little else. I became moody, but my roommates chalked it up to my being unable to get home for a weekend break. My school work began to reflect my inner turmoil, and I had more than numerous conferences with my instructors. In retrospect, I suppose I could have spilled the truth to one of them, thrown myself on their mercy, whatever. It might have been a better alternative to what actually happened. That's something I'll never know.

I turned over in Brad's narrow bed and faced the wall. I could feel the warmth of his body next to mine. Outside, the wind whistled coldly around the corner of the building. If it hadn't been for the circumstances, I would have normally felt warm and secure. Such was not the case.

"Marc."

"Sir?"

Brad laughed. "I think you can drop the 'sir'."

"Why's that? Aren't you afraid I'll slip and call you Brad in public."

"I really don't care."

"I don't believe that for a minute." I laughed ruefully. "What would people think?" And wouldn't I love to find out. Fat chance of that ever happening. Still, in the end, somehow, he was going to pay.

Brad fell silent for several minutes. Then he turned and laid a hand on my shoulder. "You know, part of me is sorry for how all this happened."

I choked back a laugh. "And what part would that be?"

Brad sighed. "The part of me who really cares about you."

I thought about letting that pass. "You have a funny way of showing it."

"I didn't mean for it to be like this."

"You mean you don't force yourself on other guys?"

"I've never had to."

"Then why me?"

He paused. "You're the first guy I've ever really cared about. I knew that from the moment I saw you step out of that limousine."

"Lucky me." I rolled over to face him.

"Like I said, I'm sorry." Brad reached up and stroked my cheek.

"Yeah, I heard you."

"Forgive me?"

I sighed. "That's going to take some doing." I stared into his eyes and then rolled back over. "It's not in the cards, right now."

"I see."

For several minutes, silence filled the room. Brad swung his legs off the bed and sat on its edge. "When are you leaving for Thanksgiving?"

"Wednesday. My train leaves at 2:40. Why?"

"Meet me before?"

Meet him? Why in the hell would I want to meet him anywhere? "Where?"

"You know the Tremont Hotel on Westchester Square?"

"No, but I've been to Westchester Square."

"You can't miss it."

Slowly, for the first time in weeks, a plan began to evolve. I rolled over to face him. "Why there?"

He looked at me and smiled. There was no sneer this time. "So we can spend some time together without having to worry about being caught. Maybe have lunch before you catch your train."

"I don't know." I was back-pedaling, thinking as fast as I could.

"I'll leave here the night before and get a room. If you leave Wednesday morning by eight, that would give us the whole morning together."

That could work. "I guess so." Having him alone could make a difference. Just maybe I could end this once and for all.

It had stopped snowing as I stepped off the Pelham Bay local at Westchester Square. The station was busy, and the light snowfall soon disappeared under hundreds of shuffling feet. I descended to street level and entered the square. Brad had been right; the Tremont Hotel was hard to miss. It was imposing in a 1930s sort of way, but, like the rest of the Bronx, had fallen on hard times.

I crossed the square, shied away from the main entrance, and entered through the less conspicuous side entry. I climbed a short flight of stairs from the street, passed a sparsely occupied coffee shop and a dark and shuttered cocktail lounge. I avoided the bay of elevators and climbed the two flights of stairs to the third floor. Room 351, Brad had told me. It wasn't hard to find.

I stood staring at the scarred mahogany door with its tarnished brass numbers. Mustering my courage, I took a deep breath and rapped on the wood panel. There was movement inside the room, and the door opened. Brad stood smiling at me, his green eyes actually softening for once.

"I thought you'd never get here."

I smiled weakly. "Sorry."

Brad grabbed the lapel of my trench coat and pulled me into the room. He kissed me fiercely and closed the door firmly behind us.

I sat on the stiff desk chair while completing the obligatory Windsor knot of my tie. I needed to get moving if I was going to make my train in Manhattan. I picked up the half-empty glass of vodka and downed its contents. Its warmth spread throughout my body, settling me, enabling me to focus.

I looked around the dingy hotel room, checking each surface for something I may have forgotten. It all looked good. I set down the empty glass and then realized I needed to do something with it. I quickly crossed to the bathroom, rinsed and dried the glass, and stowed it in my suitcase. Done. The worst that would happen would be that it would break before I arrived home. No big deal.

I pulled my trench coat over my dress blues, picked up my suitcase, and crossed to the door. Time to go. I paused and looked back at the bed.

Brad lay under one end of the sheet, his face turned toward me. Those bright-green eyes were closed, and his face was still slightly flushed. I hesitated. Should I say something? No. What was there to say?

I exited the room and closed the door. The latch fell softly into place. I retraced my route down the stairs, past the coffee shop and cocktail lounge, and out the side door. It had begun to snow again.

19

Thanksgiving 1962

IT WAS ONE OF the best Thanksgivings I can remember. Just being away from Dewey made all the difference. Being away from Brad Charles heightened the feeling. I felt an unchecked sense of freedom as I hung my uniform in my closet. The corded jeans and sweater made me feel alive again. It was so good to be home.

After my grandfather's death, Grandmother Powell ceased to entertain on her previously grand scale. Large family dinners now rotated between the five Powell siblings. This year, Thanksgiving had fallen to Uncle Fred and Aunt Harriet. As usual, there was too much of everything: booze, food, conversation. Aunt Harriet waived the black-tie requirement, and we were all much more comfortable in wools and tweeds. Times were slowly changing.

Poor George Sawyer had his hands full serving, but, at least, he didn't have to cook. That task fell to the ladies, who appeared out of the woodwork whenever they were needed.

All in all, it was a great time. I managed to garner a large glass of vodka undetected. When it came to drinking, Brad Charles had taught me well. With that under my belt, I was ready for anything.

The main dining room was only large enough to seat the Powell children, their spouses, Grandmother Powell, Granny Steadman, and Aunt Harriet's mother, Elena. The cousins were relegated to the breakfast room, but that was fine with us. It was a pleasure to be spared the constant scrutiny of our parents and grandparents as we decided for ourselves what fork or spoon to use.

All the cousins were in attendance. All were growing older now, developing their own distinct personalities. At eleven, Jane, the youngest, was beginning to blossom. Howard and Franklin, at fourteen and thirteen, respectively, had begun to gain their height. In recognition of our approaching sixteenth birthdays, Tom and I were allowed a small glass of wine with dinner. The others had to be satisfied with a fruit punch concoction created and served by our loving Regina.

Once dinner was finished, George Sawyer, with the help of the ladies, began clearing the tables. Brandy and cordials were served in the drawing room. Jane followed Howard and Franklin to the recreation room where the big pool table captured their attention. Tom and I sought refuge in his study at the top of the servants' stair off the dining room. It was the first time we had a chance to be alone since the holiday had begun.

Tom stretched out on the sofa, hands behind his head. "God, I ate too much."

I sat in the chair across from him. "Me, too," I laughed. "I could use another glass of wine."

He looked at me smugly. "I'd have thought the vodka would have been enough."

"How'd you know about that?"

He laughed. "I saw you. You're not as slick as you think you are."

I chuckled. "Guess not."

"When they finish clearing the dining room, we can sneak down and help ourselves."

"Sounds like a plan to me."

Tom paused. "How's school?"

"I hate it."

"Figured as much."

"I hate all the military bullshit."

"Who wouldn't?"

"And there's this upperclassman who keeps riding my back."

"That ain't good."

"To make matters worse, he's our RA."

"A real little tin soldier, huh?"

"You got it."

"Why don't you just tell him to lay off?"

I laughed at the absurdity of the question. "You can't begin to understand."

"I guess not."

"That's how the military works, through intimidation."

"So I've heard. Isn't there someone you can report him to?"

I laughed again. "Oh, sure. Plenty of people. But no one's going to listen to a first-year cadet."

"Have you told your father?"

"What's the point? He's pleased as punch with Dewey. Nothing I say will change his mind. I gave up on him a long time ago."

"Right."

"Tom!" George's voice floated up the stairway. "You got company!"

Tom jumped from the sofa and walked to the head of the stairs. "Send them up. Hey, guys! Come on up."

The sound of footsteps on bare treads accompanied muffled voices. Freddie cleared the stairs first, followed by Christabel. Her sudden presence took me by surprise for a moment. I knew she was seeing Dan Welch again; Tom had told me that much. So what was she doing here?

Freddie crossed the room and kissed me lightly on the cheek. "Hey, sweetie. How's school going?"

I smiled. "Hate it."

She returned the smile. "We really miss you."

"Not half as much as I miss you guys." I shot Christabel a pointed look, but her face remained impassive.

Christabel had followed Freddie into the room and sat on the sofa next to Tom. She didn't appear to be in the mood for pleasant conversation.

Tom turned to Christabel. "How was your Thanksgiving?"

Christabel shrugged. "About as usual. Had to listen to my father's drunken ramblings about his days in the service. Of course, Mother didn't say a word. She's having one of her bouts of depression."

"Fun," Tom observed.

"Yeah, I couldn't wait to get out of the house."

Freddie smiled. "We thought we might find a little drinkie-poo over here."

Tom laughed. "We were just saying the same thing. Got to wait until the dust settles downstairs. Then we'll see what we can find. Can't have George sniffing around. He'd tell Mom in a minute."

While we waited, the conversation ranged from their experiences at school to mine at Dewey. Of course, I didn't tell them the truth about Brad but simply painted him as a bully. That was close enough.

I might have shared the truth with Tom if the girls hadn't shown up, but I sure as hell wasn't about to share it with them.

When the hubbub in the dining room ceased, Tom crept down the stairs and located the half-empty bottle of vodka. Lacking proper glasses, we simply passed the bottle from person to person until it was empty.

Laughter reigned, and I took great pleasure in watching Christabel again. Her ashen hair was longer now, falling to her shoulders in a gentle flip. I still loved her laugh. There was no denying I missed her. I still ridiculed myself for my behavior last summer. Still, it felt good to be near her again, even if she was across the room, even if she was still seeing Dan, even if she wasn't mine any longer. It was good to be home.

—

The long weekend rushed to a close. Where the hours went, I'm not sure. I spent a lot of time with Tom, but I never mentioned Brad again. That moment had passed. I saw Christabel once more, fleetingly across the yard. She smiled and waved to me. I considered it a good sign.

—

On Sunday, my parents drove me to the train in Wilmington. It wasn't a pleasant journey. I was depressed at the thought of returning to Dewey. My father seemed in high spirits at my impending departure, the son of a bitch. My mother was mostly silent throughout the trip.

"I'm glad you're adjusting so well." There was a happy lilt to my father's voice.

Happy, my ass. "Yeah."

"I think you'll find it easier as time goes on."

Easier than what?

"I know it's hard mixing the military with the academic, but it provides a good balance."

Oh, just shut up.

"And I think there's something to be said for an all-male environment."

I could quote him chapter and verse on that one.

"It fosters a camaraderie you don't find at a co-ed school."

If he only knew.

"You'll make friends there who will stay with you the rest of your life."

I knew that was true of Ed and Chris. Brad, however, was a different story. My father didn't have a clue. He was so pleased with himself it made me nauseous. I wanted to reach across the seat and punch him in the face. He had no idea what he had done to me. No idea of how his master plan had gone so awry. Someday he would. Someday I would tell him. Someday I was going to throw it in his face–every dirty, sordid detail.

We reached the station. Goodbyes were said, and I boarded the train for New York. My father had arranged for a car service to pick me up at Pennsylvania Station and take me out to the school. My mother still objected to my riding the subway system alone. If she only knew.

—

The dormitory was busy with cadets arriving back from the holidays. I was checked in at the main desk by an upperclassman who I only knew by sight and then headed up to my room. The halls were filled with cadets talking and moving from room to room. There seemed to be a tension running through the entire building. I grasped some of the comments, but they meant little to me.

"On Thanksgiving day …"

"Really strange …"

"Wonder if they'll catch him."

I entered our room and found Chris and Ed kicked back behind their desks. Clay Lloyd, a friend from down the hall, sat at my desk.

"Hey, guys! What's going on?" I motioned toward the hallway.

Clay rose from my desk. "You don't know?"

I smiled. "I'm askin'."

The trio looked from one to another, and then Ed spoke. "Brad Charles is dead."

"What?" I allowed a look of surprise to cross my face.

Chris nodded. "Thanksgiving day."

"They found the body Thanksgiving day," Ed added. "He died sometime before then."

I set down my suitcase with a bang and dropped onto the edge of my bunk. "What happened?"

Ed jumped back into the conversation. "They found him at the Tremont on Westchester Square."

"Strangled with a belt or something." Clay seemed pleased with the information.

"One of the upperclassmen said so."

I did my best to feign shock. "How'd he find that out?"

Clay shrugged. "Who knows? Maybe he had something to do with it."

Chris leaned over and closed the window blind. "The commodore's going to address the school at formation tomorrow morning."

I shook my head as if to clear it. "God, I don't believe it."

Chris laughed. "I guess that lets us off the hook."

Ed glared at him. "Jesus, Chris. Don't you have any respect?"

Chris smiled. "Not for that son of a bitch. As far as I'm concerned, someone did us a big favor."

Ed simply shook his head and stared at the desktop. "That shouldn't happen to anyone, not even to a prick like Charles."

Chris sighed. "Probably picked up some hooker, and it went bad."

"A hooker!" Clay laughed. "Charles was gay."

"I know that, dummy. Guys can be hookers, too."

Clay grinned. "News to me."

The banter continued as I sat on the bunk listening. No one seemed to know how or why Brad was killed. Apparently, a chambermaid found him on Thanksgiving Day when she went to make up the room. The police were involved, but they weren't saying anything. The chances of them finding the perpetrator seemed slim. They would be interviewing all the cadets who lived under Brad's rule in hopes of finding a lead.

Certainly, Brad's alternative lifestyle had played a part in his death. Everyone seemed in agreement on that. For the rest of the details, we would simply have to wait and see. The important thing was that Brad Charles was gone. He wouldn't be bothering me ever again.

Except, perhaps, in my dreams.

20

Spring 1963 – Reprieve

WITH BRAD CHARLES GONE, the next few months flew by like a breeze. I returned home for Christmas and gloried in my freedom. Tom and I were constantly together, enjoying the company of childhood friends, especially Freddie and, occasionally, Christabel. Her relationship with Dan seemed to be holding, and I was in no position to usurp it. Being in New York held more than a few disadvantages.

At school, the stir caused by Brad's death gradually diminished. The police interviewed each dorm resident, but no one had anything to offer. My interview went smoothly. I lied, but could not summon any feelings of remorse for my actions. It had happened, and that was that. For months, the case languished in the police files and finally went cold. The investigators labeled the crime as murder by person or persons unknown.

Life took on a new feeling. I still hated Dewey, but without Brad, it became tolerable. It wasn't the place for me. I was not the type to don a uniform and blindly follow orders.

Ed, Chris, Clay, and I began to enjoy New York and all it had to offer. Clay's father had guided us to a few really good restaurants. Broadway shows became a norm, and there was always Radio City Music Hall. Afternoons were filled with museums, art galleries, and concerts. We chalked it all up as part of Ed's continuing education plan.

During one of their frequent visits to Dewey, Ed's parents had taken me aside. As it turned out, Ed had led a very sheltered, simple life. He was a trust fund baby but didn't know it. His parents were modest to the extreme but now felt it was time for him to sample the better things in life. The three of us were only too happy to oblige.

It was into this somewhat carefree existence fate decided to throw the proverbial monkey wrench.

Easter break was in the offing, and we were all making plans for our reprieve. The four of us sat around our room talking when Cal James, our new RA, stuck his head into the room. We all snapped to attention.

"Steadman."

"Sir?"

"Commodore's office. Now."

"Sir!"

I double-timed it out of the room, down the corridor, down the stairs, and out the door. The quad was busy with cadets going about their daily routines. The day was pleasantly warm, the first of many to come. I made my way to the admin building and presented myself to the commodore's secretary.

"Cadet Steadman, Ma'am."

"Have a seat, cadet. The commodore will be right with you."

I sat in an uncomfortable wooden chair and waited. What was going on? What had I done? Did this have anything to do with Brad? My mind was in turmoil.

Suddenly the door opened, and the commodore strode into the room. He was a tall, striking man with iron-gray hair.

"Come in, cadet." He held the door for me to enter. "Have a seat." He motioned to one of the chairs in front of his wide desk.

I sat, my nerves jangling.

The commodore sat in his big leather chair and looked at me. "I just had a call from your uncle, Frederick Powell."

"Yes, Sir?" Why would Uncle Fred call?

"Your father has suffered a stroke, and you're needed at home. I'm sorry for the bad news, cadet."

A stroke. My father. It seemed impossible. He always appeared to be in great physical shape. My mother was probably a mess.

"Thank you, Sir."

"Go pack your bag and get on the road. You have money?"

"Yes, Sir."

"A car will be here to take you to Pennsylvania Station at 14:00 hours. When you reach the Wilmington train station, your Uncle John will be there to drive you home. You comfortable traveling alone?"

"Yes, Sir. I've done it before."

He stood. "Then you'd best get moving."

I stood.

"And again, I'm sorry, cadet."

"Yes, thank you, Sir."

And that was that. No preamble. No fuss. Bang! Within a single instant, my life had changed again.

The trip home seemed longer than usual, but I chalked that up to the situation. Uncle John was waiting for me at the Wilmington station where he filled me in on the details, few of which were good.

My father's stroke had not been massive, but it had done some damage. His right side was partially paralyzed, and speech was difficult. His doctor felt he would recover, but the next few days were critical. A second stroke might occur without warning and could be fatal. It didn't sound good at all.

Mother was not taking it well. She had remained at the hospital from the onset, and no one could convince her to leave. She was beginning to show the effects of her vigil. Part of my duty was to convince her to go home, rest, and recharge. Getting my mother to do anything she didn't want to do was nigh on to impossible. I had my work cut out for me.

―

The next two weeks stretched on into what seemed like infinity. Through begging and nagging, I finally succeeded in getting my mother to take a break. She agreed to return home if I would stay with my father. It was a viable trade-off, and that became our routine. One of us was always at the hospital, day and night. It was only after the doctor proclaimed my father out of danger that my mother finally relented, allowing us both a good night's sleep.

I spent many hours in that dreary hospital room. Most of the time, I tried to read. When not reading, I sometimes pondered all that had happened over the past few months. It wasn't a pleasant endeavor. Too much had transpired, and I didn't exactly relish revisiting it. Still, something in my mind forced me to examine those difficult months with a stark scrutiny I didn't realize I had. I took every memory, turned it upside down, examined all sides of it, and then placed it back on the shelf of my mind. The tomes marked Tom, Freddie, Christabel, my mother, my father, Ed, Chris, Clay, and Brad sat smiling down at me.

Some of the smiles were not so nice. Brad's would likely haunt me forever.

I watched my father as he suffered with his new handicaps. He was wired to every machine imaginable. Doctors and nurses came and went with regularity. How he could begin to rest escaped me, but I didn't care about that. It honestly did my heart good to see him lying there. For once *he* was a victim. All his planning had not saved him from what fate had in store. It served him right. I hoped it humbled him a bit, but I doubted it would. That was simply too unlike my father. Even now, I could imagine him lying there planning, scheming, trying his best to put his world back in the order he preferred. Fate be damned.

I began to live for those hours when I was freed from my post. One of my aunts or uncles seemed to always be there, waiting to drive me home. There, I would forage through the big kitchen and then crash in front of the television. Occasionally, Tom would get a ride out, and Freddie called with regularity. Christabel even called once, which surprised me. I considered it a good omen.

The big question that loomed in our lives was my father's future. Would he be discharged soon? Who, besides my mother, would take care of him? How long would it be before he could return to work? Would he even be able to work? His doctors were optimistic. The stroke had not been massive, and they projected a complete recovery.

In-home care wasn't a big issue. One of the ladies would be available, if not a whole retinue of them. Regina came three days a week anyway to clean, wash, iron, and whatever else my mother could find for her to do. The companies, Steadman and Son Contracting and Steadman and Son Building and Supply, could practically run themselves, but they still needed my father's guiding hand. He had good people working beneath him and good managers at both companies. Still, he made all the major decisions. That was a hard one.

My father's stroke had one truly silver lining. It gave me an out from Dewey. Sure, I'd be home while he was hospitalized, and I was certain I could stretch that for at least another week or two. By that time, Easter would arrive, and that would mean spring break. Final exams, which I'd have to take, would then follow. But then the school year would be over. If I could manipulate the situation to my advantage, I just might be done with Dewey once and for all. It was all a matter of how well my father progressed. It was all a matter of having a plan.

My father was discharged after two weeks. His doctors were pleased with Dad's progress. My mother enshrined him in the master suite surrounded by a rotating staff of caregivers. Regina upped her schedule to five days a week, and the other ladies filled the gaps. The whole arrangement ran smoothly, as was my mother's way with most situations.

My mother moved into one of the guest suites to avoid disturbing my father. The rooms were on the second floor above the master suite and accessible by a third stairway that led from the master suite hallway to the second-floor hallway. This positioned her close enough to hear my father if he needed help, but far enough away as to not disturb his rest. Dad's physicians had stressed the need for rest as insurance against another stroke.

Granny Steadman was an emotional mess through it all. After all, my father was her only child, and all her siblings had predeceased her. She was alone in the world except for my father and me. Because of this, my mother allowed her free rein to come and go as she wished. Of course, this required someone picking her up and taking her home again. Granny Steadman had given up driving years ago, following a near miss with a deer with me as her passenger.

My mother was very strict about who visited and for how long. Friends and relatives came and went, but only with her permission and on her schedule. The company managers were forbidden to visit him for fear the aggravation of business would delay his recovery. The fact that this practice aggravated him even more didn't seem to matter. Quiet, rest, some guarded exercise of his right arm and leg became the watchwords in our house. My mother ruled over it all.

"You mustn't agitate him," she explained. "The doctors are adamant about that. It could trigger another stroke this close to the initial one."

I nodded. I had no intention of agitating him. Now that he was home, I had no intention of being around him any more than what was required. He had the ladies tending to his every want and need. My mother was constantly by his side.

"And don't bring up school. I know you're not happy there, but this is not the time to be talking about it."

"What if he brings it up?"

"Then handle it the best you can. He's already asked when you're going back."

"What did you tell him?"

"I told him after spring break." She looked at me for approval.

"Yeah, I have exams. Then it's only a few weeks before the end of term."

"That time will pass quickly."

"You're sure you don't need me here? I could come back home as soon as exams are over."

My mother shook her head. "We'll be fine. Having you come home again will only cause more concern. Hang in there for the rest of the term. We'll have all summer to talk about your return in the fall."

"I'm not going back."

"So you've said. But we're not talking about it now. We have enough to worry about without that."

I nodded. Still, Dewey was forefront in my mind. I'd had plenty; enough was enough. No way in hell was I going back in the fall. My parents were simply going to have to accept that fact. I missed my friends. I missed my family. I missed my home. I wanted my old life back.

21

Spring 1963 – Revenge

TIME MOVED SLOWLY AT our house. My father's recovery came with small steps and some setbacks. He wasn't a model patient and was easily prone to frustration and anger. When this happened, my mother became alarmed and often ended up phoning Dad's doctor. The reply was always the same: Keep him quiet. Be sure he gets plenty of rest. Be sure he doesn't overexert. No suggestions as to how to achieve all this. Simply do it. My father was, of course, of no help.

Spring break was nearing its end, and I was faced with returning to Dewey for my exams. I had only three days remaining. I'd been good to the promise I made to my mother and hadn't mentioned school; neither had my father.

My father sat in the winged-back chair next to the big canopied bed while my mother and I struggled with the sheets and bedspread. It had become a nightly ritual, this smoothing of bed linens in preparation for my father's retiring. Once finished, we helped him from the chair to the edge of the bed and settled him down for the night.

My mother pulled the sheet over him and patted his chest. She smiled and kissed him lightly on the cheek. "Get a good night's sleep."

As she backed away from the bed, he reached out his hand to me. "Talk to you?" His words remained slurred but were distinguishable.

I looked at mother in surprise. She simply nodded.

"Sure, Dad." I sat in the chair he had just vacated. "What ya want to talk about?"

"School."

My mother shot me a look of warning. I answered her with a nod. She hesitated for a moment and then walked toward the door. "I'm going up. I'll leave you two alone, but call me if you need me." Another look of warning crossed her face before she exited.

I sat in silence and waited for my father to continue. He lay on his back, staring at the canopy overhead. Then he smiled as if to himself. "School."

"Yeah, Dad. What about it?"

"Going back? When?"

"Sunday. In three days. Spring break's nearly over, and I have exams coming up."

He smiled again. "Good boy."

I laughed. "If you say so."

He laughed as well. "Make a man out of you."

Yeah, right. Some man I'd become—thanks to him.

"Like it now?"

Not a question I wanted to field. It would bring me too close to breaking my promise to my mother. "It's okay."

"Good for you."

Bullshit! Getting raped isn't good for anyone.

"Make a man out of you."

If he only knew.

"Two more years after this one."

I couldn't resist. "We'll see."

He turned his head and gazed into my eyes. "Two more years."

"I said, we'll see."

I could see the slight redness appear as it crept up his neck. He shook his head.

"Two more years." His voice was firmer now, verging on anger. I'd pushed the issue too far.

"Two more years!" His voice was almost a shout.

I didn't want him arousing my mother. That's all I needed. I rose from the chair and crossed the room to the door. Pushing it closed, I turned to face him across the room. My anger flared. "Dad, we need to talk."

—

Even with the distance separating our rooms, I heard my mother's scream the next morning. That shriek could only mean that something bad had happened.

I jumped from my bed and ran down the stairs and through the public rooms of the house. I stopped just inside the doorway to my parents' bedroom. My mother had thrown herself across the bed and lay there sobbing. My father's inert body lay under the sheet, his open eyes staring at nothing.

I crossed to the bed and lay my hand on her shoulder. "Mom…"

She shrugged my hand away and continued to cry. "What have you done? I told you not to upset him!" Her tone was nasty, accusatory.

"But, I didn't…"

Suddenly, she sat upright and glared at me. "Don't lie to me. Don't you dare lie to me!"

I backpedaled. "I'm not."

"I left you here alone with him." She motioned to my father's lifeless body. "He was fine. What did you say to him? What did you do?"

"Nothing, Mom. I didn't say or do anything."

"You just couldn't wait, could you? Always thinking of yourself! You're a selfish, thoughtless person, Marc!"

"Mom…"

"Don't lie to me, Marc. I won't have it! You've done it now. I hope you're satisfied."

"Mom," I pleaded.

She sat on the edge of the bed, face buried in her hands. "Phone an ambulance and the doctor. I…can't." She was sobbing again.

―

My father had died of a stroke. That much was certain. What prompted it was an issue only between me and my mother. It was an issue that would hang between us for the rest of our lives.

There was cause for guilt on my part, but I wasn't about to own it. The old man had goaded me, baited me, teased me. When I confronted him with the truth, he accused me of bringing Brad's attentions on myself. He accused *me* of secretly *wanting it to happen*. The son of a bitch. Him and his well-laid plans.

He had been fine when I left him; angry and arrogant, but clearly alive. I suspect he'd stewed on our meeting throughout the night until it got the best of him. I could just imagine him lying there in his king-like bed, tossing and turning, agonizing over the fact that his son was a failure. That would be just like him.

It served him right. See what it got you, old man? No more fucking up other people's lives for you. And therein lay the silver lining: Dewey was now a thing of the past.

—

The funeral was a typical Martin's Neck affair, part of the ongoing social season. Lines of expensive automobiles, crowds of people dressed in the best their closets had to offer. The service was standing room only. The by-invitation-only wake was held at our house, as was the norm in these matters.

In preparation for the event, it had fallen to me, as the surviving son, to meet with the funeral director. Once all the finer points of the service were discussed and decided upon, he led me into a large room filled with caskets. I was guided through the maze until we reached a display in the center of the room.

"This is the casket your family uses."

I stared at the black walnut box with its silver fittings. A family casket. Who knew? I suspect it was just another one of the advantages enjoyed by a family in our position. You learn something new every day.

The service was short as this was considered tasteful. There was no eulogizing, and the only music was that piped into the room prior to and following the service. Filling the first five rows of seating, the family looked its best. They had all played this role before, as they would again and again.

My mother had made it obvious that I was to give her a wide berth.

"I don't want you fawning around me like you care how I feel."

"Sure, Mom. Whatever you say."

That set the tone for the day, and I abided by her wishes.

Granny Steadman was stoic despite her true feelings. Public displays of grief were unheard of in Martin's Neck and certainly would not be tolerated by our family. I stayed by Granny's side throughout the entire day.

Granny Steadman had been staying in one of our guest rooms since my father's death, but insisted that she return home once the funeral was behind us. That would result in daily visits with her, a tradition that my father had previously fostered and maintained. Needless to say, my mother considered these visits an encroachment on her personal freedom. Fortunately for her, I would soon be licensed to drive and, thus, able to remove that burden from her shoulders.

Somehow, I survived the day. At the wake, I easily found a couple of stiff drinks at the open bar. It was a private affair, and no one really cared who drank and who didn't. At one point, I left Granny with her plate of food and sought refuge on the front porch. Tom joined me there, drink in hand.

"Sorry, man." He sat in the rocker next to mine.

"Yeah…thanks."

"I guess this means you're coming back to Martin's Neck."

"Damn right."

"At least that's one good thing."

I smiled. "Hell, yes! That's the gold ring, Tom. The gold ring."

22

Summer 1963 – Home Again

I RETURNED TO DEWEY for my exams, but that was the end of it. I unenrolled that same week, bid goodbye to Ed, Chris, and Clay, and returned to Martin's Neck. There, life continued much as usual. My relationship with my mother was still strained, but I didn't let it bother me. I was home, and that was all that mattered. The rest I could handle.

Tom and I celebrated our sixteenth birthdays–his in May, mine in July. Of course, reaching sixteen was all about getting one's driver's license. True to Uncle Fred's penchant for expensive automobiles, he bought Tom a new Austin Healey 3000, black over red. It was quite an automobile, and we were all jealous of Tom's good fortune.

Not to be outdone, though certainly not out of love for me, my mother purchased me a used 1962 Corvette–a silver blue metallic beauty with white side scoops.

Summer ushered in the opening of Powell Cottage and Tom's relocation to the Burton's Brae Beach dwelling. Both my mother and I were more than happy for me to spend as much time there as possible. I took full advantage.

Christabel was still dating Dan, so I felt no need to pursue getting her back since most of my summer would be spent at the beach. The logistics simply didn't work. I'd leave that plan until after school was back in session.

Sandy Davidson and her family were back for another season. I saw Sandy at our gatherings at the store and on the beach. After what had happened last summer with Christabel, she was reluctant to encourage my attentions. However, the arrival of my sixteenth birthday and the Corvette soon changed that.

Tom was dating Lori Sharcoff who lived next door. She was a tall, willowy girl with a great sense of adventure and humor. Lori was a perfect match for Tom. The latter part of July and all of August was filled with trips to Rehoboth Beach and Ocean City. Since neither car would hold four people, we always traveled in tandem, creating our own conspicuous caravan. In Rehoboth we tooled the Avenue, parked the cars, and walked the boardwalk. Ocean City boasted a wonderful under-twenty-one nightclub called The Beachcomber Lounge. With great bands and large crowds, it was often a favorite destination. We all loved to dance.

—

The summer months passed quickly and soon the season ended. Powell Cottage was closed, and Sandy and Lori returned home. With fall's arrival, Tom and I were soon back at Martin's Neck High. Juniors. It was hard to believe.

Christabel and Dan remained an item, but I wasn't going to let that stop me. All I needed was a plan.

I stayed as close to Christabel as possible. We were in the same classes, which made that part of the plan easy to execute. I talked to her, was polite to her, and tried to be as charming as possible without being pushy. I wanted her to feel at ease around me again. As a result, she began to rejoin our weekend soirees either at Tom's house or Freddie's. It was good to have her back, but I needed to take things slowly. As I knew from experience, one didn't rush Christabel McCafferty.

—

The annual Christmas dance was a big deal at Martin's Neck High. A semi-formal affair, it was given by the senior class in honor of the alumni. Tuxedos for the guys; short, cocktail dresses for the girls. Live music rather than the DJ that was typically hired for most of the school dances.

As much as I wanted Christabel on my arm, I knew that was impossible. She would be going with Dan. Mary Elizabeth Farmer was between beaus at the time, so we had dated on and off since my return to Martin's Neck High. Taking her to the Christmas dance was the natural next step.

It was a perfect night. The auditorium was decorated in a snow motif of blue, white, and silver. Glittered snowflakes hung from a blue and silver crepe paper ceiling. A mirrored ball crowned the center above a large, tinsel tree adorned with blue balls. Tables with white cloth and tinsel tree centerpieces were grouped around the dance floor.

Mary Elizabeth and I were seated at one of the tables with Tom and his date, Freddie and her date, and Dan and Christabel. Everyone seemed to be in good spirits, ready for what the night had to offer. About halfway through the evening, Mary Elizabeth and Freddie excused themselves to the ladies' room. Meanwhile, Dan, Tom, and Freddie's date left the table in search of more refreshments. That left Tom's date, Christabel, and me.

The band, dressed in powder blue dinner jackets, played their usual assortment of popular tunes, standards, and Christmas melodies. When they swung into "Put Your Head on My Shoulder," I stared at Christabel. It had always been one of our favorites.

"Care to dance?"

At first, Christabel looked surprised, but she soon smiled. She gazed toward the refreshment table where Dan and his friends were laughing and talking. "Sure." With that, she rose from her seat.

I followed Christabel onto the dance floor and took her in my arms. It felt so, so good. The band continued to play.

The song brought back all the memories. Memories I wanted to be part of my life again. I removed my cheek from hers and stared into her eyes. "How was your summer?"

She smiled. "Fine. You had an eventful one."

"Pardon?"

"Big birthday. New car."

I laughed. "Oh, yeah...that."

"And you didn't even bother to come by and show me your new wheels."

"I didn't think you'd be impressed."

She laughed. "You were right."

"See."

"Not to mention your new girlfriend."

"Mary Elizabeth?"

"No, silly. The girl from the beach. Dan and I saw you with her at the Beachcomber one night."

"Did you?"

"You were with Tom and some other girl."

"Lori."

"Whatever."

"We didn't see you. You should have come over and said something."

"I didn't think it was appropriate." She smiled. "After what happened the previous summer."

I laughed. "Yeah, that was a bit awkward." I looked into her cool, gray eyes and smiled. "I've missed you."

Her face clouded. "Marc…don't."

I smiled again. "Sorry."

She shook her head and looked over my shoulder at the other dancers. I pulled her close, again placing my cheek next to hers. This fool was about to rush in.

23

Winter 1964 – Fast Cars

"GET UP, YOU TWO!" Uncle Fred's voice filled Tom's bedroom. "There's something I want you to see!"

Tom and I roused, still groggy from the late night we'd had. The room was cold, and frost pock-marked the multi-paned windows.

Tom threw back the covers. "What's up, Dad?"

Uncle Fred had already left the room and had started down the stair. "Just get yourselves dressed. There's something I want you to go see."

I stretched. "What the hell's that all about?"

Tom pulled his nightshirt over his head and reached for his clothes. "Got me. Guess we'll find out soon enough."

I followed suit and, in minutes, we clamored down the rear stairway to the kitchen. It was balmy there. The cooking fireplace roared, spreading its warmth throughout the big room.

Uncle Fred stood at the kitchen counter and sipped coffee.

Tom planted himself in front of the fireplace, warming his hands. "What's going on, Dad?"

"There's been a bad accident. Couple of guys your age from Millbank."

"Who?"

Uncle Fred shook his head. "Don't know, but it's a bad one. I want you two to have a look at the car. It's out at Jimmy's Garage."

Tom looked at me and shrugged. "Okay."

Uncle Fred continued. "You need to see what can happen when you abuse the right to drive."

Tom rolled his eyes. I turned away to hide the smile threatening my face.

"Sure thing, Dad." Tom moved to the coat rack by the back door. He grabbed my jacket and tossed it to me.

Uncle Fred was right. It was a bad one. What remained of the new Chevy Super Sport coupe lay in a tangled mass in front of Jimmy's Garage. A large crowd had assembled, but the conversation was hushed and muted. Several of our classmates were present, obviously there to "learn a lesson" like us.

Dan Welch sidled over and stood with his hands stuffed into his pockets. "Damn, Sam. This ain't good."

Tom shook his head.

I didn't recognize the car and had no idea who could have been driving it. "Who was it?"

"Bill Kendal and Rick Moore. Bill got the car just this week. Guess they were trying to see what she would do."

"Dead?" I asked.

"Oh, yeah." Dan sighed. "Too bad."

Tom and I knew the boys. They were a year older than we. As Uncle Fred had said, they were from Millbank, but both had dated girls from Martin's Neck from time to time.

Tom stuffed his hands in his jacket pockets. "Where'd it happen?"

"Route 12. They didn't make the long curve there. Must have lost control. Sheared off a telephone pole about half way up." Dan pointed to the long-curved dent in the car's trunk deck. "You can see where it impacted."

Tom shook his head. "Must've really been movin'."

"Got a 409." I pointed to the insignia on the car's fender. "Plenty of power there."

Dan nodded. "Yeah, too much power."

Ironically, the accident was the first of three that followed in quick succession. The next occurred several miles south near Rehoboth Beach, where six teenagers were out joyriding. They were from Lewiston, but we all knew them by name and reputation. With this accident, there appeared to be alcohol involved and, fortunately or unfortunately, only one fatality–Lee Anne Townsend. She was originally from Martin's Neck, and we had attended elementary school together. She was decapitated.

One of the Madding Crowd

The next week, another alcohol-related accident took its toll. This time it was the elder brother of one of our classmates. He and a friend had been out drinking and met with misfortune on their way home. The accident also occurred on Route 12, but at a different curve. Instead of a telephone pole, three trees were involved. Driver and passenger were both killed instantly.

That was one of the problems with life in a small town like Martin's Neck. There simply wasn't enough to do. Of course, there were dances and parties, but with the acquisition of drivers' licenses, life became much more dangerous.

Tom and I were not the only ones with fancy cars. Most of our friends and classmates had them as well. Martin's Neck was a very affluent community, and it was the age of the muscle car. GTOs, Cutlass 4-4-2s and the like dotted the student parking lot. Even the girls drove big, flashy cars. Christabel's parents had presented her with a new Pontiac Grand Prix upon her sixteenth birthday. Our assistant principal was heard to comment, "What does it tell you when the cars in the student parking lot outshine those in the faculty parking lot?" Cars were simply a way of life. Adding alcohol to the mixture only complicated things.

Of course, as teenagers, we knew that nothing bad could happen to us. To others, sure, but not to us. We lived charmed lives, and booze and powerful cars were not going to make any difference. Yes, the odds ran out for an unfortunate few, but even three consecutive fatal weekends could not shake our sense of invincibility.

Our whole lives were ahead of us.

24

Spring 1965 – Seniors

COCOONED IN OUR PRIVILEGED little lives, time seemed to slip quickly by. 1964 and 1965 were filled to the brim with all the activities of high school life. Dances, parties, sporting events, proms, and school plays all took the forefront in our world. We were a busy bunch, and nothing could hold us back.

Numbering forty-eight, we were the largest class to ever graduate from Martin's Neck High. But we were more like a family than a group of classmates. We were always together; we depended on one another. Every activity included practically every classmate. Leaving was going to be hard. We had never really functioned independently of one another.

College was going to be a whole new world for the Class of '65.

—

By the spring of 1965, Christabel and I were back together and had been for over a year. It had happened a few months following the memorable Christmas dance. It didn't happen all at once, but I had laid the groundwork and had laid it well. By March of 1964, Dan's eyes had begun to wander. He became enamored with Jennie Simonson, another of our classmates. His infidelity gave me the break I needed, and I took every advantage of the situation. Before long, Christabel and I were reunited.

April heralded the traditional senior class trip to New York City. Three days and two nights of fun and exploration. I couldn't wait to show Christabel some of my old haunts from my time at Dewey. While there would be the obligatory visits to the Empire State Building, the UN, the Statue of Liberty, and the Museum of Natural History. That still left plenty of time for adventure.

We stayed at the Taft Hotel on Seventh Avenue and 51st Street. It was an older hotel, built prior to the Second World War in the Spanish Renaissance style. It still retained much of its original grandeur, but now catered to a somewhat lesser clientele.

Saturday night was to be the high point of our trip. The class was to attend a Broadway show, and I had promised to take Christabel to one of my favorite restaurants. While it was going to be a special night, I somehow wanted it to be more. Almost without my knowing, a plan began to formulate in my mind. I smiled to myself, confident that it would work.

Tom, Dan, and I shared a room on the sixth floor. Tom and Dan were down in the coffee shop, so I had free rein for the moment. I pulled on my overcoat and grabbed my empty suitcase. I took the elevator down to the Mezzanine overlooking the lobby. It was crowded with tourists. So far, so good; I had yet to encounter anyone from our group. From there, I descended the stairs to the side entry on 51st Street and rounded the corner onto Seventh Avenue. Acting as if I had just arrived, I entered through the main doors and walked straight to the registration desk.

"I'd like a room."

The young man behind the counter looked at me with doubt. "Reservation?"

I shook my head. "No. Unexpected trip."

He perused his listings and then handed me a registration card. "Just fill this out."

And just like that, it was done. Room bought and paid for. I had to admit I could be a clever devil when I put my mind to it.

That evening unfolded as planned. I took Christabel to Mike Manuche's on West 52nd Street, just around the corner from The Taft. Mike's was a high-end, businessmen's restaurant to which Clay's father had introduced us. It boasted a huge, horseshoe-shaped bar and was adorned with an assortment of original oil paintings depicting various sporting events. It was also frequented by an attractive assortment of expensive call girls clothed identically in fashionable, black sheath dresses, immaculate coiffures, and just the right amount of make-up.

Ironically, Christabel fit right in. She was the sort of girl at whom guys always took a second look. Tonight was no exception. Her ash-blond hair, pulled back in a severe French twist, contrasted dramatically with the black, crepe sheath with its full sleeves, and an intricate neckline that culminated in a single, pink, silk rose. She was quite a sight.

Dinner with Christabel was wonderful. We ate, we talked, and I even managed to obtain a bottle of wine to accompany our meal. Chapter one was a success.

We had plenty of time before curtain so we walked from the restaurant to the theater. Being in New York again was exciting. It made my blood tingle. I felt alive, and that all things were ultimately possible.

The show, *High Spirits*, was a huge success with our classmates. It was light and funny; the perfect show for a group of teenagers on the edge of adulthood.

We walked, en masse, back to the hotel, laughing and talking all the way. When we reached our destination, I didn't want to be herded along with the rest of our class. I took Christabel's arm and guided her into the coffee shop off the lobby.

"Let's have a cup of coffee and wait this out."

She looked at me and smiled. "Sure. Why not?"

A few others followed suit, but Christabel and I found an isolated table and did not encourage company. We continued our conversation, sipping coffee until the bulk of the crowd had thinned out.

I pushed aside my empty cup. "Ready?"

She sighed. "I guess so." She didn't seem ready for the evening to end. Neither did I.

In the elevator, I requested the eleventh floor. Christabel looked at me in surprise. "We're on the seventh floor."

I smiled. "I know. I have something I want to show you."

"Oh." She looked doubtful.

We rode the rest of the way in silence. At the eleventh floor, the attendant opened the door. "Have a good evening."

"You, too," I responded, as I led Christabel down the hallway.

At the door to room 1108, I stopped and fit the key in the lock.

"What are you doing?" Christabel sounded shocked.

"I told you." I swung the door open and stood aside for her to enter. "I have a little surprise for you."

She stepped into the room and I closed the door behind us.

"Marc, what's going on?" She stood with her back to me and surveyed the room.

I came up behind her and laid my hands on the sheer fabric covering her shoulders. I leaned down and kissed the back of her neck. "I wanted us to have some time alone together. I'm so sick of people."

She turned and wrapped her arms around my neck. She looked up at me and smiled. "You're sweet." She kissed me lightly on the lips. The single rose crushed against my chest.

"That silk rose has to go."

She laughed. "I thought you liked it."

"I do, but not when it's keeping us apart."

"Then do something about it."

I reached behind her and found the tab of her zipper. I leaned over and kissed her as I gently unzipped her dress.

College loomed. We were all going our separate ways. Tom opted on a business degree. Uncle Fred was adamant about him becoming part of the family real estate conglomerate. Tom didn't seem terribly excited at the prospect, but you couldn't always tell with Tom. Regardless, he was headed to the state university about one hundred miles away.

Freddie was off to George Madison to study education. She was excited, having planned this all her life. She dreamed of becoming a teacher and later an administrator. Knowing Freddie, everything would go as planned, as if it was preordained by some higher power.

Christabel had locked horns with her parents. They wanted her to attend the state university because the tuition was cheaper. They didn't really care what she studied as long as the price was right. Christabel, however, had other ideas. With the help of our guidance counselor, she applied to, and was accepted at, a renowned fashion design school in New York City. Her parents were less than pleased.

My lot fell to Rutgers where I would study architecture. My father had always wanted to establish an architectural design division within our corporate structure. He had simply been unable to find someone to do it. As much as I was reluctant to be a party to any of my father's plans, the idea more than appealed to me. I relished the years ahead and taking my place in Steadman and Son, which continued to thrive in spite of my father's death.

Mary Elizabeth Farmer was declared the valedictorian of our merry band. I slid in at a close second, to the dissatisfaction of my mother. My failure to garner the prime spot was a direct reflection on her, or so she felt. Of course, my mother was seldom happy these days. The business took too much of her time, but she wasn't about to lose the reins of that cash cow. Besides, she had plenty of help. My father had staffed both companies well, and they ran smoothly. My mother simply felt that she had to have her thumb on the pulse of the business. I suppose she was right in that regard. The companies never failed to post a profit.

Graduation itself was the auspicious occasion it was always meant to be. I got through my salutatorian's speech without a hitch. There was a lot of cheering and whistling, culminated by the tossing of mortar boards into the air.

Uncle Fred and Aunt Harriet hosted a graduation party for Tom and anyone else who wished to attend. That included parents as well as students. As a result, their house was full to running over.

"Hooray for me! Hooray for me!" Freddie jumped up and down excitedly.

I was reminded of how her pigtails used to bounce when she was a kid. Of course, the pigtails were long gone now. Freddie had grown into a lovely young woman very reminiscent of her mother's debutante portrait.

Tom laughed at her antics. "Careful, Freddie, you're going to bust a gut."

She smiled. "Can't help it. I'm so-o-o happy!"

I jabbed Tom in the ribs with my elbow. "Let the girl have her fun."

Freddie held up her glass. "I need another drinkie-poo."

"We're gonna have to cut you off if you continue to act like that." He took her glass and smiled. "Same poison?"

Freddie kissed him lightly on the cheek. "You're so sweet to me."

"Force of habit, I guess."

Tom left our circle of friends and headed to the bar.

Dan Welch raised his glass. "Well, here's to old times and times to come."

Freddie raised both hands in front of her. "No, no. no! You can't do that. I still don't have my drinkie-poo."

"Not to worry, Freddie. That's just the first of many." Dan hoisted his glass in a toast and then downed its contents. "Now *I* need a drinkie-poo."

I looked at Christabel and smiled. "You got a minute?"

"Sure."

"Come with me." I took her hand and led her through the crowded dining room, stopping now and again to exchange greetings with friends, family, and classmates. The adjacent drawing room was crowded as well, but there were only a few people standing around the big entrance foyer. On the other side of the foyer, the library door stood closed. I eased it open. Not a soul disturbed the peace of the book-lined room.

"Here's good." I closed the door behind me and motioned to one of the green velvet wing backs that flanked the fireplace. "Sit."

As directed, Christabel sat, and I perched on the upholstered bench in front of the fireplace. Christabel looked at me and smiled. "What have you got up your sleeve, Marc Steadman?"

I returned her smile and handed her the small black velvet box. "Graduation present."

"Marc! You didn't have to do that." She took the box and opened the lid. A look of surprise crossed her face. "Oh…my!"

"I saw you eyeing this at the jeweler's when we went shopping in Millbank last month."

"Oh, Marc. It's too much."

"It" was an unusual peridot ring. The stone was an icy green rather than the usual yellow-green. It was cut in the shape of a three-sided pyramid, about one-half inch wide on either side and faceted where the sides intersected. The stone was suspended in a raised, contemporary, white gold setting. The ring was a remarkable piece, a one-of-kind designer offering.

"Not too much for you." I smiled. "A girl like you demands nice jewelry."

She stood and crossed to sit next to me. The ring glowed on her finger as she raised her hand and cradled my chin. "You're too much, Marc Steadman." Then she kissed me, and that kiss made everything worth it.

25

1965-1967 – College

THE SUMMER OF 1965 had a certain frenetic energy about it. It was as if we were all living on the cusp of something big. I suppose we were. Summer jobs had, by now, become the norm, but the nights were filled with partying, long walks on the beach, and stolen moments alone.

―

When September arrived, we all went our separate ways. There were tears and promises, but the underlying excitement could not be curtailed. Christabel and I were lucky. Rutgers University in New Brunswick, NJ, was only about forty miles from Manhattan, where her school was located. The drive took about an hour, door to door. I brought the Corvette with me but had to keep it garaged off campus since freshmen were not allowed cars. I seldom used it, opting instead for the train, which was only a short walk down Easton Avenue.

Christabel and I commuted back and forth on weekends as our schedules allowed. We returned to Martin's Neck for all the holidays and periodic weekend visits. On those occasions, Christabel travelled by train as far as New Brunswick, I'd pick her up at the train station, and we'd drive the rest of the way. The whole arrangement worked beautifully.

Most of our weekends together were spent in Manhattan unless there was something special happening at Rutgers. I would take the train in, get a room, and we would spend the weekend exploring the city. Our days were filled with art galleries, museums, and shopping. Washington Square was always a draw, as was Fifth Avenue. In the evenings, it was the theater, a concert, a movie, or dancing. In New York, there were plenty of places for good music and dancing. One of our favorites was The Riverboat Lounge at the base of the Empire State Building. There, Monty Alexander's jazz at the keyboard of his concert grand piano was something to hear. Of course, Mike Manuche's remained a dining favorite along with Davy Jones' Locker and Mama Leone's. Life was good, and filled with fun. What more could one ask?

Tom didn't fare so well, which surprised me. He had always been the leader of our little group, always the one to take charge. To find him foundering was almost incomprehensible. Over a year had passed before I knew anything about his problems. I learned about them over Thanksgiving break in 1966.

"It's not the work." Tom sat at the desk in his study. "That's going fine."

I was immediately concerned. "Then what is it?"

"You're not going to believe this." He laughed. "I miss being home."

"You're homesick?"

He nodded. "Hard to believe, isn't it?"

It *was* hard to believe. Tom had never had much of a home life. Uncle Fred and Aunt Harriet were simply too busy to have time to raise a child. Tom had always seemed to take this fact in his stride and had looked to his two grandmothers for any outward affection. I found his relationship with our Grandmother Powell somewhat of a surprise, having always thought of her as cold and standoffish. Obviously, Tom felt differently. Such it is with families.

Uncle Fred and Aunt Harriet lived in a social maelstrom. At least two parties a month. In Granny Steadman's column, these were referred to as the "mixed bridge," though, actually, no bridge playing ever occurred. It was simply a large group of couples who met at one another's homes to drink and cavort. Referring to it as mixed bridge was simply Granny Steadman's way of making it socially acceptable. I don't think anyone was fooled, but that's how Martin's Neck operated.

There was also much traveling, with weekends in Philadelphia and New York a common occurrence. Then there was always a month in Florida at Uncle Leland and Aunt Charlene's. When Tom was younger, they would simply take him out of school for the month, but, as he grew older, they began leaving him at home with his grandmother, Elena, and George Sawyer.

I always thought Tom's hard edge came from having to fend for himself so much of the time. I realize now, it was simply a carefully constructed veneer.

"Have you talked with your folks about this?"

Tom chuckled. "When might I do that?"

I nodded.

"They're off on Saturday to a party at the Sherman's in Philly. I'll be headed back to school before they return."

"That's not right."

He shrugged. "What're ya gonna do?"

He was right. At this late date, there was no way Uncle Fred and Aunt Harriet would ever curtail their lifestyle. It simply wasn't in them.

I laughed. "I guess you could write them a letter."

"Lot of good that would do. It'd lay on the foyer table for months like the rest of the mail." He shrugged. "Wouldn't do any good anyway."

"Why not?"

With a wave of his hand, Tom tried to dismiss the subject. "You know. Stiff upper lip and all that bullshit."

I laughed. "Tell me about it."

"Yeah, I'm preaching to the choir."

"Maybe you can have a heart to heart with them over Christmas. Can you hang in there that long?"

"Oh, I can hang in there all right. I've been hanging in since day one. Another month won't make any difference."

"When did you start feeling this way?"

Tom shrugged. "I don't know, really. It just sort of crept in. Slowly at first, and then in a rush."

I was perplexed. What was there to miss? Hours and days alone with no company other than George Sawyer. How does one miss something like that? It would be different if they were one, big, happy television-like family. Of course, that was all hog wash. None of us had that kind of life. It only existed on the boob tube.

Tom looked at me and smiled. "Surprised?"

I nodded. "Yeah, really surprised." I paused, looking for the right words. "I don't mean to be cruel, but what, exactly, do you miss?"

Tom laughed. "I've asked myself the same question."

"Hard one, huh?"

"Oh, yeah." He fiddled with a pen laying on the desk in front of him. "It's hard to explain. In many ways, I don't understand it myself."

"Try me."

He smiled again. "It's a feeling as much as anything. A feeling of loss. I miss everything about my old life. I don't want that part of my life to be over."

"Okay."

"I miss all our classmates, the guys on the basketball team, our little group. I miss the hours I spent alone closeted in here." He waved his hand to indicate the comfortably appointed study. "Everything's different now. And it's like all that is gone. Like I'll never feel that way again."

I could understand his feelings. College was a lot different. Everything had changed. Those carefree years of high school were gone forever. There was no hope of ever getting them back. As for me, I still had Christabel, and that made all the difference. None of Tom's relationships had ever developed beyond some spurts of heavy dating. One girl replaced another with regularity. It was simply Tom's way, as if he didn't trust the idea that a relationship could be lasting. He viewed it as a fleeting moment devoted to pleasure and nothing more.

"Have you been coming home every weekend?"

Tom shook his head. "What's the point in that? Everyone's away at school, and Mom and Dad are always busy."

"Exactly."

"I just want things to be the way they were. And I know that can't happen."

"Afraid not."

Tom sighed. "I guess I have to just bite the bullet and make the best of things." He looked at me. "What else can I do?"

—

Christmas came and went without any change to Tom's situation. We talked some more about it over the holidays, but Tom seemed resigned to his fate. There simply wasn't a way to restore his feeling of well-being. Time was moving on, and we had to move with it.

—

It all came to a head in the spring of 1967.

Grandmother Powell had been feeling badly and had been in and out of the hospital several times. She finally suffered a massive stroke and died at home. One of the ladies found her slumped over the writing desk in her morning room when she came to clean. Her sudden death was a shock to us all.

Tom was not told of her passing. This may seem strange, and I felt it was the wrong tact to take. Aunt Harriet felt otherwise. By now, she and Uncle Fred knew that Tom was having a difficult time and they didn't want to upset him further. He had been close to Grandmother Powell, and her loss would be felt deeply. Feeling they were doing the right thing, Tom was kept in the dark about her death. Uncle Fred and Aunt Harriet agreed they would break the news to Tom once midterms were over. They thought he would be better equipped to handle it once the pressure of exams was behind him.

The funeral ran smoothly, much like my father's before. No eulogies, plenty of expensive flowers, a catered wake at our house. Of course, the whole affair was by invitation only.

Christabel and I sat on the front porch sipping our drinks. I had taken up smoking and puffed contentedly on a cigarette. I loved all the accoutrements associated with the act: refillable chrome lighters, imported cigarettes, elegant cigarette cases. It was definitely a habit intended for a gentleman. I bought into it wholeheartedly.

"Cigarette?" I flashed the gold case in front of Christabel.

She gave me one those knowledgeable smiles. "I think not."

I smiled and returned the case to the inside pocket of my jacket. "Just thought I'd offer."

"Always the gentleman."

"Got to play the role."

She laughed, and the rocker creaked. "It was a nice service."

I shrugged. "It was what she wanted. I guess that's what matters."

Christabel did not respond, and the rocker continued its creaking. We sat in silence for a few moments, the stillness broken only by the sound of the rocker. The country road on which we lived was several hundred yards from the house and buffeted by a heavy grove of trees. Still, one could occasionally hear the sound of traffic.

The quiet of the afternoon was abruptly broken by the sound of a fast-moving car eating up the asphalt. There was no mistaking the throaty roar of the Austin Healey 3000.

Christabel and I looked at each other and rose from our chairs. I tossed the remainder of the Benson & Hedges over the railing and into a flower bed.

The vehicle braked and slowed as it reached the mouth of our driveway. I walked down the length of the porch with Christabel close behind me. By the time we descended the wide, front steps, Tom's car had cleared the trees and sped into the car park. It stopped suddenly with a squeal of brakes.

Tears streamed down Tom's face as he emerged from the car and walked toward us. "Why didn't you tell me?" His voice was ragged and accusatory.

I reached out and grabbed his arm. "Your parents…"

He twisted his arm from my grasp. "Fuck my parents!" He pushed past me and mounted the steps to the porch. Christabel and I followed.

Most of the family was spread throughout the drawing room and formal dining room at the front of the house. When Tom burst through the front door, it caught everyone by surprise. The shock was quickly registered on each and every face.

Tom stopped just inside the front door. Christabel and I were close behind. I reached out and grabbed his arm again. "Tom…"

Once more, he freed himself. "Leave me alone!" He took two steps into the wide foyer with its sweeping staircase, gazing right and left for his parents.

Suddenly, Aunt Harriet appeared in the archway of the dining room. "Tom!"

He spun to face her. "When were you going to tell me?"

She strode toward him and tried to embrace him. "Tom…I'm sorry."

He pushed her roughly away. "Don't touch me!"

By now, Uncle Fred had entered the foyer from the drawing room. "Son…" He reached out to lay a hand on Tom's shoulder.

Tom side-stepped to avoid contact. "How could you do this?"

Uncle Fred moved closer to him. "Get a hold on yourself, Tom."

Aunt Harriet finally wrapped her arm through his. "We thought it was better this way." She lay her head against his shoulder. "How did you find out?"

Tom shook himself free of her grip. "I just knew something was wrong and decided to come home. When I got to the house, George told me." He glared at his parents. "Thanks a lot! Thanks a whole fuckin' lot!" The outburst was followed by more tears.

Embarrassed at Tom's inappropriate behavior, Aunt Harriet tried once more to comfort him. "I'm sorry, Tom. It'll be all right.

Uncle Fred took Tom's arm in an attempt to turn him toward the door. "Let's go home, son. You'll feel better there. We can talk about this."

Tom was having none of it. With a loud sob, he wrenched his arm away and stumbled toward the door. Christabel and I stood aside, but I tried to grab Tom's arm as he pushed through the doorway.

Between the tears and the sobs, Tom managed a "leave me alone" before stumbling down the front steps. I followed him. "Tom… Buddy…"

Tom turned and glared at me. "Some friend you are! How could you let this happen?" Then he was back in his car, revving the engine. With a squeal of tires, he left us all standing on the front porch.

Aunt Harriet was crying softly. Uncle Fred took her hand. "I think we'd better go."

She nodded silently and walked with him down the steps.

Tom didn't return to school. He didn't take his midterm examinations. He shut himself in his study and stayed there. He refused my phone calls. When I tried to see him, he locked the door. He was inconsolable. I made repeated attempts to talk with him, but he remained silent. We had all betrayed him.

Eventually, he came around. He began speaking to his parents again. It was spring break before I could actually sit and talk with him. By then, he had reordered his life. He was working daily at Powell Properties, Ltd., Uncle Fred's realty company. He had made plans to study for his real estate license. Tom seemed resigned to his choices, but I sensed a sort of relief in him. It was almost as if life had finally worked its way around to his way of thinking. At least, I told myself that.

Whether I was right or not would never actually be revealed.

26

Summer 1967 – Rodney Williams

RODNEY WILLIAMS WAS A friend of a friend who my mother had known for years. He lived in the neighboring town of Lewiston in a sprawling, antebellum mansion named The Birches. Of course, he was wealthy; most of my mother's friends and acquaintances were. She would never have given him a second look otherwise. Why she would give him a second look at all is beyond me. He was an ugly man, balding, with spaced teeth, stained from years of cigar smoking. His clothes were expensive enough; they simply never seemed to fit properly. He was loud and arrogant and generally disagreeable. He set about to dominate every conversation with an aplomb that I found disgusting.

Still, my mother agreed to go out with him, and I guess that was her choice. Rodney and my mother became a regular item, attending every party together, seen at every fashionable restaurant. My mother's friends and family appeared to tolerate him, but one could never tell about Martin's Neck society. At least to Rodney's face, they were jovial and polite. What they said behind his back could have been quite different. I guess part of their acceptance was in deference to my mother and her place in our little world.

Rodney Williams was an entrepreneur of sorts. He owned and leased several commercial properties in and around Lewiston. He dabbled in the stock market with great success. At least that was the consensus of local opinion. He showed no interest in Steadman and Son, at first. Perhaps it was part of his long-range plan.

I was celebrating my twentieth birthday. My mother had invited Christabel to dinner as sort of a birthday celebration. Of course, she invited Rodney Williams as well. Why my mother thought this was an acceptable way to celebrate my birthday escaped me for the moment, though her motive was soon to be revealed.

In lieu of a cake, baked Alaska was served. After the dishes were cleared away, we sat around the big table sipping port. The crystal chandelier was complimented by an array of candles at the table's center.

Rodney Williams picked up his glass and leaned over the edge of the table. His ever-present cigar was clamped between his stained teeth. He raised a goblet. "Here's to another birthday, young man."

I managed a forced smile and raised my glass. "Thanks."

He took a deep swallow and placed his wine glass on the table. "Your mother has something she's been wanting to talk to you about." He looked at my mother and leered.

This could bode no good. If my mother wanted to talk to me, why did she need him to introduce the subject? Couldn't it wait until she and I were alone?

My mother patted her lips with the thick, linen napkin. "Yes, dear. Actually, Rodney and I both want to speak to you."

That settled it. It had to be bad.

My mother smiled sweetly.

I looked at Christabel who sat staring at her wine glass. Poor girl. Talk about being out of place.

"Rodney and I have been talking."

Not good. Not good at all.

"He'd like to buy into the business."

Oh, no. "Which business?"

She hesitated. "Well, both of them, of course."

Of course. In for a penny, in for a pound.

"Why?"

Rodney picked up the ball. "They're two good businesses. They're doing well. I'm always looking for a good investment." He puffed vigorously on his cigar. "And your companies could do with a good financial boost."

I looked at my mother and frowned. "I thought you said the businesses were doing well."

"They are, dear, but Rodney's right. We could use a little influx of capital."

Rodney smiled broadly. "Exactly."

I was skeptical. It all sounded like a half-baked plan to me. And the thought of Rodney Williams' nose stuck in our business was far from appealing.

"You're soon out of college, and you'll be wanting to come home to start that architectural division you've been talking about." He took a long drag and stared at me. "That's going to take money—money that may not be readily available when the time comes."

"Why not?"

Rodney shrugged. "Who knows? We're talking two years here. The construction business is volatile. It can change at a moment's notice."

Unfortunately, he was right. Even though we were in a period of prosperity, one never knew what the next day would bring. I'd seen it happen before, and it could happen again.

I looked at Rodney archly. "How much are we talking here?"

He knocked an extensive ash into the ashtray provided for him. "Money?"

"No, percentage."

"Your mother and I were thinking forty-five percent. How does that sound to you?"

I pondered the point. "Seems a bit heavy to me."

"It still gives your mother a controlling interest."

I nodded before picking up the bottle of port and pouring another glass. I slowly sipped its contents.

Rodney continued to puff on the smelly cigar. "You give it some thought. Nothing's been finalized at this point. Your mother insisted that you be part of negotiations."

Big of her. I only hoped she would be more forthright with me when I had a chance to talk to her in private. Assuming that occasion ever arose. Our relationship had changed greatly since the death of my father. I knew part of her still blamed me; that wasn't going to change. Whatever closeness we had felt in our early years together had dissipated. Neither of us had tried to revive it. When we found ourselves at home alone, we were usually in different rooms of the house. I stayed closeted in my study, and my mother spent much of her time in my father's library, ostensibly working.

"Let me think about it." I wasn't going to give them anything more than that. There were too many ramifications ... too many pitfalls.

Rodney nodded and puffed. "You do that." There was a decided sneer to his voice which only I seemed to notice. My mother continued to smile. Christabel toyed with her glass, probably wishing she had never agreed to come. Who could blame her?

"I think it's a good offer." My mother looked at Rodney and smiled. "A very generous offer."

I took my wine glass and rose from my seat. "I'll think it over." I turned to Christabel who sat staring up at me. "I'd like a smoke. Join me on the porch?" I could sense her relief.

Christabel rose. "Thank you, Mrs. Steadman, for the lovely dinner. Everything was delicious."

"You're more than welcome, my dear. We're so pleased you could join us."

Christabel and I exited the dining room for the wide front porch. The waning sunlight filtered through the multitude of hanging plants that circled the porch. We sat on the porch swing and I lit a cigarette.

"Want one?" I held out the cigarette case.

Christabel stared at the gold envelope and then reached for its contents. "Yes. Yes, I think I do." She placed it between her lips, and I lit it for her.

"It was that bad?"

She nodded. "Pretty much so." She laughed her light, musical laugh. "Talk about feeling like a fifth wheel."

"Yeah, that was neither the time nor the place."

Christabel simply shook her head.

"I don't like him."

Christabel laughed. "What's to like?"

I shook my head. "My mother seems to see something in him. God knows what."

"How long has it been since your father died?"

"Four years."

"She's probably just lonely."

I laughed. "She's too busy to be lonely."

"Still..." Christabel exhaled a plume of cigarette smoke.

I nodded. "Yeah, you could be right. It doesn't change the fact that I dislike him." I drew on my cigarette. "Jesus. The thought of him at Steadman and Son makes my skin crawl."

"It really came as a surprise."

"Yeah, happy birthday to me!" I hoisted my glass and quickly downed its contents.

27

Summer 1968 – Platinum and Diamonds and Emeralds, Oh My!

1967 WOUND ITSELF DOWN without further upset. There were several more conversations about the impending sale, but my objections were ignored. My mother and Rodney Williams had made their decision. My involvement was simply to placate me into believing I was a part of that decision. In the end, Rodney purchased forty-five percent of the stock as originally suggested. I was far from pleased with the outcome.

Although Rodney did not seem to take an active part in running the businesses, I had no way of knowing what influences he brought to bear on my mother. Being at school hampered most of my involvement, and, in a way, I suppose that was good.

The winter of 1968 was uneventful. Tom had settled in at Powell Properties and appeared to be doing fairly well. He took his realtor's exam in the spring and passed with flying colors.

Freddie had become enamored with an older man who owned an air charter service north of Millbank. None of us were particularly enthusiastic about her choice in men. Still, Freddie was Freddie, and she would follow through in her own indomitable fashion.

Christabel and I continued our regular lifestyle. As schedules allowed, we traveled back and forth between New Brunswick and Manhattan on weekends, filling each hour with our own brand of fun. We were simply happy to be together.

By the summer of 1968, I had made a momentous decision. I would ask Christabel to marry me. We still had one more year of college, but I saw nothing wrong with long engagements. It would give us plenty of time to plan ahead.

When I informed my mother of my decision, she was accepting but hardly enthusiastic.

"That's nice, dear. I guess you better set up an appointment with Harold Graves."

Harold Graves, our family jeweler, had provided jewelry services for the Powell family for decades. His quaint, little shop hugged one of the side streets in downtown Martin's Neck. Soon, I met with him, described what I wanted, and awaited his call. When it came, my mother insisted on accompanying me to the meeting.

Standing at the glass showcase in Harold's shop, we waited as he spread out a black velvet cloth and then set a tray of three rings in front of us.

Harold picked up the smallest of the three and handed it to me. "I think this is what you were looking for."

I took the ring and studied it. It was exactly what I had described to him…a single, round, half-carat diamond flanked by two quarter-carat emeralds in a plain, white gold setting. "Yes. It's perfect." I held it out to my mother.

She looked at the ring and smiled. "Nice…very pretty."

Harold reached for the second ring, which was a trio of half-carat stones, again, a diamond framed by emeralds. "I ordered this one as a possible alternative. It's a bit more expensive, of course."

I laughed nervously. "Of course."

My mother took the ring before I really had a chance to examine it. "I don't like that the stones are all the same size. It's much too heavy looking."

I didn't argue. I felt my choice was the better of the two.

"Now, this ring is a bit more…unique." Harold held up the third and final offering. "Five stones: three quarter diamonds framed by two half-carat emeralds and flanked with two quarter-carat diamonds. In this case the setting is platinum. It's a beautiful piece, as you can see." The ring flared as he rotated it in the light.

My mother stared at the ring. "Beautiful."

I laughed again. "And a bit more expensive, right?"

Harold smiled. "Oh, yes. Fifteen fifty."

"Good God!" That was more than twice my budget.

Harold held up the first ring. "Of course, this *is* a very nice piece. The stones are top quality and the clarity is excellent. It's priced at five seventy-five."

I held the ring up to the light. It sparkled happily.

My mother's voice was firm. "Well, I certainly don't think there's any question about which is the right one." She was playing her role as a woman of importance.

Harold and I looked at her as I set down the ring. "Really?"

"Of course, my dear. It has to be the five stone. Anything else looks paltry by comparison."

I gazed at Harold and he avoided my eyes. "That's a lot of money, Mom."

"I know, dear, but you can't just give her anything. You're a Powell, you know. People will be expecting something spectacular."

"But most of our friends have been buying, single, half-carat rings. I thought the addition of emeralds would make it more distinctive."

"Yes, dear...but it looks a bit half-hearted. Sort of like you tried but couldn't quite pull it off." She folded her hands in front of her. "Go for the five stone."

And that was that. My mother may not have been excited about our engagement, but there were certain rules to be followed. Having her future daughter-in-law wear the right ring was one of those rules.

After our engagement was officially announced, my mother insisted on taking Christabel and her mom to Caldwell's in Wilmington. It was there that Christabel would be faced with choosing what was proper in china, crystal, and silver patterns. Following my mother's lead, she opted for the three Ws: Wedgewood, Waterford, and Wallace. My mother's work was done...for now.

While my mother seemed to treat the whole experience as a duty, Aunt Harriet appeared genuinely happy about our engagement. It was her idea to throw us an engagement party. Perched on the edge of the bay, Powell Cottage, with its wide porches and open living areas, was the perfect setting. The August affair was relatively small, with close to one-hundred attendees. Of course, the whole extended family was in attendance along with a large assortment of college and high school friends. There was ample food and drink.

The event culminated in my being tossed overboard from the observation deck. I guess I was lucky I didn't drown.

28

Winter 1969 – 311 Linden Avenue

LINDEN AVENUE RUNS PARALLEL to Constitution Avenue in Martin's Neck. Constitution runs east to west and culminates in the center of town where it becomes Commerce Street. Most of the old, grand homes are located on one of these three main thoroughfares. The house belonging to my grandparents Powell was no different. It sat upon a small rise at the corner of Linden Avenue and Hawke Street. The Hawkes were a branch of our family on my grandfather Powell's side.

Although Christabel had been in the house many times, her visits had been restricted to the public rooms on the first floor. She and I were home for the weekend, and my mother had asked that I stop in and check on the house. It had stood empty since my Grandmother Powell's death in 1967. The intention was to sell the big, brick pile, but the family had yet to get around to it.

Not intending to stay, I parked in front, on Linden Avenue. I looked at Christabel and smiled. "Won't be a minute. Just a quick walk-through."

"Can I come?"

I closed the car door and crossed to the sidewalk. "Sure. Not much to see."

Christabel joined me. "I've always liked this house."

"Well, it's certainly one of a kind."

We climbed the wide stone steps to the broad entry porch. With the help of a key, the heavy walnut door with its leaded glass swung inward.

Dust and shadows greeted us. The black and white marble floor of the entry hall stretched the depth of the house; the massive staircase rose to the left. The Linden Avenue house was built in the Victorian Italianate style. It was huge—four square with three full floors. At the rear of the main structure two wings jutted out. One contained the kitchen, pantries, and laundry room. The other contained the master suite with its dressing rooms and bath. The two were joined by a narrow, glass-roofed conservatory.

"You've been here before. Drawing room on the right with dining room behind, kitchen behind that. Library to the left with Grandmother's morning room behind that followed by the powder room and master suite. I guess there was a time when my grandparents enjoyed being close to one another."

"Marc, you're terrible."

"Facts is facts."

"I've never seen the master suite or the kitchen."

"Come this way." I led her down the length of the entry hall that terminated in an array of glass doors leading into the conservatory. A quick left took us into a small vestibule that serviced the powder room and the entry to the master suite. I opened the double doors to the bedroom. "For your viewing pleasure."

The master suite had been remodeled when my grandparents moved into the house in 1920. Little had been done to change the decor. It still sported my grandmother's Louis XV furnishings.

Christabel stared in amazement. "Goodness, what an elegant room!"

"Wait until you see the bath." I led her through another set of double doors into the large, tiled space. It was the best the 1920s had to offer. Even the tub was secreted in an arched, tiled alcove.

"Oh, my dear! I don't think I've ever seen anything quite like this before."

I laughed. "Few people have."

Next, I gave her a quick tour of the kitchen with its huge porcelain range and other antiquated fixtures. Christabel found the pantries especially fascinating. There was the predicable pantry for foodstuffs and one strictly for china and crystal.

Upstairs, I showed her through the four spacious guest rooms with their shared baths. The third floor boasted only two bedrooms and a shared bath. The rest of the space was dedicated to a playroom for the children and still accommodated many toys and keepsakes belonging to my mother and her siblings.

During our inspection, I checked for plumbing leaks, roof failure, and any signs of bird or squirrel invasion. All was tight and secure. I closed the door to the conservatory and joined Christabel at the front door. "That conservatory will need to be reglazed soon ... "

"Oh, Marc, it's a wonderful house!"

I opened the door for her. "My grandmother would love to hear you say that."

She laughed as I closed the door behind us. "I doubt that. Your grandmother never seemed to like me very much."

I helped Christabel into the car. "Not to worry. She preferred boys to girls any day. Even with that, she was a cold, old fish."

"Marc!"

Things transpired as things will do. Christabel couldn't stop talking about the house. *It was so spacious...so grand. What a wonderful place to raise children!*

With our engagement, Christabel and I knew we would be returning to Martin's Neck once college was behind us. In spite of the advent of Rodney Williams, the architectural division for Steadman and Son was a given. I had only to organize it and make it work.

Christabel, in contrast, had little outlet for fashion designing. There were no fashion houses anywhere near Martin's Neck, and its women were seemingly content traveling to Philadelphia and New York when fashion needs beckoned.

Christabel wanted children. Not at first, perhaps, but eventually. She was perfectly satisfied placing her professional aspirations on the back burner for now. I offered to set her up with a business of her own, but she replied that there was plenty of time for that.

Thus, I found myself in Uncle Fred's office while we were home on spring break. "Just what does the family want to get for Grandfather's house?"

Uncle Fred smiled and leaned back in his chair. "Well, that's hard to say. We've batted around several prices, but no one has settled on anything." There was a sly lilt to his eyes. "Why do you ask?"

"Christabel and I are interested."

"Really? That's marvelous!"

I laughed. "Only if I can afford it."

Uncle Fred righted his chair and leaned toward me across the desk. "As I said, no price has been set. What can you afford?"

I was a bit taken aback by his response. "Well...I don't really know." I paused, trying to get my feet under me. "I suppose I could swing fifty thousand."

He pursed his lips as if in deep thought. Then, suddenly, he pushed back his chair and stood. "That seems like a fair offer. Ten thousand for each sibling. I don't see anything wrong with that." He smiled and extended a hand. "Let me poll your aunt and uncles."

I stood uncertainly as we shook on it. "Well...well, that's great. You'll let me know?"

He smiled broadly. "Of course I'll let you know! But don't worry. I think everyone will be more than happy for you kids to have the house."

It was as simple as that. Everyone agreed to the terms. We had settlement one week and three days after my graduation from Rutgers. Christabel had her house.

29

Summer 1969 – Wedding Bells

CHRISTABEL AND I WERE the cause célèbre in Martin's Neck. You might have thought our wedding was the biggest thing to hit the little town in years. We had scheduled the event for Saturday, August 16. That left most of the summer for preparations. The service would take place at the Methodist church at the top of the hill on Constitution Avenue. The reception would be held at Christabel's parents' house on Commerce Street. Christabel had opted for a garden party theme in the huge backyard of the house.

Seamstresses were busy the entire summer. Of course, Christabel had designed her gown, her traveling suit, gowns for seven bridesmaids, not to mention special gowns for the maid of honor and the flower girl. We gentlemen were much easier to accommodate. Morning suits were the order of the day, and these were easily rented.

Christabel's high school friends threw her the obligatory bridal shower. She traveled back to New York for another hosted by her college roommates. My great aunt, Elizabeth Oliver, opened her big, Georgian house for a mixed bridal shower that hosted almost two hundred. It was more like a wedding reception than a shower and was truly a hard act to follow.

Gifts arrived from everywhere and everyone, even from those who weren't invited to the wedding. The McCaffertys still had numerous ties in Washington, and this generated an influx of gifts from people we hardly knew. The whole affair was beginning to overwhelm Christabel's mother. She smoked incessantly, but managed to keep her chronic depression at bay, a fact that Christabel credited to large doses of cough syrup. Her mother was a teetotaler.

When the day arrived, it was as hot as only August can be. The old church, which lacked air conditioning, was filled to overflowing with nearly three-hundred guests. The morning suits were stifling, and the wide-brimmed garden hats of the bridesmaids drooped a bit. Still, it was a beautiful wedding. Tom was my best man, and Freddie was maid of honor.

Tom and I were sequestered in a choir room to the right of the alter as my ushers guided the guests to their seats. Tom was uncharacteristically nervous. He paced back and forth and frequently cracked the door to gaze out at the growing crowd. I don't know why he felt so nervous; all he had to do was hand me the band of diamonds and emeralds on request.

For the umpteenth time, Tom cracked the door and looked out. "Damn, Marc, did you invite the whole town?"

I laughed. "Darn near. You know Mom."

"Oh, shit! You lucky devil!"

"What?"

Tom continued to stare out through the narrow opening of the door. "I just saw Christabel; she's beautiful."

I stepped to the door and pushed him aside. "Lemme see."

Tom hadn't exaggerated. Christabel looked as if she had stepped out of a Gainsborough painting. The gown was simple and elegant, all fine, white chiffon with full, billowing sleeves. The bodice was hand smocked with blue seed pearls; a blue grosgrain sash encircled the empire waist. The whole was topped with a large, white garden hat festooned with muted blue feather flowers. She was indeed beautiful.

The service was textbook perfect, and the reception ran smoothly from start to finish. Everyone seemed more than happy to be out of the stuffy church and under the shade of the many large oaks that filled the McCafferty's garden. The reception was still in full swing when Christabel and I left for our honeymoon.

Uncle Chester and Aunt Jocelyn had loaned us their St. Thomas vacation home for the week. We would drive to Philadelphia and then fly to the Caribbean. The house was a resort in itself. Located directly on the beach, it boasted a swimming pool and a small staff of servants. It made the perfect getaway and provided us with a relaxing stepping stone for the turmoil that lay ahead.

30

Winter 1970 – Rodney and Victoria

LIFE WAS GOOD TO us. We settled into the old house on Linden Avenue and set about making it our own. Christabel had her hands full, and I wasn't of much real help. Getting the architectural division of Steadman and Son up and running was no small task. Office space wasn't the problem, as there was plenty of space adjacent to the building supply division. Initially, I needed a secretary and at least one draftsman. They proved harder to find than I had imagined. Advertising also demanded my time, but our first clients came to us through the construction division. Offering design services made it easier to woo clients to our company.

In spite of all the work, Christabel seemed to be having a good time with the house. She attacked the public rooms first, painting and papering and deciding on window treatments. A lot of Grandmother Powell's belongings remained in the house. The family members had scoured it months earlier, removing whatever they wanted. Still, much remained unclaimed. Christabel sorted through it all, selling some pieces, keeping others, rearranging paintings, and buying new items. It was a daunting task, but she loved the house and would settle for nothing shy of perfection.

—

On Valentine's Day, we opted for a quiet dinner at home. Christabel had mastered the mammoth kitchen range and was enjoying the adventure of cooking. After a delicious dinner of shrimp scampi, we sat around the big dining table contemplating dessert. I lit a cigarette and poured another glass of wine.

I raised the stemmed glass to her and smiled. "Happy Valentine's Day."

"Happy Valentine's Day to you, too." She smiled and looked at the big bouquet of yellow roses on the marble-topped console in the bay window of the dining room. "Thank you for the flowers. I love them."

"Wish it could have been more."

"They're more than enough." She laughed. "Especially with all the money we've been spending on this house."

"Got to be done."

The doorbell rang. I looked at Christabel quizzically. She shrugged her shoulders, and I rose to answer the door. The lights were on in the drawing room, but the entrance hall sat in deep shadow. I flipped on the overhead light and then the porch lights as well. Two forms were distinguishable, but unrecognizable, through the leaded glass of the door.

I opened the door to my mother and Rodney who stood smiling on the front porch. My mother reached up and kissed me on the cheek. "Forgive the intrusion, dear. May we come in?"

I stood aside. "Of course."

Rodney stretched out his hand. "Evening, Marcus."

I acknowledged the greeting and followed them into the house. Rodney helped my mother off with her coat, and I hung hers, along with his, on the gothic coat rack at the foot of the stairs.

"Christabel and I were just finishing dinner." I followed them into the drawing room where Christabel stood waiting by the marble fireplace.

"Oh, I'm so sorry." Mother crossed to Christabel and kissed the air beside her cheek. "Christabel, Happy Valentine's Day. We didn't mean to interrupt."

Christabel smiled. "Happy Valentine's Day to you. We just finished. Please take a seat. It's good to see you."

My mother and Christabel sat on the two Louis XVI chairs flanking the fireplace; Rodney and I anchored each end of the tuxedo sofa in front of the leaded French doors.

My mother looked especially pleased with herself. Something was up, for sure. She smiled broadly, looking from me to Christabel and back again. "Rodney and I wanted you to be the first to know."

Oh, God, what now?

Her smile intensified. She stretched out her left hand to Christabel. The ornate Victorian ring blazed with life.

Christabel gasped in surprise. "Oh, my gosh! Are you engaged?"

Oh, shit.

My mother coyly shook her head and smiled like a schoolgirl. "Married."

Double shit.

The women stood and embraced, and I turned to congratulate Rodney. "This calls for a celebration." *Celebrating* was the last thing I felt like doing, but I really had no choice in the matter. "Let me fix you a drink."

Rodney smiled that gap-tooth smile of his. "Scotch...if you have it."

"Of course." I crossed to the fireplace and embraced my mother stiffly. "Congratulations, Mom."

"Thank you, dear."

"Wine? I just opened a new bottle."

"Of course, dear. That would be nice."

I busied myself with the drinks while the others laughed and talked. My mother seemed ecstatic, and Rodney appeared quite pleased with himself. I was less than pleased. It was bad enough having him as a business partner of sorts, but the thought of him as a step-father was almost beyond comprehension. He and I rarely agreed on anything. He loved to argue and would often take up the opposite side of a question simply for the sake of exercising his argumentative abilities. Any argument with Rodney was a dead-end street. He never budged, never relented. He was always right, no matter what. I had been in his study at The Birches and seen a sampler his deceased wife had stitched. It read, "Once I thought I was wrong, but I was mistaken." That summed up Rodney Williams in a nutshell. Life could prove to be very interesting from here on out. God help us!

31

Summer 1970 – Farewell

THE YEAR WENT DOWNHILL from there. Although my mother's alignment with Rodney didn't appear to affect Steadman and Son, there were rumblings throughout the ranks. I came to view their marriage as nothing more than a minor annoyance.

More importantly, Granny Steadman had begun to fail. She was never the same after my father's death and gradually succumbed to depression and ill health. My marriage to Christabel didn't help. It wasn't that she disliked Christabel; it simply seemed too much for her to have to deal with another "competitor" for my attention, as strange as that sounds. She felt she had lost me much as she had lost my father. In some ways, I suppose she was right. I was busy with the company and the life I was forging with Christabel.

—

By May of 1970, Granny Steadman had suddenly quit eating. She grew weak and soon reached the point at which she could no longer care for herself. We took turns staying with her until it became obvious that the situation was not going to better itself. Nursing home residency seemed the only option. At least, that was my mother's answer to the problem. Of course, Granny Steadman wanted no part of a nursing home, but my mother was adamant. She was in charge and calling the shots.

Granny Steadman lasted just shy of two months in the nursing facility. I tried to visit her regularly but didn't get there as often as I would have liked. She slept much of the time, almost in a comatose state, and died quietly one evening in her sleep.

Her funeral differed from those of the Powell family members in that no invitations were required for attendance. Granny Steadman had many friends and acquaintances of all ages. She had helped and touched countless lives in her eighty-six years. The turnout at her funeral was a testimony to that fact. She was buried between her husband, Cap Steadman, and my father in the family plot in Martin's Neck Cemetery.

My mother hosted the wake at her house in Martin's Neck. She said it was more convenient than having everyone drive down to The Birches. I knew otherwise. Rodney didn't want a bunch of strangers cluttering up his family home, especially the friends of a woman he hardly knew.

Granny Steadman's death was a sort of marker in my life. I felt the void. I felt guilty as well. Had I done enough for her when she was alive? Had I been too busy to give her the attention she wanted and needed? Had she been miserable, lying alone in a nursing home and surrounded by strangers? Should I have stood up to my mother and tried to make other arrangements that would have been more to Granny's liking? I had plenty of questions, but few answers.

As her only heir, I inherited the big house on the corner of Magnolia Street and Sheffield Avenue, its contents, her car, and the money in her bank account. The latter totaled slightly over two-hundred thousand dollars and was a huge help for Christabel and me. With the refurbishing of the Linden Avenue house and the establishing of my office, more money was going out than coming in. Granny Steadman's bequest went far in balancing the books.

I had no plans for the house. Granny Steadman had always hoped I would live there someday, but that was unlikely to happen. In fact, Granny Steadman had expressed much disappointment when Christabel and I purchased Grandfather Powell's house.

Although Granny Steadman's house was full of antiques, I had no intention of liquidating them. Her collection had been a source of great pride. I could not imagine sending the items to an auction house. Her few pieces of good jewelry went to Christabel. She was especially fond of Granny's emerald-cut, diamond engagement ring. The rest of Granny Steadman's collection remained in the house, which now sat locked and shuttered. The time would come when I would need to make a decision about its future, but I was not up to making that decision now.

32

Summer 1970 – Red Flags

UNFORTUNATELY, THE TIME FOR making decisions came sooner than I expected. The events of that summer were a shock to me, and I wasn't really in a position to deal with them. Still, I had to rally to the cause, so to speak. It was simply that I was unequipped to do so.

We were invited to dinner at The Birches. That, in itself, was somewhat unusual, but my mother had made a big deal about the four of us dining together. She decreed that it was to be a black-tie affair, which seemed strange given the small guest list. Regardless, Christabel and I dressed and appeared at the appointed time.

Cornelia, one of Rodney's long-time staff, answered the door and ushered us into the drawing room where my mother and Rodney waited. Cocktails were served, and the conversation was light, but Rodney dominated as was his habit.

Dinner was delicious, served in the huge, formal dining room by Rodney's staff. It wasn't until we had transitioned into the library for brandy and cordials that the ax fell.

Rodney stood at the fireplace, brandy snifter in hand. He puffed complacently on the ever-present cigar. "Your mother and I have been talking."

Red flag. I didn't rise to the bait.

He paused and smiled at my mother. "We've been talking about the business and thought you should be made aware of our intentions."

Not good ... not good at all.

"We're not getting any younger, and there's a lot we would like to do now that we're married."

My mother smiled warmly. "Like travel. We'd really like to travel."

I looked at her suspiciously. "Well, there's nothing stopping you."

Rodney cleared his throat. "Quite the contrary. There's a lot stopping us."

"Like what?"

He studied the end of his cigar. "Well, primarily the business. It consumes most of our time right now. It would be impossible to leave it unattended for a prolonged period."

"Well, I'd be there."

Rodney gave a short laugh. "We know that, Marc. However, you're far from ready to manage two busy companies."

"I could certainly learn."

"You've got your hands full enough with your division. Where are you going to find time to do your own work and also manage the companies?"

I had no answer. As much as I hated to admit it, Rodney was right. Still, I had to fight against what I felt was coming. "I'd like the chance to try, at least."

Rodney gave me a condescending smile. "I know you do, but it's simply not a reasonable alternative."

"Then what?" I braced myself for the inevitable.

"We've put out a few feelers for the sale of the company and have had some interest from a couple of potential buyers."

I began to panic. "But it's my father's company. He always wanted me to take it over when I was ready."

My mother's tone became matter of fact. "And had things worked out differently, that might have been a viable option. As it is..." She spread her hands to either side.

"Exactly." Rodney swallowed his brandy and crossed to the liquor cabinet for a refill. "We'll be sure there's always a place for you at Steadman and Son. That will be one of the terms of the sale. Assuming, of course, you wish to remain there."

Remain there? How should I know? Work as an employee in the firm that my father founded? What kind of a future was that? There had to be another way.

My mother smiled sweetly and placed a hand over mine. "We know this comes as a shock, but, in the end, we feel it's for the best. Just think about it."

I pulled my hand away and sipped of the stinging, amber liquid. "I'll buy it!"

My mother gave a hesitant laugh. "Why would you want to do that?"

"Because it's my father's business! He worked hard to build those companies, and I don't want to see them sold. It's my future, too, you know!"

"I know, dear, but you have to be realistic. Rodney's right. You don't have the experience to manage such a large concern."

"Then I'll just have to learn, won't I?"

My mother looked to Rodney for help.

"I think your mother's right, but I agree that you should have the chance to go it on your own. We can certainly entertain an offer."

That surprised me, but I wasn't about to let it pass. "How much are you asking?"

Rodney puffed his cigar. "Three twenty-five."

I looked at Christabel who sat staring at her hands clasped in her lap. I wasn't sure if I was doing the right thing, but pride prevented me from doing otherwise. "How long do I have?"

Rodney looked perplexed. "What?"

"How long do I have to pull together the funds?"

"Oh." Rodney drew on his cigar. "As I said, we have two interested parties. We've given them two weeks to submit a proposal."

Two weeks. Two weeks to come up with money I didn't have. Still, what option did I have? "Okay." I looked at Christabel and smiled. Her return smile was weak. I hoped I was doing the right thing. All I knew was that I had to try.

33

Summer 1970 – The Challenge

I SHED MY DINNER jacket and tie and sat on one of the blue satin benches at the foot of the bed. Across from me, Christabel sat at an ornate French dressing table. Her thin voile dinner dress lay across the bench beside her. I watched the smooth flow of her bare arms and back as she removed the hairpiece and placed it on the dressing table top. Slowly, she picked up the ormolu hairbrush and began running it over her teased and tangled ash-blond hair. She was a beautiful sight.

I inhaled deeply. "Well?"

"Well, what?" She didn't miss a stroke.

"What do you think?"

Her eyes met mine in the mirror. "Does it matter what I think?"

"Of course, it matters. You're my wife."

"Sounds to me as if you've already made up your mind." She looked away and continued her brushing.

What to say? She was right. I had made up my mind without consulting her. Somehow, I had to make that right. "I'm sorry. I shouldn't have done that. We should have had time to discuss it."

Christabel set down the hairbrush and turned around on the bench to face me. Her beige satin slip clung to her body, accenting its curves. With a wave of her hand, she tucked a stray lock of hair behind her ear. She stared at me for moment before speaking. "Would it have made any difference?"

I shook my head slowly. "I don't know."

"Can we afford it?"

I laughed. "I don't know that either. I have to work it out."

"And if you can't *work it out*? What then?"

I shrugged. "I guess I simply bite the bullet."

"If that's the case, would you stay with the company?"

"I suppose so, at least for the time being. As long as the terms were acceptable."

"Such as?"

I stared thoughtfully at the Aubusson carpet. "Decent salary, of course. Some sort of profit sharing for my division."

Christabel nodded. She rose and crossed to sit beside me on the bench. Gently, she took my hand and held it. "I guess the real question is, is this what you want?"

I squeezed her hand, and brought it to my lips, and chuckled. "You're full of difficult questions, aren't you?"

She smiled. "Just trying to help."

I sighed and took a deep breath. "I don't know. It certainly isn't what I planned."

"It's a big responsibility. Not to mention, a lot of work."

I laughed. "That's putting it mildly." I looked at her and smiled weakly. "But, I can't just stand by and watch the company being sold out from under us."

"Because it was your father's?"

I shrugged. "I guess so." I released her hand and stood. Slowly, I walked across the room and stared out the window at the backyard. All was shrouded in shadows cast by the full moon. What did I want? The shadows held no answers. "I don't know. It's just that when Rodney said they wanted to sell, my only thought was, *there's no way in Hell!*"

"It was a rotten thing to do."

I laughed. "What would you expect from the two of them?"

"I'd expect your mother to stand up for you and your interests."

"Why would you expect that?"

"You're her son, Marc. I know the two of you aren't really close, but there is something to be said for family."

I gave a rueful snort. "We haven't been a family since my father died. My mother has never forgiven me for that."

Christabel rose and crossed the room to stand behind me. I felt her soft touch as she laid her hands on my shoulders and then rested her head against my back. "Do you truly believe she blames you for that?"

"Oh, yes. She blames me alright." I sighed, enjoying her closeness. "And I guess she has every right to."

"I don't believe that for a moment."

I didn't want to talk about that night. It was behind me and I intended to keep it that way. Nothing to be gained by rehashing the past. Yet, Christabel needed to know. She needed to understand exactly the part I had played in my father's death.

"She warned me not to aggravate him," I began, slowly. "Said that he needed to rest. But then, he wanted to talk to me. Talk about school. He was calm at first, but then he started pushing my buttons. I lost it. We argued; argued violently. I knew it was wrong, but I couldn't help myself."

"You were just a kid." Her voice was soft, consoling.

I paused, still staring out the window, recalling the specifics of the conversation with my father that night–the abuse I'd suffered at that horrible school–but I wasn't about to reveal this level of detail to Christabel. It was irrelevant, at least to me. "He was flushed when I left him, but he was alive. He died sometime during the night."

Christabel tightened her grip on my shoulders but did not speak. I turned slowly and wrapped my arms around her. "Love you, babe."

"Love you, too." Her voice was muffled, her face buried in my shoulder.

The minutes passed as we gained strength from one another. I finally broke the embrace and kissed her softly on the lips. "Sorry about all this. You deserve better."

She smiled up at me and kissed the corner of my mouth. "Don't be silly."

I tightened my embrace and rested my head on top of her soft, blond hair. "I don't think I've done very well answering your questions."

"Let me be the judge of that." She took my hand and guided me to the chaise lounge next to us. Seated, she wrapped her arms around me. "I love you so much."

"And I you." I kissed her gently.

"You do what you have to do. I will always support you."

I laughed. "It all boils down to money at this point."

She pulled away and stared into my eyes. "Do we have that kind of money? It sounds like an awful lot to me."

"No, but there's a chance I can get it. We just have to wait and see."

"What's the plan?"

"I'm going to call Rae Sinclair at the bank on Monday to set up an appointment with her. She's always been good at offering me advice."

Christabel nodded and then paused, staring at her lap. After a moment, she looked up at me again. "You know, I could ask Daddy for help."

The thought appalled me. "No! No way! This is something I have to do myself. I can't look to your father for help."

She took both my hands in hers. "Marc, Mommie and Daddy love you. They'd do anything for you."

I smiled down at her. "I know, but I just can't do it this time. I have to resolve this by myself. If I took money from your father, Rodney and Mom would never let me live it down."

"Why?"

"Because that's the way they are. They'd forever be digging at me. *'You never would have pulled it off if it hadn't been for Christabel's father.'*"

"Would that be so bad?"

I stared at Christabel in shock. "Of course it would! It would only reinforce Rodney's belief that I can't stand on my own two feet. You've seen how he treats me when we're all together; that condescending asshole! I'm sure he's glorying in tonight and how he was able to put me in my place."

Christabel wrapped her arms around my neck and pulled me close. "Don't think like that! Don't you *ever* think like that."

I absorbed the smell of her and wondered what I had done to deserve a woman like Christabel. I felt the warmth of her skin through the thin, silk slip as I kissed her softly on the lips. The taste of residual lipstick and crème de menthe was intoxicating.

34

Summer 1970 – Finale

THE MONEY BEQUEATHED TO me by Granny Steadman would provide the bulk of what I needed. I planned to raise another thirty-thousand or so by selling her house. There was a small mortgage on the Linden Avenue house. Hopefully, that could be increased and extended. I would have to look to the bank to make up the rest although that, in itself, could be problematic. With little or no experience, the bank might not look favorably on such a large loan. Time would tell.

At the end of the two weeks, I found myself seated across Rodney's desk in his study at The Birches. I felt like an errant school boy facing his principal. My mother was conspicuously absent. It was obvious to me that she wanted nothing to do with the proceedings.

Rodney slowly lit a cigar and then leaned back in his chair with a grin. His wasn't a pleasant smile; it was predatory. "Tell me, how did you make out?"

"Fairly well."

"Were you able to meet our asking price?"

I hesitated. "No. I ran into a problem with the bank. They weren't willing to grant me as much as I needed."

"That's too bad." Rodney puffed contentedly. "How much did you raise?"

"Two-hundred-eighty-five thousand."

"We're asking three twenty-five."

"I know."

"Our other parties seem content with that price."

What could I say? I had done all I could do. The rest was up to Rodney.

He rose from his chair and extended a hand to me. "Well, Marc, I'm sorry this didn't work out for you, but, if anything changes with the other parties, I'll let you know."

I nodded. "When will you hear from them?"

He knocked the ash from his cigar. "Tomorrow or the next day. I should be able to give you an answer by Friday."

"I'd appreciate that." I rose from my chair.

And that was that. No negotiations. No intervention from my mother. Nothing. And why was I not surprised? It all came down to money. There was no room for personal considerations. It was all about dollars and cents.

Soon, Steadman and Son passed from our family into the hands of a man and his brother-in-law from Lewiston. There were a few negotiations, but I was not a party to them, of course. The whole deal was accomplished in less than two months. In spite of my feelings, I remained with the company. Frankly, I needed the work; I needed the money.

Striking out on my own remained in the back of my mind, but I first needed to establish myself. The best way to do that was to stay with Steadman and Son, at least for a while. The time would come. It just wasn't in the cards at the moment.

Several months later I discovered the truth about the sale of my father's business.

I was having lunch with Bill Fuller and Steve Redman, the new owners. Our relationship had developed into a fairly good one, and I appreciated all the support they gave my design division. A degree of comfort had developed between the three of us and, for the time being, I was content remaining as part of the company.

Bill Fuller sipped his cup of coffee. "At the time, Steve and I thought it was odd that you didn't take over the business."

I gave a rueful laugh. "I tried."

Steve looked surprised. "You did?"

Bill set down his coffee cup. "Really? We were told you weren't interested."

"Who told you that?"

"Rodney, of course."

I laughed again. "Well, that's a lie. I tried my level best to buy the company, but I couldn't raise enough money to outbid you guys." I smiled. "With Rodney and my mother, money talks. It's a matter of who yells the loudest."

Bill nodded slowly. "Guess you're right. Still, I'm surprised they would tell us something like that."

I shrugged. "Who knows with those two? I made an offer. It was lower than what they sought. They shot it down."

Bill shot Steve a look. "If you don't mind my asking, how much did you offer?"

"It's no secret. Two eighty-five."

Neither man spoke.

I looked from Steve to Bill. "What?"

Bill and Steve looked at one another. Neither man spoke.

I smiled uncertainly. "Come on, you guys. What's up?"

Bill looked at Steve again. Steve nodded solemnly. "We paid two seventy-five."

There it was. Proof positive that Rodney and my mother had hung me out to dry. I have no doubt it was intentional. My mother did not want me to own either company. She would have rather seen the businesses in the hands of strangers, which is exactly where they landed. I'm almost sure hers was the deciding vote.

For some reason, I felt no surprise in hearing this from Steve and Bill. I felt nothing, really, but a moment of chagrin. What do you say when your own mother stabs you in the back?

35

Spring 1972 – Miranda et al

MIRANDA McCAFFERTY STEADMAN WAS born in the spring of 1972 on the heels of an early-morning thunderstorm. Sitting by Christabel's bedside, Miranda's newborn cries were punctuated by the distant rumbles of the departing storm. It was an auspicious beginning for certain. She was born a Gemini–need I say more?

Miranda was the image of her mother, which was fortunate. No girl need resemble her father, especially at birth. Thankfully for her, Miranda would continue to favor her mother's side of the family.

We were a happy, little family. Miranda was just what the Linden Avenue house needed. Its elegant formality was now tempered with stuffed animals, baby clothes, and a proper English perambulator. Because of its proximity to the master suite, Christabel turned Grandmother Powell's morning room into a nursery, complete with hot-pink, paisley wallpaper. Grandmother Powell would have shuddered.

I was still with Steadman and Son, and the business was growing steadily. My relationship with Bill and Steve continued in a positive vein. For the first time, I actually shelved the idea of going out on my own, for the time being at least. There was always the option, but it was no longer in the forefront of my mind.

Rodney and my mother lived up to their promise. They traveled often. I had never confronted either of them about their duplicity. That day would come, but this wasn't the time for a family confrontation.

With the two of them continents away, I could easily forget their existence. They sent the occasional postcard, but these were promptly dropped into the trash.

For now, the world consisted of Christabel, Miranda, and me—and I liked it that way. I spent the weekdays at work. Christabel cared for the house. We both watched with joy every milestone of Miranda's development. Who wouldn't be happy with such an arrangement?

———

We hadn't seen much of Freddie Clifton over the last year or so. Freddie was busy getting her own life together. She currently taught in the public-school system at the state capitol and really seemed to enjoy it.

Her love life, however, was a veritable roller coaster. She survived two engagements without ever reaching the altar. Since relocating north, she had become enamored with a man several years her senior. John Allen was successful and well-established in his own airplane charter service and held several state contracts. Freddie's parents were not pleased; Bertha Mae, her grandmother, even less so. There was talk of disinheritance, but few of us took it seriously. Obviously, the threat meant little to Freddie. She and her newest love eloped one weekend, thumbing their noses at anyone who disapproved. Freddie was still Freddie, and she would live her life according to her own rules, not those of her parents.

———

Tom was a different matter. Following the debacle of college and Grandmother Powell's death, he had set about becoming one of the mainstays of Powell Properties, Ltd. Uncle Fred had always run the business with an iron hand, but that hold was beginning to falter. Having been diagnosed with colon cancer, Uncle Fred began devoting himself to his cancer treatments, allowing Tom to gain the forefront. Tom was a natural. He was a true people person and liked by all of his clients. This trait made his road to success a relatively easy one. There seemed to be nothing Tom couldn't sell.

His love life was another matter. There were plenty of girls—too many, in fact. Some of his relationships lasted only a week. It was hard for the rest of us to keep up. The issue finally reached its apex when

Christabel and I hosted a black tie, sit-down dinner for eight couples. All were old high school friends, and, of course, Tom was among them. Christabel had labored hard over place cards done in calligraphy as a finishing touch to the table. It wasn't until Tom arrived that she realized there was a problem. Instead of Terri Maitland, the daughter of a retired MGM executive, Tom introduced us to Stephanie Sessions, a former client of his. Christabel worked quickly to replace the name card, but there wasn't time to add the calligraphic touches. It was a tense and embarrassing moment, but everyone weathered it with good humor. I did, however, have a word with Tom about the infraction.

Tom's relationships continued in this fashion in the ensuing four years. Girls came and went. Each was attractive and striking in her own way. Tom always seemed happy, but I could tell there was something missing. Like the rest of us, Tom was searching. He wanted what everyone wanted. It was simply taking him longer to find it. One evening over drinks, he confided in me. "I want what you and Christabel have— a family, a proper house. I just can't seem to make it work."

He tried. I have to credit him with that. It was simply that none of the girls Tom dated filled the bill, so to speak. Yet, he kept searching. If nothing else, Tom's belief in the American Dream was firmly rooted.

36

Spring 1974 – Judith Vwater Berghoff

JUDITH VWATER BERGHOFF WAS strikingly sophisticated, gracious, and charming–just the kind of girl one would expect from a Sutton Place upbringing. She arrived in Martin's Neck along with her husband and two young children. Jeremy Berghoff was a stockbroker with Garland and Shanks, a prestigious New York-based brokerage firm. He was being transferred into the area to open and manage a branch office in Rehoboth Beach. Through some previous clients, they were directed to Powell Properties and to Tom, in particular.

As I have mentioned, Tom could sell anything. River Bend had been on the market for almost two years, but there'd been no takers. Built by a wealthy manufacturer in the early twenties, the estate was simply too large for today's market. The Colonial Revival mansion was formidable and boasted more space than most families wanted or needed. There were also garages, a stable, and a tennis court. I think it was the latter than won the Berghoffs over, as Judith was an avid tennis player. So was Tom.

Tom became enamored with the family. They were colorful and fun, just the kind of people he enjoyed. After the sale of the property, Tom continued to socialize with the Berghoffs. Jeremy was back and forth to New York on a regular basis as he worked to establish the new office. That left Judith with time on her hands, not that it was wasted.

Judith Berghoff was an artist in her own right. She and Jeremy had converted the stable loft into a studio for her, and she spent much of her time there. She had room to paint while the children played in a designated play area. Emma and Charles were five and four, respectively. They were cute children and devoted to one another. They doted on their mother and were constantly by her side. Jeremy was more distant; his work monopolized most of his time. Judith enrolled both children in a well-respected preschool, and they seemed to thrive in the new environment. Besides providing new friends for the children, the school exposed Judith to many of the young mothers in Martin's Neck. It wasn't long before she acquired several regular tennis partners and friends.

Christabel was among Judith's friends. It was through their friendship that I heard the first whisperings of concern.

—

As a means of welcoming the Berghoffs to Martin's Neck, Aunt Harriet Powell threw an elegant cocktail party in their honor. Everyone who was anyone was invited, and very few deigned not to attend.

Christabel and I stood in a group at one end of Aunt Harriet's dining room. Everything was perfect: the food, the drink, the sparkling crystal, the elegantly dressed members of Martin's Neck society. The Berghoffs fit right in.

Judith Berghoff sipped her glass of wine and smiled. "We have so much to thank Tom for. We couldn't have done it without him."

Uncle Fred, looking increasingly frail but still holding his own, laughed. "We at Powell Properties aim to please."

"Tom did so much more than that. He was there whenever we needed anything. He helped us with our application to the yacht club. He even found the kids' preschool for us."

Seeing Tom nearby, Uncle Fred grabbed his arm and pulled him into our circle. "Come on over here, son. You're being paid a compliment."

Tom laughed. "What now?"

"This lovely lady was just telling us how invaluable you are."

Tom feigned a redneck pause and shuffle. "Aw shucks! Twerent nothin'."

"Judith's right. We would never have had such a smooth transition if it hadn't been for your help." Jeremy Berghoff took his wife's hand and brought it to his lips. "And this lady is always right. Trust me."

Tom held up his hands in protest. "Please, enough!"

Judith looked at Tom and smiled. "And he's an excellent tennis player."

Jeremy laughed. "Need I say more?"

Tom dipped his head in acknowledgment. "Well, let me say it was a pleasure working with you and your family. I only wish all our clients were so engaging."

Jeremy laughed again. "Ah, flattery. I love it!"

Everyone laughed at that.

Christabel sipped of her wine. "How's the house coming along?"

"Oh, fine." Judith's voice was enthusiastic. "Tom convinced me to put the grand piano in the family room rather than the drawing room." She looked at Tom and smiled.

I laughed. "Didn't know you were an interior decorator, too, Tom."

"Well, it was just common sense. The drawing room's fine for a baby grand but too small for a full grand. Plus, they'll get a lot more use of it in the family room. That's where everyone's going to congregate."

Judith wrapped her arm through Tom's. "See what I mean? He thinks of everything!"

Uncle Fred clapped Tom on the back. "Well done, son. Well done."

Christabel was silent as we got into the car to drive home. I looked at her, sensing something was amiss. "Nice party, huh?"

She stared back at me, smiled, and nodded.

I started the engine and dropped the car it into gear. "What's wrong?"

There was a pause. "Nothing, I guess."

"Must be something."

"It's just me."

I maneuvered the sedan through the quiet streets. "Want to let me in on it?"

"I don't know…it's just…"

"Just *what?*"

We drove slowly through the center of town then up the steep rise of Linden Avenue. "Something I said?"

She looked at me sharply. "No. Nothing like that."

"Then...what?"

Christabel sighed. "I don't know." Another pause.

I pulled the car into our driveway and killed the motor.

Christabel turned to face me. "It's the way Judith treats Tom. It bothers me."

"How so?"

"I'm not sure." She shook her head as if to clear it. "It's...it's too familiar. Too personal."

I was perplexed. "Are you saying she has a thing for Tom?"

Christabel shrugged. "I don't know. Maybe. She's always talking about him. She and I had lunch last week, and all she could talk about was Tom."

"She did seem overly appreciative tonight."

Christabel sighed. "It's not that so much. It's the tone of her voice; the way she looks at him." She gazed at me pointedly. "It's not natural for a married woman to act that way."

"Oh, really?" I was taken aback. "You saying there's something going on between them?"

Christabel shook her head. "No. Not yet, anyway." She paused. "I don't get that vibe from Tom."

"Okay." I was obviously out of my depth here. "Should I ask him?"

Christabel looked at me in shock. "Good God, no! That's the last thing you should do!"

"Okay. What's the *first* thing I should do?"

"Nothing."

"I do nothing?" I was now completely at sea.

She shook her head. "This is between the two of them. We have no part in it."

I looked at Christabel in bewilderment. "If you say so. But, then, why are we having this conversation?"

She seemed surprised by the question. "We're having this conversation because you asked me what was bothering me."

"Oh, right. And...?"

Christabel reached for the handle and opened the car door. "And now you know."

37

Summer 1976 – Lucas Grey Steadman et al.

OUR SON, LUCAS GREY Steadman, was born in July of 1976. He was a happy baby and, unlike his old man, seemed to know his place in the world. Miranda was skeptical of her brother. A lot of questions and ideas swam about in her four-year-old mind. Was all this fuss really necessary? Did we actually need another member added to our family? If so, wouldn't a dog be a more reasonable choice? Still, she knuckled under and made the best of what she deemed a less-than-desirable situation.

Miranda was a never-ending joy. She was precocious to say the least, but, in her, this was an endearing quality. She was older than her four years and viewed the world with a pragmatic glint in her eye. Nothing was beyond understanding. Everything had a cause and effect. All things could be manipulated if one knew their way around a situation. And if there was a way around, Miranda would find it.

My work continued unabated. I stayed with Steadman and Son and developed a good working rapport with Steve and Bill. The idea of going out on my own remained on the back burner. I visited it from time to time, acknowledging the possibility, but never felt that the time was right to make a move.

My mother's greed raised its ugly head once again. Once more, I learned about it through Steve and Bill. Rodney and my mother had retained the fifty acres that contained our family home. They used it occasionally, especially in the winter when heating costs at The Birches were high. Beyond that, the house sat vacant with only a caretaker and a lawn service to see to its needs.

Bill Fuller plopped down in the chair across from my desk. "How's it going?"

I smiled. "Busy, just the way we like it. I got a signed contract from the Howells yesterday, so the house is a go."

"That's great news! Now tell me what's going on with your mother and Rodney."

I looked at Bill with surprise. What now? "I have no idea. What do you mean?"

Bill leaned forward and rested his arms on my desk. "Word has it that they've sold the property on Pine Bark Road. Any truth to that?"

"Damned if I know! Where'd you hear that?"

"At the bank this morning. Arnie Thompson was talking about it."

Arnie Thompson was another local realtor. Although he was a known competitor of Powell Properties, they had done business together from time to time. Arnie was also an old classmate of my mother's. He and his wife were part the Martin's Neck inner circle.

I shook my head. "News to me." Damn her. Damn them! What were they up to?

"I just thought it odd that you hadn't mentioned it."

"Trust me, I would have."

Bill nodded thoughtfully. "Sold it to some developer from up north. Maybe we can get our foot in the door with that one."

I nodded, but my thoughts were elsewhere. "I'll see what I can find out." Find out! I intended to do a lot more than that.

Bill rose from his chair. "I'll let you get back to work."

"Sure." I looked up at him. "Would you mind closing the door when you leave? I need to make a couple of calls." Couple of calls, my ass! There was only one call I needed to make.

The phone rang twice before she answered. "Hello."

"Mom."

"Marc! How nice of you to call. Did you want to do lunch today?"

"No, Mom, this isn't a pleasure call."

There was a momentary pause. "Oh. What is it, dear?"

"I just heard that you've sold the house."

Another pause. "Well, yes…it looks that way."

"When were you going to tell me?"

"Anytime, I suppose. I just hadn't gotten around to it."

"Really? 'Just hadn't gotten around to it.'"

"I didn't think you'd want to be concerned with it."

"That property belonged to my grandfather Steadman! Of course I'm concerned about it!"

A note of sarcasm slipped into her voice. "Why? Did you want to buy it?" She laughed lightly. "You have more than you can say grace over now."

"Dad always told me that one day that property would be mine! He wanted it to stay in the family!"

She laughed with more intensity. "Well, he left it to me!"

"So?"

"Let me spell it out for you, Marc. I can do with it as I wish, without your consent."

"You could have at least mentioned it."

"Why? So we could have this and many more conversations on the matter? I think not."

"So it's a done deal?"

"Yes."

"I guess they made you an offer you couldn't refuse."

"That's really none of your business."

"Well, Mother, I'm making it my business."

"How so? There's nothing you can do about it now."

I paused. She was right, and we both knew it. Any threats I might make were hollow. Legally, the property was hers, and I had no say in the matter.

"I guess it was stupid of me to think that you'd honor Dad's wishes. I'm sure Rodney had was no small influence on the decision."

"That's really no concern of yours."

"I understand now why you've always looked good in yellow. It suits you. Have a great day, Mother."

"I fully intend to," she said, in a voice that matched my own sarcastic tone.

I slammed the receiver back into the phone's cradle. As furious as I felt, my hands were tied. Once again, my mother had bested me. I was simply no match for her.

38

Summer 1978 – Tom and Judith

AS WOMEN USUALLY ARE in such matters, Christabel was correct. Judith Berghoff was attracted to Tom. I don't know how long it took for Tom to realize this, but eventually he did. The rest of the story played out over a period of several months. It wasn't long before there was talk of the Berghoff's marital problems. Jeremy moved into a condo in Rehoboth Beach. That signaled the official separation. A divorce was soon to follow. Despite the scandal, Martin's Neck seemed to accept how it had all unfolded. No one had a vested interest in the Berghoff's marriage, but Tom was another matter altogether. Tom was one of our own. If Tom was happy, then the whole thing must be okay.

Tom was indeed happy. In fact, there was an aura about him…a bright, shiny, golden aura. Tom had finally found that for which he had been searching. That he had to take it from someone else seemed not to bother him at all.

Tom moved into River Bend shortly after the divorce was finalized. He and Judith were married a few months later. Theirs was a picture-perfect wedding, held at a small chapel outside of town. It was summer. The long dresses of the bride and her attendants were carried by the wind, and a firm hand was needed on the crowns of their wide-brimmed hats. While the service was simple, the reception at the yacht club was elegant. Everyone seemed happy; most especially, Tom.

Tom and Judith were a perfect couple. Tom worked; Judith painted. They played tennis. They entertained lavishly. They traveled. They were together whenever possible. They both spent much time with Emma and Charles. Jeremy was rarely in the picture. By the winter of 1977, Jeremy had been transferred to Chicago and became a true absentee father. Tom was there to fill the void. The children loved Tom and he them. Whenever Judith was preparing for a show, Tom became the chauffeur, running the children to their various activities and play dates. To the unknowing observer, one would never know that Jeremy Berghoff had ever existed.

Christabel and I saw a lot of Tom and his family. Emma, Charles and Miranda were great friends and loved to play together. The three of them doted on little Lucas and took turns caring for him. As a group, we were often together. During the summer months, family barbeques were a regular occurrence, as were trips to the beach. Uncle Fred and Aunt Harriet considered Emma and Charles their own grandchildren. As a result, the kids spent a lot of time at Powell Cottage, just as Tom and I had done in our youth.

—

The big news came on such a summer evening at River Bend. Christabel and Judith were finishing up their final set of tennis. Tom and I lounged near the barbeque sipping Mai Tais. The children were busy playing beneath the big, old trees where Tom had erected a playhouse for Emma and Charles. Lucas was toddling by then, and much of their time was spent keeping him on his feet.

"Hear anything from Jeremy?" I asked.

Tom shook his head. "Not a word."

"Surprising."

Tom shrugged. "Not really. He's never been very attentive since the divorce." Tom rose and went to tend to the barbeque. "At least he's never late with his child support checks."

I laughed. "That's a good thing."

"I'll say." He busied himself turning the chicken.

Judith's voice broke the stillness. "That's enough. I need a break."

Christabel laughed in reply. "Oh, come on. You can stand another set."

"Enough for now. I'm done."

The two women exited the court and walked toward us. Both were flushed from their exertions. Christabel smiled and pointed to the tray of drinks. "I could use one of those."

"Sure thing." I rose, assuming the role of bartender. "Judith?"

Judith stretched out atop one of the lounges. "Not for me, thanks. I wouldn't mind a glass of water."

I smiled. "Coming right up!"

Christabel took her drink and sat in a chair next to Judith. "No drink? That's not like you."

"I'm parched. You wore me out."

Christabel looked doubtful. "Hardly."

Judith simply smiled.

I handed her a tall glass of ice water. "Here you go, Madam."

"Your wife plays a mean game of tennis."

I laughed. "Tell me about it."

"Oh, enough!" Christabel laughed. "We all know Judith's the tennis pro. She's just off her game today. Right, Judith?"

Judith smiled. "You could say that I'm a bit heavy on my feet of late."

Christabel turned suddenly, setting down her glass. "Judith!"

Judith smiled and nodded.

It took me a minute to climb aboard, but I finally connected the dots.

Christabel jumped from her chair and crossed to embrace Judith. "Oh, Judith! I'm so happy for you! When are you due?"

She returned Christabel's hug. "February. The fourteenth to be exact."

Christabel laughed. "Valentine's Day. How perfect!"

I stood and offered Tom my hand. "Congratulations, old man!"

Tom grasped my hand and smiled. I could tell he was genuinely happy, and that made me happy. Tom had earned the right. He had waited too long for his idea of life to unfold. Finally, it was happening.

39

Fall 1978 – Passings

UNCLE FRED POWELL SUCCUMBED to his prostate cancer in October. He had responded well to treatments for a time, but his time had run out. Although we all knew it was coming, his death was still a shock. Tom was hit particularly hard. For years he and Uncle Fred had worked side by side at Powell Properties; now he was alone. Sure, he was now head of the firm, but that was little consolation. At least he had Judith and the kids, as well as a baby on the way.

Uncle Fred's funeral was the typical Powell production. Because of his many friends and business associates, "by invitation only" was omitted from the proceedings. As a result, the turnout for the viewing and the funeral was overwhelming. Who knew Uncle Fred's influences had reached so far and wide?

The wake was a slightly smaller affair, but Aunt Harriet opted for the yacht club as opposed to having it "in house." It was a wise decision on her part because the wake was still very well attended. Preparations for that crowd at home would have been overwhelming even with a caterer. As it was, the cocktail hour, dinner, and memorials stretched into the early evening. I was glad to see it end. I sensed that Tom experienced the same sense of relief.

—

In the months that followed, Tom knuckled down to running Powell Properties. Business was good, and the company took up much of his time. He had plenty of help. The company had run like the proverbial well-oiled machine for years. Uncle Fred's passing was felt, but Powell Properties continued to grow and prosper.

Aunt Harriet remained in the big house with only George Sawyer as company. She adopted an informal period of mourning, part of which was scaling back on social events. Tom, ever the dutiful son, stopped in daily to check on her well-being. It wasn't that she needed anything specific; it was simply the need for company.

Tom was executor of Uncle Fred's estate. It took him a while to sort through all of Uncle Fred's holdings, but Uncle Fred's penchant for record keeping made the task easier than most. As was expected, Uncle Fred left everything to Aunt Harriet and promoted Tom to president of the company. No surprises there. It was simply a question of picking up the pieces and then moving forward.

Judith's pregnancy was uneventful. Her doctor deemed her and the baby to be healthy and on schedule. Nothing could have made Tom happier. Emma and Charles were surprisingly excited at the prospect of a new brother or sister. Of course, having watched Lucas grow and develop, they were well aware of what was in the offing.

Judith had commandeered one of the guest rooms for the nursery. It was a bright, sunny room that faced the wide lawn and the river beyond. Following her artistic acumen, Judith embarked upon painting a series of Winnie the Pooh murals for the room. They were delightful.

The fall of 1978 was unusually cold, and the first snowfall arrived just prior to Thanksgiving. That event set the tone for the months to come. We had more snow than we had ever experienced. Where it normally would rain, it snowed. It took a while for us to adjust to the sudden change in climate, but we did. Boots, mufflers, hats, gloves, and snow tires became the norm. The little town of Martin's Neck had its hands full dealing with snow removal. As a result, much slipping and sliding occurred, and occasional fender-benders were not unusual.

The kids loved the snow. Sledding, snowmen, and snowball fights filled their days. The big radiators in our house were constantly draped with drying coats and gloves. Emma and Charles were often at Linden Avenue, and Miranda and Lucas were regular visitors at River Bend where the long, sloping yards made for perfect sledding. Christabel and

Judith rode herd on all the proceedings. Their days were full. Still, Judith managed an occasional art showing and would be out of town for days at a time.

As the Christmas holidays approached, the snow continued. By now, we were all adapting fairly well.

Judith was at an art exhibit in Wilmington, and Tom awaited her arrival home in the comfort of our library where a fire burned brightly. The children played together down the hallway in the conservatory. They had never enjoyed the big playroom on the third floor; it was too far away. With time, their toys migrated, one by one to the conservatory which soon became their center for playtime activity.

I splashed some Scotch into my tumbler and looked over my shoulder at Tom. "Ready for a refill?"

He laughed and downed the remainder of his drink. "I am now." He held out his glass, and I took it.

"Judith picked a hell of a day to be in Wilmington." I liberally filled the glass and handed it back to Tom.

He took a sip. "You can say that again." He glanced at the walnut case clock in the corner of the room. "Shouldn't be too long now."

Christabel entered the room and crossed to sit on the needlepoint bench in front of the hearth. She carried a half-full goblet of wine. "Dinner should be ready by the time Judith gets here."

I sat in one of the wing-backed chairs flanking the black marble fireplace. "How are the kids?"

"Fine. I just checked on them. No disagreements as of yet."

Tom laughed. "The night is young."

The harsh clanging of the doorbell, which was original to the house, rang abruptly. The raucous sound startled us and we jumped in reaction.

Tom was the first to regain his composure and rose from his chair. "Must be our girl now." He crossed the room and entered the wide foyer.

"It's unlocked." I called after him.

There followed the sound of the heavy door being dragged open. Then a pause. The tone of Tom's voice was uncertain. "Sam. What are you doing here?"

"I thought I recognized your car parked out front."

I looked questionably at Christabel who rose from her seat and headed toward the foyer. I followed.

"Yeah. Come in."

As we entered the foyer, Tom stood to one side to allow the tall, young man to enter. "What can I do for you?"

Sam Reynolds was an old classmate of ours who now served as the chief of police for the Martin's Neck Police Department. Sam removed his hat and shook free the newly fallen snowflakes.

"Well..." he stammered hesitantly, eyes roaming from Tom to Christabel to me and then back to Tom. Sam's discomfort was palpable. He spoke suddenly in a rush. "There's been an accident. I'm sorry."

Christabel rushed to Tom and pulled his arm close to her. "What's happened?"

Given his lead, Sam continued. "A rig jack-knifed out on 26." He paused again, looking at Tom. "I'm afraid your wife's car was involved as well."

Horror flooded the foyer and settled its look on each of our faces. Tom was the first to recover. "Is she...is she alright?"

Sam's face spoke volumes. "She was either passing the truck, or it was passing her. We can't be sure."

Tom's face became etched in sorrow. "And the baby?"

Sam looked down at his feet and sadly shook his head. "I'm so sorry."

"Is that my mommy?" Emma's squeal filled the space. She left the conservatory door open as she ran into the hallway.

I shot Christabel a look as she dropped Tom's arm and turned to intercept the little girl. Taking Emma by the shoulder, Christabel guided her back toward the conservatory. "No, honey. It's just a man come to talk to us."

"But when is Mommy coming?"

Christabel offered no reply. She ushered Emma into the conservatory and followed her into the room, closing the door behind them. A heavy silence ensued. I glanced at Tom. A single tear ran down the left side of his face.

—

And so the nightmare began to unfold. There was nothing simple about it. The situation was too complicated for that, and everything seemed to move at a break-neck speed. Tom did his best to keep the wheels from dislodging, but with only marginal success. How do you explain death to two young children? How do you make them understand that their lives have suddenly been changed forever? Tom tried, and we did our best to support him. It was far from easy, though no one expected it to be otherwise.

Although Tom hoped that he and the children would continue to live at River Bend, it was not to be. The house had been bequeathed to Emma and Charles and would have to be sold.

Jeremy arrived two days after the accident and made it very clear that the children would be coming to Chicago to live with him. No one really expected otherwise; each simply hoped for an alternative that would never come.

Emma and Charles were in shock. They clung to Tom for support. Even their father's presence made little difference. Tom was their anchor, and they looked to him to make everything right again. Unfortunately, that was beyond Tom's ability.

Upon realizing that they would soon be leaving Martin's Neck, the children panicked. They wanted to remain at River Bend with Tom. It was their home. They didn't want to leave. These wishes, once vocalized, were silenced by their father and grandparents. The decision had been made. They would be moving to Chicago with their father.

Christabel tried to get the children to stay with us until after the funeral, but Tom insisted that they return to River Bend. He felt they needed familiar surroundings. Of course, the house was filled with visitors. Jeremy took one of the guest rooms, as did Judith's parents who arrived shortly thereafter.

There were arguments. Each contingent felt it had the authority to make decisions where the funeral, wake, and burial were concerned. No one was thinking straight. They were simply voicing their opinions and trying to force them on one another. Progress was slow and complicated.

In the end, the service was simple. The wake was held at River Bend, but the burial would not occur until the following week. The remains were being sent to New York so that Judith and the baby could be buried in her father's family plot.

It seemed that everything was being taken away from Tom. His family was gone. His home was gone. Now, he would not even be allowed the consolation of visiting the grave of his wife and unborn child. It was almost as if that brief period of his life had been erased, had never occurred at all, or had all been a dream.

40

1978-1983 – Train Wreck

TOM STAYED ON AT River Bend long enough to ready it for the market. Jeremy had insisted that Tom handle the listing even though Tom would have preferred otherwise. Having to deal with the property only irritated the already painful wounds. Once the movers had emptied the house, Tom relocated back home and took up residence with Aunt Harriet and George Sawyer. They were a pathetic trio of sorts, knocking about the big, old house, seemingly with no real purpose in life.

Although his realtor work occupied his time, clearly Tom's heart was no longer in it. He went to work every day. He sold properties with the same regularity as before. He smiled. He joked. He put up a good front, at least for a while.

Tom had always been a heavy drinker. We all drank to excess. Cocktails at five had been as much a religious experience as church on Sunday morning. One simply didn't miss it. Nightly cocktails gave one an opportunity to relax and refuel in order to face the next day. Now, however, Tom took it one step further.

For a while, we became regular dinner guests at Aunt Harriet's home and witnessed Tom's nightly rituals firsthand. Those evenings were often awkward, but the children's laughter and antics helped soften the otherwise somber mood. Both Tom and Aunt Harriet seemed to enjoy having the young ones around, but Christabel and I were cautious. They were a constant reminder of what Tom had lost.

In May of 1979, at one of our dinner gatherings, I talked for a while with George Sawyer. Dinner had ended, and Christabel, Tom, and Aunt Harriet were in the library enjoying after-dinner drinks. I lagged behind, watching George clear the table. George busied himself and seemed oblivious to my presence.

"How's he doing?"

There was no response.

"George?"

He paused in his work and stared at me. He then averted his eyes and returned to the task at hand.

I inhaled deeply. "How's Tom doing, George?"

George hesitated and then shook his head. "Not good, Marc. Not good."

I hadn't been expecting a positive response, but George's tone was disturbing. "How so?"

George looked at me for a moment and stared at the cluttered table. "Him and Missus Powell always has their drinks before dinner in the drawing room. Then, I serve them dinner here in the dining room. There's always a bottle of wine."

I nodded. This was nothing new.

George picked up the tray of dishes and headed for the kitchen. I followed. As he began to unload the tray, I sat on one of the bar stools at the counter. George remained silent.

I forced a laugh. "Well, Tom has always liked his drink."

Without looking at me, George continued. "What's left, he takes with him to the library. I keep a fire there most days."

"Yes, I know."

"Missus Powell, she goes upstairs and watches television."

"I see."

George turned and looked at me. "When I finish cleaning up the dishes, I check on him. By then he's got the whiskey bottle out. He's always got that old, sad music playing. I leave him be and come back here to watch TV."

"That's not good."

George shook his head. "No. Not good." He paused for a breath. "Before I goes up to bed, I check on him again. He's usually asleep in his chair. Sometimes, I try to get him upstairs, but most times I just let him be."

I sighed. "That's every night?"

George nodded. "Most nights."

"Well, I'm glad you're here to take care of him."

George turned back to the dirty dishes. "Just not much I can do to help someone that unhappy."

Christabel regularly invited Tom to our house for dinner. Sometimes he came; sometimes he didn't. On those occasions when Tom was MIA, he rarely called to make excuses, and the evasion would go unmentioned by all of us. This lack of accountability was becoming part of Tom's new persona. He was drifting. There seemed to be no objective in his life now, and it became obvious that he didn't know how to handle that fact.

Aunt Harriet never alluded to the change in Tom. The subject was obviously taboo to her. I recalled my conversation with George Sawyer. That things were "not good" should have told me that Tom was on a never-ending, down-hill slide. It could only be a matter of time before he reached bottom.

Christabel did her best to include Tom whenever we entertained. Her efforts, however, were rarely successful, and, at times, became embarrassing, depending on Tom's frame of mind and demeanor.

By the spring of 1982, our relationship with Tom had truly begun to suffer. I returned home early one Friday and was greeted by the sound of china and crystal as I entered the house. Following the source of the noise brought me into the dining room where I found Christabel busily setting the long, mahogany table.

I paused at the archway separating the dining room from the drawing room and watched her for a moment. "Aren't you the busy one?"

She turned and smiled. Abandoning her work, Christabel paused and kissed me softly on the lips. "You're home early."

"Thought I'd give you a hand, but you seem to have beat me to the punch."

Christabel turned her attention to the table. "Oh, we're in good shape, but I'm sure I can find something for you to do."

"Who's coming?"

"Johnsons, Simplers, and Welches."

"Sounds good." I paused. "No Tom?"

Christabel stopped her work and turned to look at me. "No. No Tom."

"Begged off again, did he?"

"No, Marc, I didn't ask him."

"How come?"

Christabel sighed and sat on one of the high-backed, William and Mary dining chairs. "To be honest, I'm tired of asking him. Half the time, he doesn't respond, and, when he does, it's a fifty-fifty chance that he'll show up."

I nodded. "I know."

"I've done all I can do. Twice I've invited eligible women, only to have him ignore them. It's embarrassing."

I sighed. "I know, sweetie."

"I don't know what else to do. It's obvious he doesn't have any interest in developing a new relationship."

"Maybe it's too soon."

Christabel stared at me in shock. "Too soon? Marc, it's been four years."

What could I say? She was right.

As time passed, it seemed that Tom had almost divorced himself from me and my family. Our contact with him dissipated to the traditional family functions that graced the holidays. We'd sometimes see one another at the occasional wedding or funeral, but, even there, our interaction was minimal.

—

Great Uncle Henry Powell died unexpectedly in the fall of 1982. To say his death was unexpected is perhaps erroneous. He was eighty-five. It was at Great Uncle Henry's wake that I found myself standing beside Tom in a small alcove off Uncle Henry's drawing room.

The room was filled with friends and family members, most pausing to offer Great Aunt Eloise their condolences. The dining room beyond was filled as well. As was usual, there was plenty to eat and plenty to drink.

Tom's stance indicated that he'd already downed a few by the time I encountered him. His right hand held a tumbler filled with amber liquid.

I placed a hand on his shoulder. "Hey, buddy. How you been?"

Tom shrugged. "Same as ever."

"Haven't seen much of you of late."

He shrugged again. "Been busy."

"Office busy?"

He nodded. "You could say that."

"Sure would like to see you. Christabel and the kids really miss you. So do I."

Tom took a long swallow of his drink. "One of these days."

I knew when I was being put off, and I didn't like it. I grabbed Tom's arm and tried to turn him to face me. He resisted. "Hey, man, I'm serious. What's going on?"

Tom glared at me and shook free of my grasp. "What do you think?"

His retort shocked me. For a moment, I was speechless. "Well..."

Tom cut me off. "Don't you know how painful it is for me to be around you and your family? Don't you know that every time I see you, I'm reminded of what I lost? I have nothing. Nothing. Is that so hard to understand?" He turned and walked away.

What could I say or do? Tell Tom that he was right? Agree that his situation was hopeless? Affirm that he'd lost all purpose in life and had no reason to go on living? No. I couldn't say those things, even though I knew them to be true. Tom was a lost soul. As much as I loved him, there was nothing I could do to alleviate his pain.

—

Shortly after the new year of 1983, I learned that Tom had drifted into a fast-moving summer crowd from the DC area. Most of them were single, and they were known for their wild parties and heavy drinking. There was talk of drug use and unbridled sex, but I marked that up to mere gossip. The truth was, I had little or no evidence of any of Tom's activities except through the rumor mill. On a few occasions, photos of Tom with his DC clique, taken at some society-driven affair, would show up in the local newspaper. Once or twice I commented about this to Tom who merely replied, "Oh, that wasn't me." I never understood why the denial was so important to him, or why he would even bother to dispute a published photograph. It made no sense to me. When I mentioned it to Christabel, she simply shook her head sadly.

—

As the years passed, Tom began to show the physical effects of his lifestyle. He actually began to age. We were all aging, but there was something about Tom's decline that differed. His once shiny, blond hair appeared dull and lifeless. Tom's clothes seemed to hang on him, and he seemed to have no inclination to update his wardrobe. His skin tone changed, taking on a sallow, unhealthy color His eyes, those bright, blue orbs, were now dull and faded. Christabel said it was the result of his lifestyle, and I grew to accept that as fact.

———

The truth came late one morning in my office during the summer of 1983. The phone rang; it was my mother. Her voice was curt and businesslike. "Your Aunt Harriet just phoned. Tom's in the hospital in Milbank."

"What happened?"

She sighed. "I'm not sure. Harriet was upset. I'm not really sure she got everything straight. You know how she can be."

"What did she say?"

"Something about a fundraiser in Lewiston. Apparently, he passed out, or maybe he fell. You should check on him."

———

The news was surprising. Had Tom's collapse been a result of excessive alcohol consumption? It was surely possible. But would it have put him in the hospital? I started to speculate. Perhaps he'd hit his head when he fell. Perhaps Tom's alcohol use had damaged his liver.

I phoned the hospital. After two transfers, I was connected to Tom's room. After several rings, Tom finally answered with a weak and emotionless "Hello."

I sensed something was truly wrong. "Hey, Buddy, your mom just called. What's going on?"

He didn't reply.

"Are you okay?"

"I was…I was in Lewiston, helping out at a fundraiser, and I blacked out."

"Were you dehydrated? Have you undergone any tests? What did the hospital staff say?"

Silence on the end of the line.

"Tom?"

Tom cleared his throat, his voice nearly a whisper. "Yeah, I've undergone tests. Marc, there's something you should know. I have AIDS."

41

Summer 1984 – Tom

TOM'S BATTLE WITH AIDS was long and difficult. Aunt Harriet was the general in charge. She pushed and pushed and pushed. Since there was no treatment for AIDS at the time, Tom was given a variety of experimental medicines and holistic alternatives as he and Aunt Harriet visited numerous hospitals and clinics in search of some respite from the illness. However, nothing seemed to retard the hunger of the disease. It appeared that Tom's heart wasn't in the fight. He looked almost resigned to his fate. He put up a good front, but one could tell that Tom wasn't showing all his cards.

As Tom's condition worsened, Aunt Harriet became more and more ashamed of her son's illness. It was a time when few of us really knew anything about the disease. Much of what we did know was based on rumor rather than fact.

Regardless, scions of prosperous, important families did not contract such diseases. It was scandalous; unheard of. As recourse after recourse failed to pan out, Aunt Harriet became more protective. Whether she was protecting Tom or the family name remained to be determined. I think she regarded them as one and the same.

Fraught with confusion and worry, Aunt Harriet began restricting Tom's contact with the outside world. She moved Tom into the downstairs guest room, and then left him largely to himself. Aunt Harriet played watchdog and depended on George Sawyer for back up. She also hired a formidable woman of African descent named Katherine

Collins. Katherine took over the meal preparation. She also coordinated the cleaning–and general running–of the house. As a result, George had more time to help with Tom's care.

It wasn't until I received a phone call from Freddie Clifton Allen in mid-September that I realized how extreme Aunt Harriet's behavior was becoming.

"Freddie! How are you?"

"Just fine, sweetie. Just fine."

"How are the boys?" By now Freddie and her husband, John, were heading up a family consisting of three active boys.

Freddie laughed. "They take after their father."

"That can't be good."

"Depends on which day of the week it is."

I laughed. "We've got to get together."

"I know. It's been too long."

"Give Christabel a call and see if you girls can't work something out."

"I will." There was a pause. "Have you seen Tom lately?"

"Not for the last week or so. Why?"

Freddie hesitated. "I stopped by the house yesterday; they wouldn't let me in."

"Who wouldn't let you in?"

"It was George, actually, but Aunt Harriet was behind it."

"Are you sure you're not overreacting to something George said?"

"I went to the back door. As I was about to open it, George opened it for me. Though not really. He blocked the doorway so I couldn't enter."

"Did he say anything?"

"I told him I'd come to visit with Tom. He said that Tom was sleeping. I asked to see Aunt Harriet, but George said she was lying down and didn't want to be disturbed."

George was not the epitome of tact. He was good at following orders but did only a minimum amount of thinking for himself. His recitation of Aunt Harriet's directive was somewhat true to form. "And?"

"And he wouldn't move. I was going to go in and wait, but George said no one could enter the house without Aunt Harriet's permission. I finally gave up."

"Strange. I don't know what to say."

"Well, I thought you ought to know."

"I'm sorry that happened, but I'm not sure I can do anything about it. Aunt Harriet certainly isn't going to answer to me. In her mind, Tom and I are still kids."

"I'm sure. But I thought you'd want to know."

"Yes, thanks. I'll talk to Aunt Harriet. I'm sure she didn't intend anything by it. Probably just a misunderstanding between her and George."

"It really upset me."

"I'm sure it did."

"Let me know what she has to say."

"I will. Be sure to get in touch with Christabel soon."

"I will, Marc. Thanks."

It was unlikely that Aunt Harriet would have anything to say to me about the incident. Most likely, she'd simply tell me to keep out of her business. Still, I couldn't let George's treatment of Freddie pass without notice, though I knew better than to accuse Aunt Harriet of being behind it. That would have been Uncle Fred's obligation, but he was no longer around to run interference. Aunt Harriet had grabbed the reins of leadership bequeathed to her in widowhood, and she was not about to relinquish them to anyone.

42

Fall 1984 – Damaged Goods

IF THERE WAS ANYTHING positive about Tom's illness, it was the fact that we began to see more of him. Aunt Harriet kept him sequestered as much as possible in the downstairs north bedroom. Occasionally, with George Sawyer's help, Tom escaped to the library next door. George would build a fire, secure Tom on the Chesterfield sofa, and set the stereo to play Tom's favorite vinyl. He wasn't allowed to drive, and he was never seen in public. Christabel and/or I tried to visit Tom at least once each week. Those visits, though sometimes painful, were often filled with tales of our childhood memories, wishes, and unfulfilled dreams. The first of October was such a day.

"As you can see, Mom's put me in here with Beatrice." From his place on the big canopied bed, Tom waved a hand to indicate the portrait above the mantle. He laid aside a paperback copy of *On Death and Dying*. "It was easier than having me upstairs in my old room. At her age, Mom doesn't like to climb stairs any more than she has to."

Christabel sat in the Chippendale chair to the right of the bed. "I'd think she'd let George and Katherine take care of that."

Tom shook his head in mock seriousness. "Oh, no! Mom's on a mission. Gotta take care of her kid."

I studied the portrait. "Beatrice is aging well, all things considered."

Christabel looked at me askance. "What are you talking about?"

I looked more closely. "I can still see a faint imperfection."

Tom laughed. "Don't let Mom hear you say that! She thinks Beatrice is perfect, and, for what the repairs cost, she should be!"

Christabel sighed. "Obviously, I'm not party to this conversation."

Tom laughed. "It was a long time ago. Marc and I were test flying those little balsa flyers in the living room."

Christabel looked skeptical. "Oh, that was smart!"

Tom smiled. "At the time, we thought it was. Anyway, Beatrice was a casualty of our shenanigans. Back then, she had the place of honor above the fireplace in the drawing room, where that big landscape hangs now."

I laughed. "And the rest is history."

Christabel shook her head. "I can only imagine."

I turned from the portrait and sat on the end of the bed. "How are you feeling?"

Tom shrugged noncommittally. "A little nausea, depression. Some anxiety."

Christabel smiled. "I'd think that's to be expected."

"It's the medications, especially the antidepressant." Tom picked up the book he had been reading. "Here's a partial list of its side-effects: 'possible euphoria, increase of appetite, alertness, sense of well-being, weight gain, depression, loss of appetite, weight loss.'" Tom looked up at us. "What does that tell you?"

Christabel shook her head. "Seems pretty inconclusive to me."

I chuckled. "Yeah, pay your money and take your choice."

Tom set the book aside. "Exactly. Supposedly it takes three or four weeks for the antidepressant's effects it to kick in. I've been on it for two weeks. I do feel a little better, but we'll see."

I took a breath. "Freddie stopped by here the other week."

Tom looked surprised. "Here? I didn't see her."

I forced a laugh. "She said you were sleeping. George wouldn't let her into the house."

"You're kidding."

"That's the story according to Freddie."

"Where was Mom?"

"According to George, she was resting and didn't want to be disturbed."

Tom sadly shook his head. "Bunch of old people creeping around this place. It's like a morgue! Did you know Katherine is going to be seventy next week?!"

I laughed. "God! That must make George…"

Tom joined the laughter. "…at least a hundred!"

"He was seventeen when he came here. We were only ten."

Tom nodded. "So that makes him forty-two. Seems older than that to me. The fuckin' live-in babysitter! God, I hated that!"

I smiled. "I thought it was great! Your folks would go off somewhere, and I'd get invited for the weekend."

Tom sighed. "To me it seemed like *every* weekend. If it wasn't George, then it was Grandmother Helena. Or I'd be shipped off to your house."

I nodded and smiled.

"I don't know how old I was before I began to wonder why we weren't like other families. You and your folks always did things together...everyone did." Tom sighed deeply at the memory. "For some reason, my parents had to be socialites. If they weren't in the city for the weekend, it was party *here*, party *there*."

"I always envied you your freedom, Tom. Your parents never cared where you were or what you were doing."

Tom gave a rueful laugh. "Seemed like to me I was put on a shelf and forgotten."

Christabel shook her head. "That's sad."

Tom sat suddenly upright, grasped his robe, and swung both feet off the side of the bed. "You'll have to excuse me..." He took a faltering step.

Christabel jumped from her chair and held his arm. "What is it? Do you need help?"

I rose from the bed and crossed to them. "You okay?"

Tom smiled with a hint of embarrassment. "I have to use the bathroom. I'm not usually this weak."

I took Tom's other arm and helped him toward the bathroom. "Not a problem."

"I've been having some diarrhea, no doubt another one of the fun side-effects."

Christabel nodded. "That's common with a lot of medicines."

As we passed the fireplace, Tom faltered and stopped. Looking up at the portrait, he smiled. "Did you notice that I'm sharing a room with Beatrice?"

Christabel glanced at me and I returned a sad smile.

Tom chuckled. "Good old Beatrice. She's seen a lot."

We continued our walk to the bathroom as Tom began to reminisce. "Do you remember the day we bought those gliders? Bea was hanging in the front room then..." He laughed at the memory. "That was quite a day. The restoration guys did a good job of fixing her, but boy, was Mom pissed!"

I forced a laugh. "She sure was."

Christabel dropped Tom's arm and I steered him into the bathroom. "Just yell when you're ready." I closed the door behind him and turned to look at Christabel. She stood at the window and wiped her eyes. I walked slowly to her and rested a hand on her shoulders. "Are you all right?"

Christabel bit her lower lip and shook her head. "It's too much."

"Come here." I led her to the bed and sat beside her, my arm around her shoulders. "It'll be fine." As I pulled her close, she seemed to crumble.

"He's always been like a brother to me." Christabel sobbed.

I sighed. "Me, too. I only wish he had told us sooner."

She nodded. "I never imagined he was so advanced." Christabel sat up suddenly, eyes circling the room. "I hate him living like this. He's right; it's like a mausoleum."

"He really needs some vitality around him...something to take his mind off the situation."

"I wish he could come stay with us. It would be so good for him. He could have the whole third floor. He'd have the kids when he felt like it. You and I would be sure he got plenty of activity."

"Aunt Harriet would never go for it. You heard Tom. She's on a mission."

"Oh, please!" Christabel's tone was sarcastic. "The only mission she's ever had is Harriet Powell!"

Christabel was right. Aunt Harriet was a self-contained admiration society. That she would sacrifice for anyone seemed ludicrous. This was all about keeping up appearances—a subject Aunt Harriet knew by heart. She had devoted her life to it. Tom's illness was simply another hurdle for her. And this, too, would pass.

Christabel brought my hand to her lips. "Marc, there's something I need to tell you. I hope you won't take it wrong."

I squeezed her hand tightly. "Not to worry."

"Whenever you and I had trouble, I always thought that if worst came to worst, I could always go and live with Tom."

I gave a short laugh and kissed her softly on the cheek. "That was always my option, too."

She smiled sadly at me. "That's not going to happen now."

I nodded. "I know."

43

Spring 1985 – Finale

TOM'S HEALTH CONTINUED TO deteriorate. The medicines ostensibly helped, but he was beyond saving. He grew weaker and weaker, and his weakness ushered in a level of disorientation that bordered on dementia. Some days it was more than painful being around him. On other days, Tom would occasionally rally and almost approach being his old self. But these day grew more and more rare as time passed.

He lost weight. His once-beautiful hair thinned and began to fall out. His face took on a haunted, gaunt look that only reflected the tragedy that had befallen him. Some days it was all I could do to look at him.

Powell Properties was eventually sold to Arnie Thompson. Tom could no longer work, and Aunt Harriet was too old to manage the company. My uncles, Tom and John, brokered the deal, but most of the negotiations were kept from Tom. He simply was in no condition to participate.

Christabel and I continued to visit Tom regularly. Some days were good, some were bad. His mind wandered and he cried often. I never asked him why. Was he crying because death was approaching, because of all that he had lost, or because of everything he'd never gotten a chance to accomplish? Who knows? As I said, I never asked, and Tom never told.

It tore at our hearts to be with him, to see him failing so miserably. We were powerless to help. There was simply nothing to do but sit, wait, and watch. Those were the longest days of all.

I recall April 30 well, for Tom was particularly lucid. Christabel had been unable to accompany me, and I sat by his bed alone. He had been reminiscing; it was one of his few pleasures now. He had been going on and on about his trip to England with Judith shortly after they were wed. It had been an extremely happy time for them. They had rented a small house in the country and spent a month there with the kids. In the midst of this reflection, Tom suddenly stopped and looked at me. "Will you do something for me?"

The sincerity of his voice frightened me. "Of course. Anything."

He smiled wistfully. "I don't know who else to ask."

I smiled in return. "Shoot."

He turned and looked into my eyes. I found the stare disconcerting.

"Will you get me something?"

I laughed nervously. "Sure! You name it."

He smiled sheepishly. "Pills."

Caught off guard, I laughed again and pointed at the bedside table. "You've plenty of pills."

He grew more serious. "Not those. Something to…something to end this."

Shocked, I swallowed with difficulty. "What do you mean, *something to end this?*"

"Something to end this, Marc." Tom suddenly grabbed my hand. "I can't stand this anymore!"

My lower lip quivered as tears came to my eyes. "I can't do that. Tom, I can't do that."

Tom laughed. "Of course you can. You must know someone."

"That's not what I mean."

"I know, but I'm ready. I'm tired, Marc. Tired of the constant pain, the middle-of-the-night nausea and vomiting, the tremors. I'm tired of fighting this thing. This isn't a life; it's a life sentence."

I brushed my eyes with my free hand. "How could you ask me to do something like that?"

Tom grinned. "Because you're my best buddy."

—

The Scotch provided me with a warm sensation as it pooled in my stomach, but it did little or nothing to ease my anxiety. I heard the

One of the Madding Crowd

heavy front door open and close as Christabel entered the house. The sound of her heels on the marble floor echoed as Christabel crossed the entry hall. I turned from the library fireplace and waited. I was soon rewarded with her smile.

Christabel glanced at the glass in my hand and then at me. "Hard day?"

"You could say that."

She crossed the room and kissed me softly on the cheek. "How was he?"

I sighed as I sipped the amber liquid. "Actually, not too bad…all things considered." I sat on the bench in front of the fireplace. "He seemed to enjoy talking about their time in England." I paused, trying to collect my thoughts. "We laughed a lot. Cried a lot, too."

Christabel rested a hand on my shoulder. "I'm sorry I couldn't be there today."

I nodded thoughtfully. I wasn't going to tell her the rest. As much as I wanted her opinion and support, I couldn't expose Christabel to the anxiety and guilt I was feeling. This was another truth to which she could never be party.

Of course, I would do as Tom requested, and sooner, rather than later. Tom would see to that. Now that he had broached the subject, he would worry it until it was resolved. And he was right. He would do as much for me if asked.

I got the dealer's name from a coworker of Christabel's named Keith Mahoney. Christabel had recently taken a part-time position as a designer and seamstress for a local theater company. The job had sounded like a challenge to her, and she found it truly enjoyable. Through the company, we had met several new friends including Keith. As an actor/director, Keith was talented. As a source for things "out of the ordinary," he was invaluable.

―

The parking lot of the vacant restaurant was as dark as only such places can be. I looked nervously at my watch. He was late. It was cold out, but I lowered the window and lit another cigarette. What was keeping him? He had specified 9:30. It was now 10:00 p.m.

As I finished the cigarette, a sleek, gray BMW slipped into the deserted parking lot. It slowly circled the building and then pulled up beside my car. The passenger's window was lowered, and I had the view of a young man with stringy blond hair. His features were barely distinguishable in the muted dash lights. "You got the money?"

I nodded. "Right here."

He extended a hand. "Let's see it."

I held up an envelope but didn't pass it to him. "It's all here."

"I want to see it."

I opened the envelope and ruffled the stack of bills. "Two hundred fifty, just like you said."

"Hand it over."

"Let me see the pills."

He cackled. "Shit! How's that goin' to tell you anything, man? Pills is pills." With a graceful nonchalance, he tossed a pill bottle through the open window and onto my lap. "There you go, old man. Now make with the cash."

I held the bottle and stared at it for a moment. I had no idea whether I'd been given lethal pills or baby aspirin. I relinquished him the money envelope. "They're what I asked for?"

"Yeah. It ain't Coke-a-Cola, but it's the real thing."

"And they'll do the job?"

The stranger held up his hands. "I don't guarantee anything, pops. I don't even want to know what you plan to do with them. Understood?"

I nodded. "Understood. Thanks."

"Yeah, right." The BMW's window slid shut with a whirr, and as quickly as the stranger had arrived, he disappeared into the darkness.

For a moment I sat unmoving. I started the car. The sudden influx of heat comforted my cold legs. My car's window was still down, and I lit another cigarette. The acrid bite of the smoke felt good to my throat. Our "business transaction" was complete. Now for the rest.

I maneuvered the car through the quiet streets of Martin's Neck. At this hour, the roads were practically deserted. A few lights burned in the houses that abutted the roadway, but most were dark and silent.

Minutes later, I slowed the vehicle into Aunt Harriet's tree-shaded driveway. The house was dark, as I expected it to be. The Powells had been, of late, early to bed. The exhaustive burden of Tom's illness was contagious. Tom, however, slept fitfully and with much discomfort.

I found the key to the front door under a nearby urn. Tom's room was closest to the front of the house, which saved me from having to enter through the kitchen and then traverse a multitude of rooms. With luck, I wouldn't disturb anyone else.

After closing the door quietly behind me, I tip-toed down the stair hall. The library was the first room on the left; Tom's was the second. The door to his room was ajar, and I eased it open. The well-oiled hinges made not a sound.

The lamp on the bedside table burned softly under its rose-colored shade. Tom lay atop the big canopied bed, only a sheet and light blanket covering his legs. The door clicked shut behind me, and Tom's eyes opened. "That you, Marc?"

I approached the bed and sat on its edge. I took Tom's hand in mine. "Yeah. You okay?"

Tom released a short, sarcastic laugh. "What do you think?"

I squeezed his hand but said nothing.

"Did you get them?"

I nodded.

He smiled. "I knew I could rely on you. Let me have them."

I fumbled with the bottle before placing it in Tom's hand. "You sure you want to do this?"

Tom sighed. "God...do I ever! Especially after today."

"Bad one?"

He nodded. "One of the worst. I've been so weak...can't even get to the bathroom anymore. Have to use a damned bedpan." Tom grasped the bottle and struggled without success to open it. His hand trembled. His fingers couldn't grasp the container with any strength. He finally dropped the bottle, and it fell to his lap.

I reached across the bed. "Let me help you." I took the pill vial and popped off the cap with a single motion.

Tom looked at me and smiled. "See what I mean?"

I didn't reply.

"The water glass is on the nightstand." He indicated the marble-topped table beside the big bed.

I reached for the glass and gently handed it to Tom. Again, his hand shook, and the contents of the glass danced erratically. As Tom fought to retain the glass, I reached out my hand to help steady it.

Tom sighed deeply. "I'm so fucking tired of this."

I couldn't find words. I was on auto-pilot. If I let myself think too much about what we were doing, I might run screaming from the house. I had to concentrate; get the job done.

I dumped four tablets onto the palm of Tom's hand. Tom stared at them for a moment and then slowly brought them toward his open mouth. At the last moment, his hand spasmed and the pills fell, coming to rest on Tom's boney, shrunken chest.

Tom stared at the tablets forlornly. "Damn it." He looked at me. "This is so fucking humiliating. You're going to have to feed the pills to me." The look in Tom's eyes was one of uncertainty. I think he was afraid I would refuse.

At that moment I *wanted* to refuse. I wanted out of this situation. I wanted to go home and pretend that none of this had ever happened. I thought of Christabel and the children, safe and warm in the house on Linden Avenue. I envied them their comfortable innocence. I wanted a drink, a warm fire, a cigarette. Most of all I wanted Tom to be well again. In my panic, I knew that would never happen. There was only AIDS and its inevitable outcome.

Slowly, I lifted the pills toward Tom's mouth and pushed them, one by one, through his wrinkled lips. The water followed, and he swallowed.

I felt a tear run down my face, but I repeated the process until the vial was empty. When we had finished, Tom lay back against the pillows and sighed. "Now that wasn't so hard, was it?"

I wiped my eyes and stared at him.

He smiled weakly. "Sorry to put you through this."

I simply shook my head.

Tom reached out and took my hand. "Come here." He pulled me toward him and I leaned over, my head resting against his bony shoulder. Claw-like fingers caressed the back of my neck. "Thank you."

There was nothing I could say. I could only cry.

44

Spring 1985 – Left Behind

I SAT IN MY OFFICE…waiting. The computer screen in front of me glowed contentedly, its face filled with intersecting lines and numbers defining the floor plan of a future building. To the casual observer, I would appear to be trying to fathom its intricacies. That wasn't the case. I was simply waiting. Waiting for the phone to ring.

It was nearly 9:00 a.m. I would be hearing soon. The call would come from either Christabel or my mother. I was sure of that. Aunt Harriet, George, and Katherine would not be making the calls. Their world had been turned upside down. Aunt Harriet would phone one of the Powell siblings, and they would take it from there.

When the call finally came, it was my mother's voice on the other end of the receiver. She fed me the details like a self-important newspaper columnist, peppering the facts with her own editorial slant. Tom had passed. Unexpectedly. In the night. What a blessing. Poor Harriet was finally free from the burden. She could get on with her life.

Her smug voice lit a fire, and my mind raged. Fuck you, Mom! And your proverbial horse! Fuck Aunt Harriet, too, for that matter! Old bitch! She could have done so much more to make Tom's final years more pleasant. But not her! No! She had an agenda, and she stuck to it!

I swallowed and let out a deep sigh. "How's she doing?"

"How's *who* doing?"

"Aunt Harriet, of course. How's she holding up?"

"Harriet's a strong woman. She'll manage just fine. Of course, we'll all be here to help her."

I nodded silently. "I suppose you're right." Aunt Harriet rarely faltered, and, when she did, it was only for a few steps.

My mother's business sense stepped in. "No plans yet. Too early for that. Harriet wants services at the Episcopal church. Tom was an altar boy there."

"I know, Mom."

"Well, I'll keep you posted."

"Yeah, you do that."

There was a pause as my mother shifted gears. "Feel like lunch today?"

I sighed. "No. Not today."

As it turned out, Tom's prior services mattered little to the Episcopal church. Father Woodrow told Aunt Harriet that the diocese had enacted a policy that forbade people of "questionable lifestyles" from being buried by the church. Aunt Harriet was furious.

The whole thing saddened me. Poor Tom. Not that he would have cared particularly. It just seemed that he had put up with enough. And now this fiasco.

The funeral service was ultimately held at the local mortuary with a fundamentalist preacher in attendance. How that happened, I'll never know. He was probably recommended by the funeral home staff. Regardless, I'm sure Tom saw the humor in it. That the arrogant Powell family would deign to step outside the confines of organized religion was well worth a good laugh. The family made multiple comments about how inappropriate the whole thing looked. More than anything, it was simply sad. Those who knew Tom could tell that the speaker had never met him and that he had no clue about the real Tom Powell. Tom deserved better than that. If I shed a tear, it was over the injustice of the whole thing.

The biggest upheaval came with the guest list. Aunt Harriet adamantly restricted attendance to only first cousins and above. That eliminated a large segment of the family as well as all of Tom's friends and business associates. In my mind, I could see Tom, sitting off to one side, sadly shaking his head at his mother's shenanigans.

In the days that followed Tom's death, my phone rarely stopped ringing. For many of our friends, I became the customer complaint executive. Everyone felt the whole thing was unfair, and many regarded it as a personal affront. Freddie Clifton Allen headed that list.

"Marc! You simply have to do something!" Freddie's voice was piercing.

"Have you talked to Aunt Harriet?"

"Talked?" Freddie bellowed. "I've talked. I've pleaded. I've begged. She won't budge."

"That's ridiculous! She can certainly make an exception where you're concerned."

"Oh, no," Freddie said, mimicking Aunt Harriet's authoritative tone, "if I make an exception for you, then I'll have to make it for others, and I'm just not going to do that."

"I'm really sorry."

"Will you talk to her, Marc?"

I sighed. "It won't do any good. I've already tried to intervene for a couple of people, but she's not listening. I'm afraid her mind's made up, and that's how it's going to stay."

"That bitch!" Freddie sounded close to tears. "It's just not fair! Tom and I grew up together. He was like a brother to me!"

"I know. I'm sorry."

Freddie sobbed.

I sighed. "Maybe we can have a separate memorial service for him later. Maybe down at the beach. Invite anyone who wants to come."

"Oh, Marc, do you think we could?"

"Let's think about it. See what happens."

"Love you, sweetie," Freddie said, a glimmer of hope in her voice.

"Love you, too."

———

By the time the funeral commenced, my sadness had turned to anger. I was angry. At everyone. I was angry at my mother for being so nonchalant about Tom's death. I was angry at Aunt Harriet for being such a bitch. I hated the way she treated Tom's death as simply another hurdle to be mastered and put behind her. I was angry with myself for not standing up to them. I was angry that I couldn't gain any comfort from Christabel for the part I played in his passing. I was generally in a dark, foggy place that seemed to envelop any ray of hope that might enter.

We dropped Miranda and Lucas at Christabel's parents' house and made our way to the funeral. As one would expect, it was a somber affair. The impeccably turned-out Powell clan sat at rigid attention while the fundamentalist minister rambled on and on about redemption and accepting Christ as one's personal savior. His words fell on closed ears. Through it all, I sat fuming in silence.

I was one of the selected pallbearers, along with the other male cousins. These included cousin Jane's husband who seemed out of his element among the rest of the family. He was too nice a guy to fit well in that mix.

We managed to make it through the funeral service and the internment. When the latter was complete, Christabel and I stood staring at Tom's grave.

My youngest cousin, Franklin Powell, turned and walked away from his family to join us. "Too bad."

I simply nodded.

Christabel was more forthcoming and actually gave him a weak smile. "Yes, it is."

Frank looked at me as I lit a cigarette. "I didn't even know that Tom was gay."

Christabel gasped. I drew heavily upon the cigarette and glared at Frank. "No one said he was." My tone was cold and unfeeling.

Frank was taken aback. "Well … I mean … the AIDS and all."

I started to retort, but Christabel cut me off. "You don't have to be gay to get AIDS!"

Frank looked like a schoolboy caught late to class. "Oh, yeah … I know. But…"

I puffed angrily on the cigarette. "But what?"

Frank hesitated. "Nothing."

"That's right! Nothing!" I grabbed Christabel's hand and yanked her away from Frank. "Come on! Let's get out of here."

Christabel gave Frank a fleeting look and followed me to the car. I climbed in, lowered the window, and inhaled deeply on my cigarette. Next up, the wake. It was being held at Aunt Harriet's house because the size of the gathering was small. Oh, joy; oh, bliss. I could hardly wait.

Christabel reached out and laid her hand on mine. "I'm sorry."

I shook my head. "Not your fault."

"I know that hurt you."

I nodded.

Christabel sighed and settled back in her seat. Around us, the rest of the family made their way to their vehicles.

Taking one last draw, I tossed the cigarette and closed the window. "I'm not going."

Christabel looked at me. "Not going where?"

"Aunt Harriet's."

"Marc! You can't do that. What will Aunt Harriet say?" She paused. "Better yet, what will your mother say?"

"I don't give a damn. I need a drink." I started the car and put it in gear.

"There'll be plenty to drink at the reception."

"Not enough!"

45
Fall 1985 – Remorse

TOM WAS DEAD.

There was nothing I could do about that. Somehow, life continued on its merry way. Everyone picked up the pieces and forged ahead. Reluctantly, I followed suit. Business remained good, and I still had no inclination to leave Steadman and Son. We were busy, almost too busy, but I guess that was a good thing. It allowed me to throw myself into my work and to put what I could behind me.

Miranda and Lucas grew. They were great kids, good in school, caring and loving. No parents could ask for more. Lucas appeared to be developing an interest in architecture, which genuinely pleased me. He often dropped by the office after school to hang out. Eventually, he would have a job working at Steadman and Son in the summer, but that was yet to come.

Miranda was the free spirit of the family. She was artistic like her mother. While she dabbled in painting and drawing, her true love was the stage. The theater company for which Christabel worked developed a children's division, and Miranda found herself quite at home there. As she grew, her roles developed, and she devoted much of her time to singing and dancing. Hers was a busy schedule, but she was happy, and we were happy for her.

As a family, the Powells lumbered along, adding, each year, to their monetary and social success. Aunt Harriet, George, and Katherine continued to rattle around the big, old house, each becoming more dependent on one another. My mother and Rodney stayed on at The

Birches. They were immersed in their life together: traveling, entertaining, pretentiousness. The rest of the family followed suit, and life was often a never-ending array of cocktail and dinner parties. All in all, life was good, and I suppose I shouldn't complain. It certainly could have been much worse.

Still, Tom's death and the memory of that night continued to haunt me. I had experienced death before, but it had never felt like this. I felt empty and alone. Sure, everyone knew I was hurting, but so were they. Tom's death affected many people. Their loss was not going to disappear overnight. I could share my sorrow with others, but that did not lessen my loneliness. I suppose that was because of the part I had played in Tom's passing.

—

It was a gray, overcast Saturday afternoon in October. Christabel and Miranda were at the theater, and Lucas was off with his buddies. I was depressed. That's the only word I could find to describe my feelings. Tom had been dead for five months, and I still felt an aching void deep within me.

The big, old house was quiet around me. It was filled with shadows and memories. I had given in to the depression and sought refuge in the library with a bucket of ice cubes and a decanter of Scotch. One of our many photo albums lay open in my lap. Many of the photos simply reinforced my depression.

I was fixated on a series of shots taken at Powell Cottage shortly after our marriage. It was dusk. We were all on the beach, ranged around a brightly burning bonfire. Tom was laughing and holding up his beer bottle in a mock toast or salute. For the life of me, I couldn't remember the occasion or the reason for Tom's actions. I'd probably had too much to drink by the time the photo was taken. But that didn't matter. What mattered was the firelight on Tom's face and his shiny blond hair. He was happy. It showed in his smile. We *all* looked happy. That was life back then. Now a series of images rendered on Kodak paper.

The memorial service on the beach that I had proposed to Freddie had yet to take place, and it probably never would. My heart simply wasn't in it. It would open old wounds, and I didn't need that. Of course, Aunt Harriet would have been aghast at such an idea, and I was in no condition to do battle with her. Fortunately, Freddie had not mentioned it again, and I was perfectly willing to let the idea die its own quiet death.

I sighed and took a deep drink from my glass, rested my head against the high back of the leather wing back, and closed my eyes. I inhaled deeply and emitted a big sigh. God, Tom, why did it have to end this way?

I had just begun to drift when I heard the front door open, followed by the sound of clogs across marble tiles. Christabel and Miranda were laughing as they entered the foyer.

I smiled to myself and sat upright in the chair. "I'm in here."

"Hey, Dad!" Miranda appeared in the doorway of the library and smiled. "Whatcha been doing?" She crossed the room and plopped down on the leather ottoman in front of my chair. Christabel followed her into the room and stood next to me.

I sipped my drink. "Reminiscing. Looking at some old pictures."

She smiled. "And drinking."

I laughed. "And drinking. How was rehearsal?"

"Great! It's going to be a terrific show. Keith says it's the best we've done so far."

"Keith?" I feigned surprise.

Miranda nodded. "Yeah, Keith ... Keith Mahoney. He's the director." She paused a moment in apparent confusion. "Dad! You know Keith."

"Oh, I know Keith. I just didn't know you all were on a first-name basis."

"Dad, everyone calls him Keith."

"Really?"

Christabel rested a hand on my shoulder. "Marc, quit teasing her." She looked at Miranda and smiled. "Pay no attention to your father."

"Hey, can't I kid with my daughter?"

"Your daughter was wonderful today. You would have been so proud of her."

Miranda suddenly looked embarrassed. "Ah, Mom ..."

"Ah, Mom, nothing. You were very good today."

I laughed and feigned a fist to Miranda's right shoulder. "I'm sure she was."

To save face and to cover her embarrassment, Miranda rose from the ottoman and kissed me on the cheek. "Love you, Dad. I've got to go upstairs and call Stephanie."

I smiled. "Of course, you do."

On her way out of the room, Miranda paused long enough to kiss Christabel on the cheek. "Love you, too, Mom." Then she was gone like the will-o-the-wisp she was.

Christabel laughed and took Miranda's seat on the ottoman. I looked at her for a moment and smiled. "She's quite a girl."

"Oh, yes," Christabel laughed, "you can certainly say that."

There was a pause as Christabel looked at me. Then she reached out and took my hand. "Reminiscing with old photos?"

I nodded and took another sip of my drink.

"Feeling sorry for yourself?"

I issued a weak smile. "I guess you could say that."

"I wish you wouldn't do this."

"Do what?"

"Beat yourself up like this." Christabel sighed. "You did everything anyone could do for Tom." She placed a hand on my knee and gave it a gentle squeeze. "Cheer up ... you hear me?"

I placed a hand over hers and nodded. There was nothing I could say because the truth was something I could never share with anyone ... not even Christabel. Her support would have helped ease the pain and guilt of what I had done, but I could never burden her with what had transpired that night. It was too much to ask. This was a burden I alone would have to endure no matter how it made me feel. I was alone. There was no way of avoiding that fact.

I would simply have to accept it.

46

Spring 1986 – Upheaval

RODNEY WILLIAMS DIED SUDDENLY of a heart attack on May 17.

It happened at one of the frequent, formal affairs he and mother hosted at The Birches. We were all seated in the drawing room partaking of pre-dinner cocktails. Rodney, as usual, dominated the conversation. He stood in front of the fireplace, drink in one hand, cigar in the other, expounding some inane opinion that he felt everyone should hear and appreciate. He stopped suddenly in mid-sentence, set his glass on the mantle, and collapsed while still clutching his ever-present cigar.

My mother screamed his name, jumped from her chair, and knelt on the floor by his side. I followed, kneeling on the other side of Rodney's prone body.

My mother looked at me and pointed to Rodney's still-smoking cigar. "Grab that. I don't want carpet burns; it's an antique Sarouk, you know."

Confusion followed as everyone tried to find some way to help. An ambulance was called, but it was too late. Rodney was dead before it ever arrived.

Rodney's death left my mother a very wealthy woman. There were stocks and bonds. There was property. There was plenty of money. She was well able to continue her preferred lifestyle unabated. And she did. She shopped. She played bridge. She dined, she lunched, and she breakfasted. Her traveling ceased, however. She claimed it was no fun traveling alone. She had few truly close friends to join her.

The Birches was her base of operations for most occasions. It was the perfect venue for entertaining. But it was big and entailed significant upkeep and expense. She managed for a while, but soon began to grow weary of the responsibility. Of course, she was getting older. There was no denying that.

—

Mother, being Mother, had a plan. She hit us with it one night in December over dinner at our house.

She set down her fork and picked up her wine glass. "I have something I want to run by you two." She looked at us and smiled.

I felt the first ripple of warning but brushed it aside. "And what would that be?"

"Well, as you know, The Birches is just too big for one person."

I looked at her in surprise. "No. I didn't know that."

Christabel looked at my mother questioningly. "I always thought you loved that house."

"Oh, I do. It's a magnificent house!" She paused to sip her wine. "It's just so much to take care of."

I laughed. "I can't argue that point."

"And the expense!" She rolled her eyes.

"Well, that hasn't stopped you up to now." My tone was a bit sarcastic but restrained.

My intent was not lost on her. She looked at me archly. "Well ... if you want to know the truth, I'm lonely."

Christabel looked surprised. "But you have Lucy, Gabriel, and Hank."

My mother dismissed her with a wave of her hand. "What company are they? They're only the hired help."

Christabel was taken aback. "Well, I'd certainly think it would be better than being completely alone."

"That's easy for you to say."

Lucas adopted his best ten-year-old adult voice. "You can come live with us, Mom-Mom Powell." He looked at his mother and smiled. "Right, Mom?"

Christabel motioned for him to be quiet. "I don't think that's what your Mom-Mom has in mind, darling."

I jumped back into the conversation at this point. "Just what *do* you have in mind, Mom?"

My mother sat back in her chair, cradling her wine glass. A self-satisfied look crossed her face. She reached over and grasped Lucas' hand. "Would you like Mom-Mom to come live with you, Lucas?"

"Sure thing!"

"How about you, Miranda?"

Miranda looked surprised. "Live here ... with us?"

"Mom, be serious. Don't bait the kids like that."

She gave me a feigned look of innocence. "I'm not baiting them. I *am* being serious."

"Oh, Mom, you've got to be kidding! That would never work!" I looked at Christabel and rolled my eyes.

"Why not? You've got that whole third floor just sitting vacant. It would make a perfect apartment for me."

"I don't think so."

"Why not? I'd have a place for myself without being in your way. Of course, we could dine together from time to time." She reached out and patted Christabel's hand. "That is, if Christabel would want that." She smiled sweetly.

Christabel smiled uncertainly and looked at me.

"Mom. Think about it."

"I *have* thought about it, and I think it's a marvelous idea. I'd use my own money to refurbish the third floor. I would help with the mortgage and the utility bills ..."

"We'd drive each other crazy, Mom. You know that as well as I do."

"I know no such thing! I think it would all work out quite nicely."

"That's cool!" Lucas beamed. "Mom-Mom is going to live with us. Yay!"

I looked at him and smiled. "No, son. She's not. We just have to talk about this some more."

Lucas looked confused. "Why?"

"Because that's what adults do when there is a decision to be made."

Lucas appeared unconvinced.

My mother laughed. "Now who's baiting who?"

"Mother! Please!" I looked angrily in her direction. Dear God, where was the door that led out of this nightmare?

47

Spring 1987 – The Sideboard

AS WAS HER LOT in life, Victoria Powell Steadman got her way. Christabel actually felt sorry for her; she disliked the thought of mother having to live alone. I weakened and, in the end, relented. Lucas was excited at the prospect. If Miranda shared her brother's excitement, she never voiced it.

I worked with my mother to reconfigure the third floor for her use. The original playroom morphed into a large living area that comprised a kitchen, formal dining space, and ample living area. The two large bedrooms and bath were transformed into a single master bedroom, a luxurious bath, a dressing room, and a small study. My mother was ecstatic with the changes and busied herself with decorating the new spaces.

Of course, we contracted Steadman and Son to do the work. That only made sense. The construction took only two months, but the disruption was huge. The workers arrived each morning at seven. It meant that getting ready for work and school, eating breakfast, and cleaning up all had to be accomplished with builders running up and down the stairs.

Although the construction was restricted to the third floor, sawdust and plaster dust managed to find its way as far down as the first-floor foyer. The workers did their best to mitigate this incursion, but, in the end, it was hopeless. Fortunately, Miranda and Lucas were still in school. Christabel was in the midst of a large, musical production, and I went to the office each morning. That left my mother to ramrod the construction process. For the most part this worked, but there were times when the train jumped the tracks.

On the afternoon of April 24, I parked in front of the house and entered through the front foyer, having received one of *those* phone calls from my mother. "You need to come home and talk to this man!" Rather than belabor the issue over the phone lines, I stopped what I was doing and headed toward Linden Avenue. It was going to be one of those days.

As I entered the house, my mother was coming down the front stairway. She was not happy. I closed the door behind me and smiled. "What's up?"

She paused halfway through her descent. "It's that man. You need to talk to him."

"*What* man?"

She waved a hand up the stairs and completed her descent. "That plumber fellow … he won't listen to a word I say."

"How so?"

"I told him I want the dishwasher to the right of the sink … not to the left."

"So?"

She placed her hands on her hips. "He won't do it!"

I was perplexed. "Why not?"

"He says it's shown on the left on the plans, and he won't change it without your approval."

"Oh, for goodness sakes!" I ascended the staircase to the second floor with my mother in tow and then continued onto the third.

Bryan Howard was a big, burly man with sandy-red hair. He was one of the best plumbing contractors in the business, but he did have a rough edge to his personality. I crossed the vast open space to the kitchen alcove where Bryan was working. "Hey, Bryan. How goes it?"

He laid aside his wrench and extended a hand. "Marc! Howya doin'?"

I smiled. "Fine, thanks." I looked beyond him to the kitchen. "I've been told we have an issue with the dishwasher. Bring me up to speed?"

Bryan nodded seriously. "Sure. The lady tried to get me to move it." He waved a hand in my mother's direction.

My mother glared at him. "*The lady* wants it on the right side ... not the left." The disdain and arrogance in my mother's tone was unmistakable.

"Just a minute, Mom." I motioned for her silence and looked at the sink area. I then looked at Bryan. "Any reason we can't do that?"

"Only if you give the go ahead. It's shown on the left on the plans so, you know, gotta stick to the plans unless you tell me otherwise."

I nodded. "Then let's change it."

"Sure 'nough."

My mother continued to look upset.

I sighed deeply. "That suit you, Mom?"

My mother stood stiffly, her arms crossed in front of her. "Yes."

Though she had gotten her way, her tone was frost cold. I paused for a moment. How best to handle this situation so that it didn't happen again? I had better things to do than run home every time my mother decided to go off script.

I turned to Bryan and gave him a knowing smile. "Bryan, it's *her* apartment. *She's* writing the checks. If she wants to change something, it's all right with me ... unless there's a good reason not to."

Bryan nodded. "Understood."

I smiled. "Good."

In the distance, my mother smiled broadly. What kind of monster was I creating? Only time would tell.

By the time construction was complete, we were all exhausted. It was June, and we all wanted life to return to normal. Unfortunately, what had passed for our "normal" no longer existed. Mother saw to that, and she did her job well.

One evening, shortly after my mother's official move, Christabel met me at the front door as I was returning home from work. The look on her face was conflicted ... almost as if she didn't know whether to laugh or cry.

"What's wrong?"

She gave a short laugh and turned to walk back along the corridor. "I'm not really sure." Christabel stopped at the dining room door and looked at me. She motioned me to enter. "Come look at this."

I followed her into the room. The sudden light from the chandelier dispelled the shadows. I didn't need the light to see what Christabel was showing me. Since my childhood, the big bay window at the end of the dining room had housed my Grandmother Powell's marble-topped, Italian sideboard. Now it was empty.

I was astounded. "What the hell?"

Christabel gave a controlled laughed. "You tell me. I came home from the theater, and it was simply gone."

"Well, at least whoever took it was nice enough to leave you the contents." I indicated the array of silver, crystal, and linen spread out on the dining room table.

"Yeah ... and just where am I going to put all that stuff?"

I shrugged and issued a weak smile. "The butler's pantry?"

Christabel managed a laugh, though it was a bit forced. "Yes ... of course ... there's plenty of room in there."

There was only one, viable explanation for the mystery, and its name was Mother. I looked at Christabel and sighed. "I'm sorry, honey." Christabel simply shook her head.

As she was my mother, she was my issue to handle. I felt the frustration growing within me. Jesus Christ, I hoped this wasn't the sign of things to come. I strode out of the dining room, down the foyer hallway to the foot of the stairs. "Mom!" I yelled at the top of my voice.

There was no response.

I took a couple of steps up the staircase and yelled again. Still nothing. Finally, I sighed and trudged up the flight of stairs. "Mom! Can you hear me?!" The response was muffled; I couldn't discern its content. "Mom! You need to come down here!" I skirted the gallery to the foot of the third-floor stair. "Mom! Do you hear me?!"

"Yes, dear. What is it?" Her tone was too cheerful for my liking.

"Need to see you downstairs for a moment." I turned to retrace my steps.

"Can't we just talk up here?"

I wasn't having it. "No, Mom. Downstairs ... in the dining room."

Christabel had seated herself at one end of the dining table. I took up station beside her. Together, we waited.

My mother took her time. She was not accustomed to being ordered anywhere ... least of all by her son. She would dally and then make her entrance when she felt she had made her point. Long minutes passed before the sound of her heels echoed on the oak stairway signaling her approach. Her pace was slow but steady. Then, down the hallway to the dining room doorway. She stood there smiling. "What is it, dear?"

I motioned to the vacant bay window behind me. "What do you know about this?"

She smiled sweetly. "I commandeered it."

"What?" I was practically speechless. I looked at Christabel who simply shrugged her shoulders. The expression on her face said it all. I looked back at my mother. "Why the hell did you do that?"

"It fits perfectly in my dining area." She made motion to turn and leave. "Come see."

I took a step toward her. "No ... wait ..." I was flabbergasted. "What made you think you had the right?"

She turned quickly to face me. Her curt voice cut me off. "Well, it was *my* mother's sideboard. I'd say I have as much right to it as you ... more, actually."

I was astounded. "Then why didn't you take it when we were emptying the house?"

She answered smugly. "I didn't want it then."

I took a step toward her, and Christabel laid her hand on my arm. "Marc ... it's alright."

I paused and looked at Christabel. Her eyes said simply, *don't go there*.

I retreated a step and stared at the empty bay window. "I don't believe this. I don't fuckin' believe this." I turned and glared at my mother. "Jesus, Mom ... next you'll be taking our bedroom furniture."

She smiled sweetly. "Not to worry, dear. I never shared my mother's love for French furniture."

I looked at Christabel and rolled my eyes. "Oh, lucky us!" I slammed a fist against the top of the dining table. The assortment of crystal and silver rattled and clanged. "I just can't believe you'd pull a stunt like this!"

"Marc, it's alright. I never liked it much anyway." Christabel shot my mother a "so there" look.

My mother smiled in response. "See ... it's no problem. I'm sure Christabel will be able to find something more to her taste. Right, dear?"

Christabel smiled archly in the old woman's direction. "Absolutely."

I glared at my mother. "And you'll pay for it."

That comment ruf-fled her feathers. "I think not! I have as much right to that sideboard as you have!" She turned on her heel and started to leave the dining room.

"Where are you going?"

She glared at me over her shoulder. "Upstairs … where it's quiet … and where I'm better appreciated."

I gave a rueful laugh. "Yeah … and ten cents will still get you a cup of coffee."

48

Summer 1987 – Conflict

THE INCIDENT OF THE sideboard was but the tip of the iceberg. My mother continued her reign of terror unabated. If it wasn't something Christabel or I had done, it was one of the kids.

Christabel and I gave up entertaining at Linden Avenue. We had tried to make it work, but it was a futile battle. Whenever we entertained, everything was fine and ran smoothly as long as my mother was part of the mix. The moment she was not included resulted in a tirade of mammoth proportions. The days after these events were filled with bilious comments such as, "God! I thought they'd never leave!" and "The noise! I never heard so much noise! Please don't invite them again."

Although I tried to placate her, my explanations were never accepted. Only *her* protestations held any weight. "It's my home, too, you know. I'm not as young as I used to be. I need my rest." She was the one being victimized, and it was very obvious that neither Christabel nor I cared how she felt. As a result, we moved private entertaining to local restaurants and the yacht club. At least there we could enjoy our friends without bearing the brunt of my mother's ire.

Of course, these conflicts did not impinge on my mother's personal entertaining. She continued to socialize with avid regularity. Her smaller functions were confined to her apartment, but these were few compared to the overall volume of her activities. On other occasions, she would simply take over the first-floor public rooms at will. Bridge parties filled the drawing room and lunch was served in the dining room. Of course, there was never a request on her part. It was, as she was quick to remind us, her home, too. Christabel or I often arrived home to find the house filled with my mother's friends. On those occasions, we were treated as guests, with her as the grand dame hostess. I had never imagined that she would take over our home, but she was doing her best to do so.

I fumed about this treatment but to no avail. Christabel seemed to take it in stride, but she was always willing to commiserate with me on the direction our life was taking. Whenever my mother decided to take charge, one simply stood aside and let her have her way. That was the easiest way to survive.

The children were another matter. Their constant comings and goings seemed to infuriate my mother, and she complained regularly: They were too busy. They were overindulged. Miranda's love affair with the theater was unrealistic. She needed to concentrate on her studies. Lucas' friends were loud and annoying. They turned the house into a zoo. They played soccer in the backyard and trampled the planting beds.

It was something new every day, and it never ended. For some reason, I think my mother gloried in it. Whenever she complained, she wore a smug smile that said, "I've got something on you." I suppose it was her way of maintaining control of what she considered to be her kingdom.

There were many incidents, though one in particular comes to mind. Christabel and Miranda had returned home from an afternoon rehearsal at the theater in July. Christabel was doing costumes, and Miranda had a supporting role in the summer comedy.

I stood at the bar in the library fixing myself a pre-dinner Scotch when Christabel joined me, flopping down onto one of the chairs by the fireplace. I looked at her and hoisted my glass. "Join me?"

"Certainly."

I busied myself fixing her a vodka and tonic. "What time are we meeting the gang tonight?"

"Seven o'clock reservations at the yacht club."

"How was the rehearsal?"

Christabel sighed. "Long. You know how Keith can be sometimes."

I handed her the drink. "A perfectionist."

She smiled and sipped the drink. "That, too."

A sudden slamming of doors and heavy footsteps erupted from

above. Christabel and I looked at one another and shrugged. The noise was followed by silence.

I laughed. "Mice ... large mice."

"You can only hope."

"Did she have a hard time this afternoon?"

"No, not especially." Christabel paused, thinking. "No, actually she made out quite well."

Another door slammed, and the sound of heavy footsteps sounded along the second-floor gallery and quickly grew louder. In a matter of seconds Miranda burst into the room. Without a word, she crashed onto the sofa facing the fireplace.

I watched and then shot a look at Christabel, who simply shrugged. "What's up?"

There was no response.

"Miranda, honey ... what's wrong?" Christabel's voice was soft and soothing.

Miranda picked up of the sofa pillows and buried her face in them. "I hate her!" Miranda's voice was muffled but curt.

I sighed. "What's she done now?"

Miranda lowered the pillow and glared at me. "Disconnected my stereo."

"Why did she do that?" It was a pointless question, but I asked it anyway.

Miranda tossed the pillow aside. "My music is too loud. It gets on her nerves."

Christabel sighed. "Here we go again."

"And it's just noise ... not really music at all." Miranda crossed her arms and scowled. "I hate her!"

It was my turn to sigh. Would this constant bickering never end?

Christabel moved to sit beside our daughter. "She's old. We have to make allowances for her."

"I'm sick of making allowances for her!" Miranda glared at me. "Why does she have to live with us? She's *your* mother ..."

I took a big swallow of my Scotch. "Please don't remind me."

A brief moment of silence ensued. The tension was maddening. Christabel and Miranda looked to me for answers, but I had none. I felt as much a victim as they.

Still, Miranda was right; she was my mother. Realistically, I should be able to handle these situations. But I was tired ... tired of the constant conflict, tired of feeling powerless and at fault. If only I had redirected her when she proposed moving in with us. But I hadn't. I had taken the course of least resistance, telling myself that we, as a family, could make it work. I'd been wrong, and I didn't know how to undo this vexing situation. I truly doubted there was a viable solution to the problem.

I poured another drink and sat across from Christabel and Miranda. "I'm sorry, sweetie. I never expected it to be like this."

Miranda sighed. "I know."

"Can you sort of control the volume on your stereo?" It was a lame request ... weak ... without any resolution.

"But I wasn't playing it loud. The volume was only set on four." Miranda, seemingly defeated, sighed deeply. "I don't think she can even hear it. She's just trying to boss me around. She does it all the time! Lucas, too! He told me his friends don't even want to come over to the house anymore." She sighed again. "Who can blame them?"

I was at a loss. It was a no-win situation and I was doing a poor job of resolving it. "Tell you what ... when you want to play your stereo, why don't you use the one here in the library?"

Miranda rolled her eyes. "Yeah, right!" She glared at me. "It's not the same, Dad! I like to listen to my music while I'm doing my homework, getting dressed, putting on make-up. It's just not the same."

"I realize that ..."

"Really? You could have fooled me!"

Christabel rested a hand on Miranda's knee. "Honey, we all have to make adjustments."

"Well, when does Mom-Mom make adjustments? Never! That's when. The rest of us adjust and adjust, but she gets to do whatever the hell she wants, whenever she wants. It's not fair!"

Christabel smiled weakly. "I didn't say it was."

Miranda glared at me again. "Then do something about it!"

I shook my head. "I wish I could."

Miranda looked shocked. "And that's it? That's all you can say? Won't you even talk to her about how unfair she's being?"

I nodded. "Yes ... I'll talk to her, but don't expect too much."

Miranda rose and crossed to the doorway. Her tone was sarcastic. "Great! Big help that'll be! God, Dad, you're a grown man! Can't you stand up to her for once?" With that, Miranda left the room. Her angry footsteps echoed through the big foyer as she retraced her way upstairs.

Christabel and I sat looking at one another. What could I say? Miranda was right. What she didn't realize was that I was simply a sixteen-year-old boy with a family who was incapable of standing up to his mother. Allowing my mother to have her own way had always seemed like a birthright. Nothing I could say or do could possibly change that fact. Still, I had to think of my family. I couldn't stand to see them continually torn apart like this.

I would talk to my mother. I would be firm.

I would do my best to make her understand.

And, in the end, I would undoubtedly fail.

49

1990 – The War Drags On

THREE YEARS PASSED, BUT nothing changed. The conflict continued unabated. My mother's presence remained a blemish on our family life. Of course, I talked to her. I talked to her repeatedly. After each incident, we would lock horns over what she had done or not done, over what she had said or not said. She would never admit fault. It was always something Christabel had said, Miranda had done, or Lucas had neglected to do. It was their fault, and she "would have none of it!"

We did our best to avoid her whenever possible, but she had a way of seeking us out and instigating confrontations. There wasn't a safe place in the house. She'd appear at the most inopportune times flaunting some transgression that had been committed. Birthday parties seemed to be one of her favorite venues. She was always invited, but never did such occasions end without some snide comment being dropped or someone's feelings hurt. Mother only seemed happy after one or the other occurred. Miranda's performances, Lucas' soccer victories, graduations, proms, each occasion was marred in some way by her interference.

Among the worst was Miranda's graduation from high school in June. We were proud of her. She was a good student and ranked fourth in a class of two-hundred twenty-seven. Following commencement, our family adjourned to the yacht club to celebrate the occasion. We sat at a round table with a view of the river. Everyone was in good spirits. Once drinks had been served and champagne poured, I rose from my seat to propose a toast. "Here's to Miranda. We are so proud of you, honey, and all you've accomplished. We know that you're going to do well at college next fall."

Miranda smiled and blushed.

My mother, sitting to my left, snorted. "Really."

I glared at her. "Did you want to say something, Mom?" I should have ignored her, but I didn't. As a result, Miranda would pay the price.

My mother sipped her champagne demurely. "No dear, I think you've said quite enough already."

I sat and swallowed the contents of my flute. "What's that supposed to mean?"

She laughed gaily. "Why, I was valedictorian of my class! Even you were salutatorian, although you couldn't match me." She laughed again. "What's Miranda have to brag about? Fourth in her class ... big deal." She shot Miranda a wicked smile.

Miranda's reply was ice cold. "Thanks, Mom-Mom."

I glared at my mother. "Mom ... enough."

My mother smiled one of her knowing little smiles and sipped champagne. "Whatever you say, dear."

Dinner progressed with a strained silence. Poor Lucas tried to lighten the mood, but no one was having it. My mother had struck again.

Later that night, Miranda left the house to attend a graduation party at one of her friend's homes. By then, Lucas was out as well. My mother had retreated to the seclusion of her apartment. Christabel and I sat in the library seeking solace in one another's company.

I'd had plenty to drink for one evening, but my mother's actions dictated the need for more. I poured a snifter of Drambuie and sat in the chair beside the fireplace.

Christabel looked at me with concern. "Don't you think you've had enough for one night?"

I laughed ruefully. "Undoubtedly." I sipped the thick, rich liquid.

Christabel sighed. "What a night."

I simply nodded.

"What are we going to do with her?" It was a plea rather than a question.

"I don't know."

"Does she enjoy hurting others?"

"Apparently. Did you see that smile of hers?"

"Who could miss it? I'm sure Miranda didn't."

"Poor thing. I felt so badly for her."

Christabel looked at me archly. "Then why didn't you say something?"

"I did."

"Really?" Her tone was sarcastic. "I must have missed something."

"What would you have had me do?"

"Well, you could have shown more support for your daughter." She glared at me. "Maybe, actually, defended her?"

"What was the point? The damage had already been done."

Christabel was right. I had brushed it off without really addressing the insult. That seemed to be my way where my mother was concerned. Smooth it over and keep moving. Problem was, that strategy never solved anything.

I sipped my drink and sighed. "I need to talk to her."

"Who?"

"Mom. Tonight was inexcusable."

Christabel stifled a laugh. "And what good will that do? You've gone down that road before, and it's never made any difference."

I finished the Drambuie in one gulp and set the snifter on the little table beside my chair. "Maybe this time will be different." I rose from my chair and crossed the room.

Christabel laughed. It was a harsh, jarring sound that expressed her sadness and frustration. "Somehow, Marc, I doubt it." The tone of her voice said it all. We were victims, each of us confined to a trap from which there was no escape.

I left the library and climbed the wide staircase to the second floor. With the kids gone, the second floor was quiet ... no music, no muted conversation, no laughter. I paused at the foot of the next flight of stairs and gazed upward. A faint light spilled into the third-floor gallery from my mother's sitting room. She was still awake. Probably glorying in her recent victory.

My footsteps left a hollow sound on the bare treads of the stair. At the top, I paused again and looked toward the open doorway. I dreaded talking to her. Over the last years, my mother had become a monster. Maybe she had always been a monster. Maybe my father and Rodney Williams had borne the brunt of her sarcasm and ire in silence. Who could say? They were gone, and my mother had no one other than me and my family on whom to feast. Regardless, I didn't recognize her anymore, nor did I want to.

The door to the sitting room was open. My mother had changed into one of her many peignoirs and sat on the sofa leafing through the latest issue of *Cosmopolitan*. She looked up in surprise as I entered the room. "Why Marc, what brings you up here at this hour?"

I sat in a chair facing the sofa, and she set aside the magazine. "We need to talk."

"Really? What about?"

"I think you know."

"I'm sure I don't." Her sweet smile was fake, as always.

I took a deep breath. "Mom … those comments at dinner were totally out of line. You had no right to embarrass Miranda like that … especially on the day of her graduation."

She feigned surprise. "I don't know what you're talking about."

I sighed. "Mom … you were there. We were all there. There's no denying what you said."

"I didn't say anything that wasn't true, did I?"

"That's not the point."

She crossed her arms and glared at me. "Then what is the point?"

I exhaled deeply. "Why would you choose to hurt Miranda, your own grandchild, like that?"

"I wasn't trying to hurt her … I was simply making a point."

"Well, it did hurt her … it hurt us all. You ruined what otherwise would have been a nice family celebration together."

With a flip of her hand, she dismissed me. "Don't be so dramatic. The dinner was fine."

My ire rose. "For you, maybe. For the rest of us, it was a terrible evening."

My mother shook her head in disdain. "You make too much out of things. I was simply commenting on the fact that Miranda did not make a showing while I, and even her father, did. It was as simple as that."

"God, Mom! She graduated fourth in her class!"

"So?"

"Fourth in a class of two-hundred twenty-seven! Remind me, what was the size of your graduating class?"

She was silent for a moment. "Thirty-six."

I gave a short laugh. "There!"

"That doesn't change the fact that I was valedictorian. I was still at the top of my class!"

"A class of thirty-six? Big deal! Who cares?"

My mother stared down her nose at me. "Well, I care ... and Miranda should accept the fact that she wasn't number one."

I rose from the chair in disgust. "Jesus Christ, Mom! You are impossible! Don't you care about anyone's feelings but your own?"

"I believe in being forthright and honest. There's nothing wrong with that." Her voice was smug.

I turned to look at her. "There is when it hurts someone."

"That was not my intention."

"Intention be damned! You just don't care!"

My mother glared at me. "I don't like the tone of your voice."

I smiled cruelly. "Nor I yours."

"You and Christabel have simply overindulged Miranda and Lucas. I have tried to be a leveling influence in their lives. I've tried to show them what life is really like."

I turned away from her. "Oh, please!"

"It's true. You've allowed Miranda free rein with this theater thing. And now you're sending her off to that actor's college."

"It's not an *actor's college*. It's one of the best schools in the nation."

"And just where do you think that's going to get her?"

I turned and glared at her, close to my breaking point. "I guess we'll just have to wait and see, won't we?"

"Yes, we will. But, to me, it's money wasted."

I shot her a cynical smile. "Why am I not surprised? With you, it's always about the money."

"What's that supposed to mean?"

"I means that you care about money more than anything else."

"That's not true!"

"You married Rodney for his money, didn't you?"

"What a terrible thing to say!"

"Terrible but true ... and you earned every penny of it." I walked toward the doorway. "He was a miserable bastard!"

"Marc! I will not have you speak ill of the dead!"

"It's hard to speak otherwise where Rodney is concerned."

She shook her head sadly. "I can't believe these words are coming out of my son's mouth."

I laughed. "And I can't believe you and Rodney sold the company right out from under me ... and then turned around and sold my grandfather's land without even mentioning it to me."

"Rodney and I gave you every chance to purchase the business. You weren't able to raise the funds. It's as simple as that."

"So you sold out to Bill and Steve for ten-thousand less than I offered."

For an instant, she was speechless, but she soon rallied. "Can you prove that?"

I laughed. "Of course I can prove it! Steve and Bill told me themselves."

"They had no right to share that information. That was a private negotiation."

"Gee ... they didn't seem to think so."

Silence took the floor. I stood by the doorway; my mother stared at her lap.

Finally, I sighed. "This is obviously going nowhere. You're a hopeless cause."

She looked at me sharply. "I've told you how I feel."

I gave her a wide, pasted-on grin. "Yes, you did. But you know what, Mom? I don't give a flying fuck how you feel anymore!"

50

Spring 1993 – Climax

IN 1992, LUCAS ENROLLED at Drexel University to study architecture. Over the years, he had spent many hours working in my office and seemed to have found his true niche. Still, in the end, it was his decision, and that's what mattered.

Miranda was completing her junior year at the North Carolina School of the Performing Arts and was doing quite well. Christabel and I had made several trips to Winston-Salem to see her on stage. She had also met Phillip Morrison, a tech major, who seemed to consume much of her time. All in all, it seemed like a good thing.

With the kids at college, home became a bit less stressful, but my mother still managed to strike, python like, from time to time. It was simply that her targets were now primarily limited to Christabel and me. Naturally, the kids, when home for holidays and breaks, provided a diversion for her.

Christabel spent much of her time at the theater; I was very busy at the office. I suppose my mother spent all that downtime plotting where and how to strike next.

With the kids' exodus, Keith Mahoney became somewhat of a regular fixture at Linden Avenue. He and Christabel were working closely together, and Keith had even succeeded in getting Christabel on stage. It was becoming clear where Miranda had inherited her talent, and it certainly had not been from her father.

Keith had dinner with us on a regular basis, and much of the time was spent talking shop. On several occasions, my mother joined us, feigning her enjoyment of Keith's company. Keith had a quick wit and seemed to be able to keep my mother entertained. At least, she laughed a lot and appeared to enjoy Keith's flattery. One could never be sure about my mother as so much of her personality was a sham. She had had many years of experience perfecting the art of the fraud. Personally, I didn't worry too much about its effect on Keith. He was a grown man, skilled in the art social interaction. Very little got by him. Keith had a way of being able to delve to the core of people, thereby determining how best to handle them. He approached my mother in the same way.

As I've said, with my mother, you simply never knew what was going to happen next. Such was true of her relationship with Keith Mahoney. On the day she struck, she struck hard.

———

It was April and a typically busy Friday afternoon at my office. We were readying three projects for bids and were immersed in a flurry of activity. Drawings were checked and rechecked and finally run off as blueprints. I had intended to make an early day of it, but that didn't happen. It was after 6:00 p.m. when I let myself into the house. Two suitcases sat at the foot of the wide stairway. The house was silent.

I closed the door slowly behind me. "Christabel?"

"In here." Her muted voice floated out of the library.

Christabel sat to one side of the fireplace, her hands folded calmly in her lap. I could tell she had been crying. I crossed the room and squatted down beside her chair.

"Honey? What's wrong?"

She looked at me with sadness and slowly shook her head.

I took her hand. "What is it?"

She sighed deeply. "Your mother. As always."

I took a deep breath. "Oh, Jesus Christ! What now?"

Christabel looked at me intently. "She threw Keith out."

"What?"

"She threw him out … told him to leave."

I shook my head as if to clear it. "I can't believe it … she always seemed to like Keith. What happened?"

"Keith and I came home from the theater around three. He was going to stay for dinner. We were having a drink here in the library when your mother burst into the room. She verbally assaulted him."

I stood slowly and crossed to the liquor cabinet. "Verbally assaulted him?" I poured myself a stiff glass of Scotch.

"Yes. She said, 'Don't you have a home of your own?'"

"What did Keith say?"

"Nothing. He just looked at me in shock. Then she went on. 'You spend entirely too much time hanging around here with my daughter-in-law. It's not proper; people are beginning to talk.'"

"What people?"

"I don't know! You know … people. The people your mother is always talking about."

I nodded. "Then what?"

"Keith didn't say a word. He just looked at me. Finally, he shrugged, set down his glass, and left. Your mother simply stood there and stared at him with that look of hers … you know the one I mean."

I nodded again. Yeah, if looks could kill.

"As soon as he left, she turned on me. 'This has just got to stop! You've become an embarrassment to me … and to Marc.'"

"I've never said anything about your friendship with Keith."

Christabel smiled sadly. "I know that. But it doesn't change what she said. She went on like that for several minutes. Accusing me of having an affair with Keith, dragging the family name through the mud, setting a bad example for our children. You name it." With that she broke down and cried.

I crossed to her chair and rested a hand on her shoulder. "Honey … I'm so sorry."

Christabel wrapped her arms around me and sobbed. For the moment we took comfort in one another's embrace.

"I'll go talk to her." It was a lame solution, but the only one I could think of.

Christabel pulled away from me and brushed her eyes. "Lot of good that will do! The damage is done." She paused and looked at me intently. "This can't be undone, Marc. This is too much."

"We have to do something."

Her anger flared. "Not *we*. *You* have to do something! I've taken all I can take. I can't take anymore!" She walked past me to the doorway.

"Where are you going?"

"Philadelphia." She paused in her exit without turning to look at me. "I'm going to go see Lucas … do some shopping …" She turned to glare at me. "I may even get drunk."

"Honey ..."

"Marc, I'm not coming back until she's out of here. I can't live this way any longer. Life is too short. I've done my part ... I've done the best I can to tolerate her cruelty and your indifference to it."

I was floored. "What do you want me to do?"

Christabel started to pick up the suitcases but paused. "Do? You heard me! I want her out of here! I don't care how you do it ... that's your problem. She's your mother."

I stood staring stupidly at my wife. I couldn't believe this was happening. What to do? What to do? We'd had these problems before, but it had never been anything like this. Before, we had always banded together ... gained strength from one another. This was different ... this was serious.

I stood watching as Christabel picked up the bags and turned to the door. I made a move toward her. "Let me help you with those."

Christabel jerked her arm away and shouldered open the front door. "No! I can do it! You just take care of your mother!"

The door slammed behind her, and I stood staring blankly at the leaded glass panes. I guess I was in shock. I felt totally helpless. Totally alone. Abandoned. Bereft. Yes, that was the word for it. Bereft. I was bereft. The word felt good to my tongue, and I savored it for a few moments. For some reason I felt a degree of comfort from the thought.

Swallowing the last of the Scotch, I turned slowly back to the library. I needed another. Probably more than one. I filled the glass and sat heavily on the sofa. What now? How to fix this? What to do about my mother?

Where was she? Upstairs, I guessed. Christabel had not said otherwise. I guess I had to talk to her, but what to say? I needed a plan before I spoke with her. I had to know what I was going to do. My father had always said, "You've got to have a plan." Right now, I needed one. A good one. One against which my mother could raise no objection. I laughed aloud and took a swallow of my drink. No objection? Did such a plan exist? My mother objected to everything that wasn't her own idea. What made me think I could come up with a solution? She would laugh me right out of the room. God, I hated her for this!

I swallowed another gulp of the burning liquid. Its fire felt good to my throat. Its rawness soothed my nerves. A plan. Yes, I needed a plan, but where was I going to find one? My only ally was gone. I was on my own now ... sink or swim ... this whole mess lay in my lap and my lap alone.

I nursed the drink until the glass was empty, and then I poured another. False courage. That's what my mother always called it. "All alcohol gives you is false courage," she often said. Well, I needed that right about now. Courage ... false or otherwise. I'd take what I could get.

I returned to my seat on the sofa and cradled the glass in my hands. Okay. Let's look at this. Where could she go? What would appeal to her? A little cottage all her own? No. My mother was not the little cottage type. One of those new, elegant condominiums on the beach front? That was more her style. Plenty of room. View of the ocean. Maybe. Retirement living? I shook my head. Probably not. Too restrictive, and she'd have to admit to her age. My mother's vanity would never allow that. She was always younger and better than anyone else her age. She found comfort and security in her arrogance.

I swallowed another mouthful of Scotch. I had to talk to her. That much was clear. But what to say? Confront her with her behavior? Demand some answers? Answers to what? She had done what she had done. There was no questioning that. It was up to me to find a solution. What that solution was, I had no clue. Still, I had to talk to her. There was no avoiding that.

Seeing no other alternative, I climbed the two flights of stairs to my mother's apartment. The lights in the sitting room were lit, and my mother sat in an overstuffed chair doing needlepoint. I stood in the doorway and stared at her. The bitch! I cleared my throat, and she looked up from her work.

"Marc! I didn't hear you come in." Her face wore her usual self-satisfied smile.

I stepped into the room.

She motioned toward the chair next to her. "Come in. Sit."

I sighed deeply. "No. This isn't going to take long."

She studied the needlepoint. "What's on your mind?"

I laughed dryly. "As if you didn't know."

She looked up at me. "I'm sure I don't."

I glared at her. "Christabel ... Keith ... your accusations."

"Oh, that." She looked back at her work. "Well, it was obvious you were never going to say anything to your wife. I merely said what needed to be said."

"Really?"

"Yes, that relationship had gone far enough. It was time someone put an end to it. Besides, it was getting embarrassing."

"For Christ's sake, Mom. There's nothing going on between Keith and Christabel! Keith's gay."

My mother looked smug. "Gay or otherwise, he's a man, and men have needs and desires."

"Jesus Christ!" I shook my head sadly.

"I'm simply saying the whole situation doesn't look good. It reflects badly on our family."

"Mom, you're being ridiculous."

"You're entitled to your opinion."

For a moment I was at a loss for words. There was no talking to this woman. As far as she was concerned, she was right. Always was, always would be. About anything and everything. I was no match for her and never had been. But my marriage was in jeopardy now. I had to do something.

My mother returned her attention to her needlework. "I assume your wife has gotten you all upset over this."

"My wife is gone."

She looked up at me. "Gone? Where?"

"Philadelphia ... to see Lucas. She's not coming back until we resolve this issue."

"Resolve? There's nothing here to resolve. Keith simply needs to spend less time here. It's as simple as that."

I shook my head. "It's not that simple."

"Oh?"

"She's not coming back until we make other living arrangements for you."

My mother laughed harshly and tossed aside the needlepoint. "Really? And what makes you think there's going to be any change?" She glared at me as if I was a small child. "I'm not going anywhere."

I took a deep breath. "You have to, Mom. We can't go on living like this."

"Like what?" She feigned innocence. "I'm perfectly happy here."

"Well, we aren't!"

"I'm sorry for you, then. However, I have no intention of moving now or later. You can forget that and make the best of things because nothing is changing."

"I thought you'd be happy in one of those new condos on the beachfront. They're like living in a luxury hotel."

She snorted disdainfully. "I don't think so."

Why was I not surprised? If it had been her idea, it would have been fine. Since it was my idea, that automatically made it a bad one. "Well, we have to do something."

"Yes, you do. You and Christabel are going to have to accept the fact that I live here, too. It's my home. I grew up in this house, and I have no plans for leaving."

"It's our home, too."

"Yes, it is, and I'm perfectly willing to share it with you."

I shook my head sadly and stared at the floor. Silence flooded the room. It puddled around the legs of the furniture and seeped into the thick carpeting. God help me, I had no idea of what to do or say next. We were at an impasse, plain and simple. I was at a loss. I stood there for several minutes waiting for something to happen. I kept praying for an answer, but none came. Once again, I had been bested. And why was I not surprised? I was no match for my mother. I never had been. What made me think I was going to be successful tonight? I felt suddenly foolish for having even considered that possibility.

My mother's voice broke the silence. "Well?"

I sighed deeply. "We have to do something. We can't go on like this."

My mother laughed lightly. "Of course, we can!"

I felt the weight of the situation bowing my shoulders. The fight left me, replaced with a stone-cold anger. "Well, we're not!" I turned and crossed to the doorway. "Sleep on it. We'll talk more tomorrow."

My mother actually smiled. "Whatever, you say, dear. Goodnight."

I left the room without a reply. Tomorrow. What more could be said tomorrow? I descended the wide staircases and sought refuge in the library. I filled my Scotch glass and flopped down in one of the chairs next to the fireplace. Tomorrow. Tomorrow would simply be a replay of tonight. She wouldn't give and inch and would find much delight in goading me with her answers. Nothing would be different tomorrow.

I took a deep swallow of the amber liquid and rested my head against the back of the chair. What to do? Where to go? Where to hide? I had no answers.

I wished Christabel would call, but that was unlikely to happen. I didn't even know where she was staying. Fool! How could I let something like this happen? Why had I ever agreed to my mother moving in with us? This was all my fault. There was no one else to blame. I tossed back the remainder of my drink and poured another. The warmth spread throughout my body. What to do?

I sat in the chair and continued to berate myself. I had caused this mess and now felt powerless to fix it. The one thing my wife had requested of me seemed impossible. I was a failure, pure and simple. I was caught in a trap. I could see no way out. My mother had had me under her thumb all my life, and that's where I remained now. I felt hopeless.

As my thoughts escalated, the Scotch began to take effect. I finished the glass and had another. The chair was comfortable, and my body hurt. It hurt all over. The Scotch soothed the aches, and I drifted close to sleep. There had to be an answer ... somewhere.

—

When I awoke, little had changed. The Tiffany lamp on the library table glowed softly. The Scotch glass sat empty on the table next to my chair. The mantle clock read 2:30 a.m.

I stretched, and suddenly the whole futility of my situation cascaded over me. What in hell was I going to do? My whole life was threatened, and I seemed powerless to save it. I thought about Christabel. I thought about the children. I thought about everything we had accomplished together. And here I was, ready to let it all slip away. Ready to let my mother jeopardize my life and my family. Anger at the thought boiled within me.

No.

I had to make this right regardless of my mother. If it took a court order, I would see to it that she left this house. I laughed at the thought. The bitch! Her friends would take great delight in seeing her evicted from her own home. It would certainly do my heart good.

Okay. That was that. This couldn't nor wouldn't wait until tomorrow. This had to be resolved now. Tonight.

I rose from my chair and retraced my steps to the third floor. All was dark. My mother, long since in bed. I crept through the shadowy sitting room and eased open her bedroom door. The moonlight filtered through the thin draperies illuminating the surface of the bed. My mother slept soundly on her back, her profile facing upward. God, how I had grown to hate that face. She breathed softly, barely making a sound.

I hesitated. "Mom?"

There was no response. I reached down to shake her shoulder but stopped suddenly. I stared at the thick, down pillow that lay beside her on the bed and ran a hand slowly over its silky surface. I slowly picked up the pillow and hefted it as if to test its resilience. Nice and thick. Thick yet soft. I gazed at my mother's sleeping form and smiled.

Slowly I bent over her. The thick, soft pillow adhered nicely to the contours of her sleeping face.

Epilogue

WITH MY MOTHER'S SUDDEN death, Christabel returned home to Linden Avenue to play the dutiful wife. The kids came, too, as would be expected. The funeral and burial were swift and without fanfare.

Life became a joy without my mother's constant harangues, and we all continued our merry march to the grave.

Life in Martin's Neck changed little in the ensuing years. Several old habits and institutions waned and disappeared, but the little town remained basically the same. Black tie dinners fell out of fashion and life took on a more relaxed atmosphere.

I remained with Steadman and Son. When Steve Redman decided his interests lay elsewhere, I bought out his share of the business. Once again there was a Steadman at the helm.

Christabel continued her interest with the theater both on and off stage. Keith Mahoney continued to be a regular fixture in our home. He seldom ever mentioned my mother. Neither did we.

Lucas graduated cum lade from Drexel and returned to Martin's Neck. He married his high school sweetheart and took her to live in Granny Steadman's big, old Victorian house. The house had stood empty since Granny's death. I'd never emptied nor rented it, but had kept it in constant repair. It was like a time capsule, and Lucas' wife, Doria, loved it. With some extensive remodeling, it made the perfect home for them. Of course, Lucas continued to work with me, bringing the whole Steadman and Son issue full circle.

Miranda married Phillip Morrison soon after graduating from college. Phillip had a job awaiting him on Broadway, which meant their relocation to New York. Miranda found moderate success as an actress. Most of her roles were in off-Broadway productions, but she landed a few minor roles on the Great White Way. After two children and several years in New York, Phillip and Miranda grew weary of the city and returned home. They purchased the defunct movie theater in Martin's Neck and worked hard to build it into a fully operational theater. It took time, but, with help, they succeeded.

———

By the time Phillip and Miranda returned to Martin's Neck, the big house on Linden Avenue was becoming too much for the two of us. With age, entertaining had slackened, and most of the house stood empty. We passed the dwelling along to Phillip and Miranda and settled ourselves in a vintage, three-bedroom Tudor cottage on one of the lesser side streets in Martin's Neck. It had everything we needed and was more than enough for the two of us.

———

Christabel was diagnosed with the first stages of Alzheimer's shortly after her seventieth birthday. Her doctors were optimistic and felt that, with recent advances and medications, she had a good amount of time ahead of her.

Still, the news shocked us. Christabel deplored the idea that she would grow to a point of not recognizing her children and grandchildren. At present she is doing well, and is exhibiting very little sign of the disease. However, we both know it's only a matter of time.

When it happens, when lucidity wanes and her memory begins to fail, I will take care of her. I will see that Christabel doesn't suffer the indignities so common to the disease.

Of that, you may be certain.

David W. Dutton

DAVID W. DUTTON is a semi-retired residential designer who was born and raised in Milton, DE. He has written two novels, several short stories, and eleven plays. David's writing credits include the musical comedy, *oh! Maggie*, written in collaboration with Martin Dusbiber and produced by the Possum Point Players and the Lake Forest Drama Club. He also wrote two musical reviews for the Possum Point Players: *An Evening With Cole Porter*, in collaboration with Marcia Faulkner, and *With a Song in My Heart*. His one-act play, *Why the Chicken Crossed the Road*, was commissioned and produced by the Delmarva Chicken Festival.

In 1997, David was awarded a fellowship as an established writer by the Delaware Arts Council. The following year, he received a first-place award by the Delaware Literary Connection for a creative non-fiction work entitled "Who is Nahnu Dugeye?" This piece was subsequently published in the *Terrains* literary anthology.

David, his wife, Marilyn, and their Rottweiler, Molly, currently reside in Milton.

Made in the USA
Columbia, SC
17 June 2021